Cries in the New Wilderness

T0151453

Cries in the New

FROM THE FILES OF THE MOSCOW

translated and introduced by

Eve Adler

 PAUL DRY BOOKS *Philadelphia 2002*

Mikhail N. Epstein

Wilderness

INSTITUTE OF ATHEISM

First Paul Dry Books Edition, 2002

Paul Dry Books, Inc.
Philadelphia, Pennsylvania
www.pauldrybooks.com

Originally published in Russian as Novoe sektantstvo: Tipy religiozno-filosofskikh umonastroenii v Rossii, 1970–80-e gody.

Parts of the present work appeared in a different version in the New England Review 18, no. 2 (Spring 1997): 70–100.

Text type: Palatino and Meridien families
Display type: Monotype Albertus
Designed by Adrianne Onderdonk Dudden

1 3 5 7 9 8 6 4 2
Printed in the United States of America

Library of Congress Cataloging-in-Publication Data
Epstein, Mikhail N.
    [Novoe sektantstvo. English]
    Cries in the new wilderness : from the files of the Moscow Institute of Atheism /
by Mikhail N. Epstein ; translated and introduced by Eve Adler.
        p.   cm.
    ISBN 0-9679675-4-6 (cloth : alk. paper) — ISBN 0-9679675-5-4 (pbk. : alk. paper)
    1. Religion and culture—Russia (Federation)—Fiction.   2. Sects—Russia
(Federation)—Fiction.   I. Title.
    PG3479.7.P74 N6813 2002
    891.73'5—dc21
                                                                            2002016994

ISBN 0-9679675-4-6 (cloth)
ISBN 0-9679675-5-4 (paper)

Contents

. . . . .

Selected reviews of The New Sectarianism

Epilogue to **The New Sectarianism**

Atheism as a Spiritual Vocation: From the Archive of
Professor R. O. Gibaydulina

Afterword: The Comedy of Ideas

Acknowledgments

I want to express my deepest gratitude to Professor Eve Adler whose inspiration and dedication made possible the publication of this book. Eve did everything a friend, a colleague, and a co-thinker could do to bring this project to a full realization. Her translation is elegant, inventive, and fully congenial to the style and intention of the original. I am also thankful to my friend Dr. Thomas Epstein who has checked the text of the translation against the original and made valuable editorial revisions.

Translator's Introduction

Since the fall of the Soviet Union, we have heard plenty of postmortems on the communist economic and political project. But the Soviet Union was also the first great attempt to realize the ancient dream of an atheist society. How did that experiment turn out? Did Soviet atheism take root in Russian souls? Did it manage to form a radically new type of human being, to change the landscape of the human heart, to replace the typical spiritual experiences of Western civilization with unheard-of novelties? Do today's Russians still belong to the same spiritual world as today's Americans, today's Europeans?

On these questions there has been a resounding silence. We can read statistics and anecdotes bearing upon church attendance in today's Russia, the ups and downs of the reconstituted Russian Orthodox Church, the pros and cons of the 1997 Law on Freedom of Conscience and Religious Organizations. But, since the fundamental question concerns people's inner lives, all this information remains dumb without a special sort of guide to make it speak to us intelligibly. Mikhail Epstein is such a guide, with the sympathetic heart of a participant, the erudition of a scholar, and the cool eye of a curious observer. But above all—Mikhail Epstein hears voices, and his literary art enables us to hear those voices for ourselves.

In *Cries in the New Wildernesss*, Epstein takes us inside the disintegrating Soviet Union by sounding the voices of a whole orchestra of late-Soviet types. This is satire, but of an unusually loving and revealing variety, more in the line of Horace or Musil, say, than of Juvenal or Swift. Epstein is representing people who are on or over the edge, but he does it with a delicate touch that shows not only the wildness and absurdity but also the pathos and plausibility of the everyday half-madness in the hearts and minds of ordinary people, its connection to things heard on the radio and read in forbidden books, seen in the street and daydreamed in the kitchen. There is a striking absence here of wickedness, vice, or monstrosity, and correspondingly a striking absence of indignation; instead, ordinary confusion and everyday hopes and longings are represented in all their disorienting connections to the most spectacular ambitions, surmises, and claims of the philosophic and Biblical traditions. The voices Epstein hears speak in a luxuriant interplay of styles: the everyday, the poetic, the Marxist-Leninist-scientific, the romantic-literary, the bureaucratic-Soviet, the mystical-paranoid, the foreign-Western-bourgeois, the literary-critical; they brood portentously on implausible etymologies, on half-cracked, half-revelatory antics with allusions, associations, quotations; they attribute an ineffable significance to stray bits of terminology or snippets of forgotten manifestos and anthems. Under Epstein's direction, these voices add up to an intimate drama of the inner worlds of ordinarily confused and striving people.

The core of *Cries in the New Wilderness* is an annotated handbook of underground sects brought to light by the vigilant efforts of the fictitious Moscow Institute of Atheism. In this imaginary handbook the reader has a compilation of selected citations from the writings of the sectarians themselves, writings catalogued and analyzed by Professor of Scientific Atheism Raisa Omarovna Gibaydulina in a classified document intended for internal use by the Institute of Atheism. Copies of this classified document, however, were somehow smuggled to the West in the mid-eighties, and the version before us includes an appendix of responses from the bourgeois press, where we hear several Western intellectuals trying to come to grips with the late-Soviet realities described in the handbook. The imaginary documents of *Cries in the New Wilderness* crystallize these realities with rare literary power.

While some of these Western reviewers are most impressed by the splashy collective voice of the sectarians piercing through the numbing insistence of the scientific-atheist commentary, the voice of the commentator herself, Professor Gibaydulina, finally becomes most mysteriously compelling. With her respectable resolve to be a credit to her profession, her struggle to keep her scientific cool in the face of unspeakable folly and depravity, her occasional outbursts of righteous indignation, her optimistic instructions on the most efficient methods of rooting out error from the human heart, her wooden insensibility to everything playful or diabolical in the unruly materials she must reluctantly catalogue—Raisa Omarovna gradually emerges as a fascinating character in her own right, and I always wondered what became of her after the collapse of the Soviet Union took scientific atheism the way of the planned economy. For this Paul Dry edition, Mikhail Epstein has added a special epilogue of materials from her personal archive, in which we can follow the vicissitudes of her career and her inner world up to the time of her death in 1997.

Note on the English Edition

On 15 December 1995 I had my first telephone conversation with Mikhail Epstein, and on the next day, in my first e-mail to him, I wrote: "I am still somewhat amazed that 'Mikhail Epstein' did not turn out to be a figment of the imagination of some comedian at the 'National Council for Soviet and East European Research.'"

This is what had happened. On 25 November 1995 I ordered some titles on religious sects from "Panorama of Russia," an excellent Boston outfit specializing in Russian scholarly literature. When my order arrived in the early days of December and I started leafing through my new books, one of them, called *Novoe Sektantstvo* (*The New Sectarianism*), somehow kept resisting my efforts to categorize it. It seemed to be a publication under the name "Mikhail Epstein" of a previously classified document of the Moscow Institute of Atheism, describing seventeen new sects discovered by that Institute in the waning years of the Soviet regime. But something about it didn't add up—the amateurish printing, the cover illustration of a black cat and a Soviet worker in angel-wings and earmuffs, the crackpot index with its entries for "fire" and "Feuerbachian," "Dante" and "dietology." . . . It had been published in Moscow in 1994 by a house called "Labyrinth," with the following note, in English, on its title page:

> The preparation of this manuscript for publication was supported from funds provided by the National Council for Soviet and East European Research (USA) which however is not responsible for the contents of this book.

Eventually I called the National Council for Soviet and East European Research, and was told that there was another, perhaps fuller text, copies of which were held in restricted collections of only two U.S. libraries: the Library of the Department of State and the National Defense University Library. Still, works from these restricted collections could, in some cases, be ordered by private citizens upon submission of a special application form requiring not only U.S. government clearance but also written permission from the author. But who *was* the author, and where could I reach him? The National Council for Soviet and East European Research gave me a telephone number in Atlanta, with a warning that I'd better hurry up since the government was about to shut down because of the budget deficit. It was Friday, 15 December 1995, and indeed the government did shut down the following Monday. But by that time I didn't need government help with my search anymore, since I had made direct telephone contact with the real Mikhail Epstein. My surprise at his existence was as nothing next to his surprise that I was looking for his work in restricted collections of U.S. government libraries.

Cries in the New Wilderness is the fruit of my initial confusion about the genre and author of *The New Sectarianism.*

NOTE: Biblical verses have been translated from the standard Russian (Synodal) Bible, drawing on the King James Version (and other standard English versions) where possible.

Cries in the New Wilderness

From the Author

Let me add that the reader will find in *Russian Nights* a pretty accurate picture of the intellectual life lived by the young people of Moscow in the twenties and thirties, a life of which there are practically no other records. That time had its own significance: thousands of questions, doubts, and surmises were seething, all of which have awakened again, even more vividly, in our own time: the questions of pure philosophy, of economics, of private and national life that occupy us now occupied people then too, and very much of what is being said now, directly and indirectly—even the new Slavophilism—all this was already stirring in embryonic form at that time.

V. F. Odoevsky, notes to *Russian Nights* (1862)[1]

Times repeat themselves. Prince Odoevsky's recollection of Nicholas's era of stagnation during Alexander's era of glasnost is fully applicable to the present spate of new Russian ideologies, which were just beginning to stir during the Brezhnev era. And, in fact, isn't "stagnation" a kind of pregnancy, when the restless life of the next generation is being invisibly nurtured in the maternal womb? The national, religious, mystical, philosophical, and literary ideas that are now propagated at every street corner and kiosk were already perturbing many minds back then, though at the time there was no public outlet for them.

This book too is about "Russian nights," that is, the various intellectual movements that were secretly maturing in the 1970s and early 1980s and, in the usual Russian manner, taking on the character of insular, sectarian worldviews. Since it was always the case in Russia that only the one "correct" ideology had the right to a government monopoly, all the others had to crowd into back alleys where they surreptitiously enticed passersby with their forbidden underground intellectual wares, their "sedition," "heresy," "contraband." Such trafficking was illegal; you had to pay extra because of the risk, and thus these underground ideas developed into something priceless and even

3

world-redeeming. After many years of unanimous thought in Communist Russia, it is no wonder that in the 1970s and especially in the 1980s, thought involuntarily took on a sectarian tendency, veered off toward particularity, partiality, eccentricity, sharply diverging from the beaten path set before it. The very fact that thought was moving obliquely, going to extremes, verging sharply to the right or to the left, sometimes raving and raging without ever converging on any one position, was a true sign of its accumulating strength.

Over a century ago, Herzen wrote:

The pestilential streak, running from 1825 to 1855, will soon be completely cordoned off; men's traces, swept away by the police, will have vanished, and future generations will stand bewildered before a bulldozed wasteland, seeking the lost channels of thought that were actually never interrupted. The current was apparently checked; Nicholas tied up the main artery, but the blood flowed into side-channels. . . . [These] are the rudimentary germs, the embryos of history, barely perceptible, barely existing, like all embryos in general. Little by little, they form into groups, attracted by various center points; then the groups start repelling one another. . . .[2]

Couldn't these words describe twentieth-century Russia? If you change the 8s in the years to 9s, don't the implications become even sharper and more prescient? Yes, that's how it was with us too. If you superimpose the two centuries, you see that for us too those same thirty years are a burnt-out crater, a wasteland pounded into the earth with iron boots; and nevertheless the paths never converged but swerved clear out of reach, onto roundabout ways, into garrets and cellars, into sects.

This book was written in Moscow in the mid-1980s. It describes the spectrum of religious views then widespread among the intelligentsia in the capital, though not limited to them. The author himself was active in several Moscow discussion clubs and intellectual associations[3] and found himself under the intersecting influences of all their views; in certain parts of his soul, he even belonged to some of the new sects. In addition, in 1985 and 1987 he participated in expeditions sponsored by Moscow State University to study various popular religious beliefs and sectarian developments in southern Russia and Ukraine, which enabled him to amass plenty of material for a general characterization of the religious quests of the period.

This is not, however, a documentary book; it is written in the special genre of the "comedy of ideas," which the reader will find explained in the Afterword. It would be futile to look in existing dictionaries for the names of such sects as "Steppies," "Folls," "Arkists," etc. These names are used by the author of the present study as conventional designations for those religious-ideological types which, though so prolific in the society of that time, were just at the point of conception and not only had no publications, but had not even worked out a terminology in which to express themselves. How often was it the author's lot to converse with Foodniks and Thingwrights, Arkists and Bloodbrothers, Atheans and Good-believers, Domesticans and Pushkinians, and how many remarkable ideas he encountered, how many germs of new theological and philosophic systems passed before him! These ideas flashed by in a word, a phrase, but were almost never to be met in a developed form, as a grounded system; so it seemed that the spiritual experience of a whole generation would leave its imprint only in these countless passing conversations and finally come to nothing, vanish into the air of club gatherings and friendly arguments. Thus arose the need to write, in the name of these sectarian movements, entire treatises and sermons, excerpts from which constitute this book. Although the author takes full responsibility for everything he has written, he regards this book as the fruit of a collective labor, where his role has been that of the "wandering rhapsode," stitching together in his own peculiar way the motifs diffused in social consciousness.

True, this religious "folklore" is unusual in its somewhat learned and speculative character. It sings not of heroes but of ideas. But such is the bookish character of the new sectarianism, just like the earlier sectarianism that had sprung up on the heights of Russian culture when it was consciously seeking schismatic lines of separation from the state ideology. Here we may refer to the views of A. S. Prugavin, the great scholar of Russian sectarianism, who at the beginning of the twentieth century had already noted the social displacement of Russian sectarianism and emphasized the prominent role played in it by the educated classes:

Among us there is a widespread view that religious sectarianism is the exclusive property of the masses, and that the nests of various religious sects are to be found only among peasants and the urban poor. . . . This view does not correspond to reality at all. Religious quests have long been typical of the Russian people, and not only of its lower depths, its peasants and workers, but also of the middle classes, the intelligentsia and the bourgeoisie, and even of the highest aristocratic circles. . . . Nowadays, the ranks of various sects more and more often include the intelligentsia, people with a higher education, who are beginning to play a visible role in the sectarian world. New religious doctrines, new sects, have arisen under the influence of persons from the intelligentsia whose followers are now organizing themselves into special societies.[4]

The grounding of sectarianism in the intelligentsia was further strengthened during the late Soviet period, after half a century of the ideological dictatorship that had given our culture an even more dogmatic character. All ideological movements, even those in opposition to the ruling ideology, started from above, from various circles of the intelligentsia, and trickled down from there to the masses. Almost all the ideological movements of the 1970s and 1980s started among the intelligentsia, who in fact formed the cardinal class of this ideocratic government. The government took its ideological foundations from the intelligentsia and brought down upon the intelligentsia the whole monolithic weight of its own ideas, so that the intelligentsia under ideocracy emerged as both the most privileged and the most persecuted class. What I call the "new sectarianism" is in essence the ideology of our intelligentsia as expressed in religious concepts or, rather, the sum of such ideologies, radiating out in all directions from the "center" of the government ideology.

Such is our spiritual tradition, going back to Chaadaev and the Slavophiles, Dostoevsky and Tolstoy, the thinkers of the Silver Age: religion as the expression of the extreme limits of urgent, importunate thought. Social, national, aesthetic, philosophic, even scientific ideas, as well as mere preferences in the way of life: each of them, taken to extremes, acquires the form of a spiritual absolute and a religious credo. That is why every Russian ideology sooner or later turns into a theological doctrine of the ultimate meaning of human life, and every social movement that fails to seize power turns into a heresy, a sect. Absolutism of content and particularity of form are the two complementary marks of a sect. The form of sectarianism shows both the weakness of our intelligentsia, its social segregation, its isolation in narrow "kitchen" circles of freethinking, and simultaneously its strength, its moral maximalism, its readiness to think every thought through to the end and to devote itself to ideas not reflexively but with its whole being, to "live by the idea." Evidently, sectarianism is the predestined Russian form of the "survival" of thought under conditions of terrible government oppression. The chief goal of this book is to convey to the reader the new *summa theologica* that developed under the unprecedented conditions of the communist experiment, where one of the former sects came to power and others started rising up in opposition to it, although partly in its own image.

Just as pre-Revolutionary Russian sectarianism cannot be understood outside the system of the official Orthodox Church, so the sectarianism of the Soviet period cannot be understood outside the system of government atheism. In essence, everything that deviated from this system became sectarianism—the inversion of the ruling ideology, the same but with a minus sign. The government dogma, in its turn, lived and flourished precisely by eradicating even the slightest glimmer of free religious thought, which it would breathlessly blow up and exaggerate, since it saw in every such spark the threat of complete disintegration and destabilization of the foundations of the government. The atheism of this period and its sectarianism together form a kind of ideological symbiosis, which must be interpreted as a whole.

This is the origin of the formal conventions of this book. It appears as a publication "for official use only," where the views of the sectarians are presented to select reader-propagandists from the perspective of the atheistic worldview. This form of publication, known as *spetsizdat* (special publication), was widespread during the Brezhnev era and served as a natural complement and counterweight to the better-known *samizdat. Spetsizdat* circulated in runs of a few tens or hundreds of numbered copies assigned to responsible leaders and closed libraries (spets-collections). And, of course, the only way sectarian ideas could be collected and published at that time, even as material for the atheist slaughterhouse, was in the form of a *spetsizdat* anthology, not unlike those published for its own staff by the Committee on Religious Affairs, where secret facts were disclosed about the numbers of believers, their distribution by national and social groups, their changing attitudes, etc.

For American readers, it may perhaps be useful to describe in more detail this Soviet triple-think system of publication. Alongside the official mass publishing system there existed two other types: non-official (i.e., *samizdat*) and non-mass (i.e., *spetsizdat*). Publication by the regular method was limited to those areas in which the government and the people were supposed to share full mutual understanding. But as cracks in their unanimity developed, forms of publication in which the people could hide something from the government and the government could hide something from the people became more and more prevalent. One set of works was circulated in typewritten copies among friends and acquaintances; the other set was printed or typeset, but in miniscule quantities, so that only a limited circle of trusted administrators and specialists had access to them. One would think there could be nothing in common between the contents of these two sets of publications, since each was trying to avoid publicity on the other side: what the *samizdat* people feared above all was that their productions might become known to the "organs," and what the *spetsizdat* people were most anxious about was the secrecy of their publications, each copy of which was individually numbered and assigned to a named recipient.

Nevertheless, it soon became clear that there was a growing identity between the productions of *samizdat* and those of *spetsizdat:* exactly what society was trying to hide from the government was what the government was trying to hide from society. A symmetrical figure of silence was operating on both sides, each of which knew very well what the other side was hiding. The works—mystical, political, satirical—that people were copying by typewriter for their friends were the very same works being issued in numbered copies "for official use only." Hence the publication of Solzhenitsyn and Marcuse, Orwell and Zinoviev, Freud and Garaudi, psychoanalysts and existentialists, dissidents and revisionists, the new left and the new right—everything that society wanted to read in spite of the government, and the government wanted to read secretly from society. Thus this book serves up a *samizdat* filling (the sectarian views) in a *spetsizdat* crust (the atheistic denunciation). It is in this carnival of ideas, constantly hailing one another and transposing themselves from one system of world-views to the other, that the reader is herein invited to participate.

The third important ideological factor of the period was the potential reaction from abroad, from "reactionary" circles—"bourgeois," "emigré," and "revisionist." So, in this book, the presentation of a *spetsizdat* anthology of *samizdat* materials is followed by a set of reviews showing the possible reaction of *tamizdat* (publications from abroad) to the new sectarian movements.

Finally, the religious-atheistic debate of the 1970s and 1980s needs to be reassessed from the radically different perspective of the 1990s. What happened with this "invincible" Marxist-atheistic monolith, as presented in Professor Gibaydulina's introductions to the *spetsizdat* edition, after the entire Soviet system crumbled? This new prism is added through the commentaries and confessions of Gibaydulina herself on the complicated evolution and gradual dissolution of her atheistic beliefs up to her death in 1997.

Thus the phenomenon of the new sectarianism is presented in five dimensions: the compositions of the sectarians themselves; the presentation of their views in a neutral, encyclopedic manner; the atheistic prefaces; the assessments of Western observers; and post-Soviet perspectives on the fates of "scientific atheism" (Epilogue).

As for the sixth dimension, the author's own understanding of the new sects and ideologies, the reader will find that in the Afterword.

The religious revival in late Soviet Russia took place in the wasteland of mass atheism that occupied one sixth of the globe and, with the successful expansion of the "world socialist system," finally covered almost half of it. The lonely voices of faith that resound throughout this book are truly "cries in the wilderness"—the new wilderness of the late twentieth century, which may have prepared the rebirth of traditional beliefs and, most importantly, the birth of new, post-atheist varieties of religion. Hence, the title of this book follows the prophet Isaiah, who speaks of "The voice of him that crieth in the wilderness, Prepare ye the way of the Lord, make straight in the desert a highway for our God." (40.3).

Institute of Atheism
of the U.S.S.R.

THE NEW SECTARIANISM:
A Reference Manual

***

Moscow 1985

***

Published under the auspices of the
Editorial Council of the Institute of Atheism

Facsimile of the title page of the original 1985 edition

General editor and author of introductory essay:

Professor R. O. Gibaydulina, Ph.D.

Contributing editors:

M. P. Kondakov, *Candidate in Philosophic Sciences*

S. I. Levin, *Candidate in Philosophic Sciences*

N. I. Ryumina, *Candidate in Philological Sciences*

P. M. Smilga, *Candidate in Philological Sciences*

Consultants:

I. P. Rumyantsev, *Doctor of Philosophic Sciences (Philosophy)*

Y. B. Sorokin, *Doctor of Philological Sciences (Sociology)*

D. K. Ryadenko, *Candidate in Art History (Aesthetics)*

V. M. Spirin, *Candidate in Philosophic Sciences (Ethics)*

B. A. Rogov, *Candidate in Philosophic Sciences (Scientific Methodology)*

G. A. Sviridov, *Candidate in Psychological Sciences (Psychology)*

Literary editor:

M. N. Petrov

This manual contains the first publication of information on a series of new sectarian groups in the U.S.S.R.: **Foodniks, Sinnerists, Arkists, Khazarists, Good-believers, Steppies,** etc. It includes extensive excerpts from the writings of sectarian preachers and ideologues, and definitions of little-known religio-mystical concepts and terms. It is based on sources held in the manuscript collection of the Institute of Atheism, and materials collected in the course of religiology expeditions in the 1970s and early 1980s.

This manual, the first of its kind released in the U.S.S.R., is intended for specialists in Scientific Atheism and Contemporary Non-traditional Beliefs.

THE NEW SECTARIANISM AS A PROBLEM FOR RELIGIOLOGY

by Professor R. O. Gibaydulina

The approach taken in this reference manual on contemporary sectarianism is dictated by the urgent tasks of atheistic enlightenment in our country.

Our scholars and propagandists have long been in the habit of restricting themselves to the critique of the traditional religions, proceeding from the dogmatic assumption that it is impossible for new religious movements to arise on socialist soil. Reality, unfortunately, has refuted these superficial prognoses and dogmatic illusions. The dying out of religion as a type of social consciousness by no means excludes the possibility of spasmodic outbreaks of individual and collective religiosity, especially against the background of acute new problems of social-historical development. The sunset of religion can be accompanied by an especially fantastic play of colors, by the birth of the most preposterous and ambitious ideas, losing all contact with reality.

Since the mid-1970s, the Institute of Atheism has been conducting a series of research projects and expeditions departing from earlier patterns in the following ways.

1. The main objects of study were manifestations of individual and so-called non-traditional religiosity, whereas previous expeditions had collected data on the established world religions and the traditional sects of our country.

2. The study was conducted mainly in large cities where a significant proportion of the population belongs to the scientific-technical and literary-artistic intelligentsia. Our questionnaires were composed with a view to the undergraduate or graduate/professional education of the interviewees.

3. The study included not only believers but also selected strata of the intelligentsia, with the goal of bringing to light their lifestyle priorities, their philosophico-ethical positions, their views on the relationship of belief and knowledge, belief and morality, belief and art. Where previous expeditions began by establishing the believer's membership in a given confession and proceeded to explore his membership in a profession, here we took the opposite approach, investigating how the representatives of certain professions, certain creative and scholarly collectives, define themselves with regard to religious belief.

As a result of three expeditions (1975, 1979, and 1983), we now have at our disposal numerous documents and materials: (1) manuscripts, some from the pens of the believers themselves, some from their private libraries—articles, sermons, manifestos, entire treatises and anthologies; (2) notes made by our researchers on writings that the believers, for one reason or another, could not or would not turn over to us directly; (3) written responses to the questionnaires; (4) tapes of interviews. It should be noted that most of the believers talked with us willingly and shared their views openly, but they usually requested that we not use their names in case of publication—a request that we honor here.

The picture that has taken shape before us as a result of these research projects is most unusual. We have discovered many new concepts, ideas, and terms never before registered by historians of religion.

Sectarianism has had a long history in our country. In the past, it often took the form of mass social protest, especially by the serfs against the exploitative oppression and violence of the serf owners and against the monopoly of the Orthodox Church. But this does not mean that sectarian ideas cannot find a friendly environment in socialist society:

the very crisis of religious consciousness often drives people to seek an outlet in non-traditional forms of religion.

Up to now it has been standard to distinguish two stages in the development of Russian sectarianism. The first stage, associated with the schism in the Russian Orthodox Church, saw the spread, in the seventeenth through nineteenth centuries, of the so-called old-Russian sects, the roots of which can be traced to the old feudal system: Khristovery, Dukhobortsy, Molokane, Khlysty, Skoptsy, etc. Ultimately, these sects barely survived, and nowadays they have no discernible influence.

After the liberation of the serfs in 1861, sects of the Protestant type began to spread in Russia: Baptists, evangelical Christians, and later Adventists, Pentecostals, Jehovah's Witnesses. Their popularity, like that of Western European Protestantism at the zenith of its expansion, was caused by the rapid development of capitalistic relations in post-reform Russia. Until recently, these groups have occupied the dominant position among the Christian sects in our country.

But in the mid-sixties of our century there arose a new type of sectarian group, the systematic study of which, unfortunately, was not begun until a decade later, and even then was pursued rather ineffectively at first. Some of these weakly organized groups preached views conventionally designated "non-traditional" by contemporary religiology. Their doctrines mostly have a syncretic character, eclectically combining elements of various religions and philosophic systems, which gives some basis for their occasional characterization as "postmodern."

It is important to note that the vast majority of these sects are unrelated to the non-traditional cults that have become so widespread in the West since the 1960s: "Crusade for Christ," "Hare Krishna," "Mission of Divine Light," "Transcendental Meditation," "United Church of Reverend Moon," etc. Attempts to transplant these religious movements from their capitalist countries of origin were usually ineffectual. Those few of our young people who may have felt some superficial attraction to such movements were soon enough weaned away by vigorous educational-atheistic programs and by the very conditions of socialist reality itself. Such foreign sects do not come into the purview of our study, since their ideology has already been adequately studied and critically analyzed in the Marxist literature on the major Western religious confessions. The situation is different with regard to our so-called homegrown sects: although they are undoubtedly influenced by mystical breezes blowing in from West and East, their doctrines must nonetheless be recognized as quite independent and in need of a separate investigation.

Also beyond the bounds of the sects under study here are those holding the type of mystical views connected with false interpretations of the facts of natural science (parapsychology, extrasensory perception, UFO lore, etc.). The natural sciences have always been surrounded by all sorts of parasitic pseudoscientific speculations and fantasies, the refutation of which belongs to the concrete scientific disciplines and to the general task of promoting the scientific worldview.

The material under study in the present book is, then, distinct from foreign or borrowed religious currents on the one hand and, on the other, from the para-scientific and pseudoscientific theories more appropriately treated in the corresponding scientific subspecialties.

What, then, are the sects considered in this book? Their very names sound exotic: "Bloodbrothers," "The Red Horde," "Arkists," "Domesti-cans," "Sinnerists," "Good-believers," etc. However, there is nothing surprising in this. After all, the names of the old-Russian sects also sounded rather strange: "Child-bearers" and "Non-child-bearers," "Dumb nay-sayers" and "Singing nay-sayers," "Fugitives," "Tremblers," "Pray-nots," "Good-for-nothings," and so on.

The key feature of the new sectarianism is the fact that it has arisen in the socialist era, in the midst of mass atheism. Since we do not yet have a scientific literature dealing specifically with the activities of the new sects, it would seem useful to give a brief account of the specific ways in which they differ from traditional sectarianism.

First of all, the new sects, unlike the traditional ones, are found primarily not in rural areas but in big cities with highly developed cultural and educational infrastructures. As our research has shown, non-traditional beliefs find their most fertile soil among specialists with a college education and higher. This, then, is the source of the actively professional orientation of the new sects: they attempt to give a religious interpretation and "sanctification" to man's activities as a professional. "One practices holiness by practicing one's profession" is one of the "aphorisms" from a manuscript of N. A. entitled "On Religio-Professional Unions." Indeed, professional specialization as such is an area of intense sectarian self-consciousness and self-definition. Thus, the new sectarians often group themselves around the specific attributes of their profession, though of course they may also include amateurs who simply have an interest in that profession. For example, there are sectarian groups of writers, historians, physicians, and physicists, who try to give a religious interpretation to the facts of their respective disciplines. Sometimes they formulate their religious doctrines in the guise of professional instructions and prohibitions, reinterpreting the technical terms of their disciplines in a religious spirit. Thus, among philologists, the cult of the "incarnated" Word takes on a peculiar meaning as they try to show the "divine intellect" or the "grammar of providence" in action in the laws of language. Physicists who attribute special significance to the categories of "light" and "energy" have succeeded in reconciling the data of contemporary science with interpretations of light and energy found among certain "Church Fathers." A "Sacripathology" movement has been observed among physicians who strive not only to cure the sick but to "adopt" their sickness, becoming "co-invalids" with them. Historians and writers compose treatises on ethnic roots in hopes of proving the "God-bearing" mission of this or that group.

Surveys conducted by investigators at a variety of research and teaching institutions show that many academics, without holding any traditional religious views and without belonging to any of the existing confessions, nevertheless take an interest in what they call "mysteries." It goes without saying that no one can forbid a professor of mathematical physics or romance philology to engage in theoretical studies at the very boundaries of those disciplines in which they can be considered competent—and sometimes even beyond those boundaries, in the sphere of the "unknown." But we must not close our eyes to the fact that once this stage is reached, people may find themselves on the road to sectarianism, to a break with mainstream science and a corruption of the very fabric of scientific knowledge into occult "mystery-knowledge."

It should be emphasized that the phenomenon of sectarianism is both broader and narrower than that of religion. Religion can occur in the most varied organizational and confessional forms, of which the sect is the most particular, discrete, and transient. On the other hand, sectarianism can appear altogether outside the sphere of religion—in science, art, politics—although here too it always contains a potential, "latent" religiosity. The isolation of sectarians—of scientific sectarians from mainstream science, of artistic sectarians from mainstream art, of political sectarians from mainstream politics—inevitably leads to religion. Let us not forget that it was precisely among the Liquidators, who occupied a far-left sectarian position in the political struggle, that the "God-building" movement began. The sectarian isolation of scientists from mainstream science led to the embrace of mysticism in Nazi Germany, where "Aryan physics" enjoyed official support. In the final analysis, all these specialized "scientific" or "political" forms of sectarianism end up swelling the ranks of religious sectarianism.

A characteristic feature of contemporary sectarianism, arising from its high educational level, is its *bookishness*, its abundance of literary sources. If, as Engels puts it, among Protestants every rank-and-file believer becomes a priest, then among the new sectarians almost everyone considers himself a "theologian" and writes extensive doctrinal treatises, theoretical analyses, sermons, and manifestos.

Huge quantities of individually typed and hand-bound works called "leaflets" or "florilegia" circulate among the sectarians. Ranging in size from a few to a few score and even a few hundred pages, they contain religio-philosophic, religio-journalistic, and religio-artistic texts in the form of sermons, instructions, manifestos, essays, treatises, monographs, legends, proverbs, letters, reports, etc. This literary exchange of information is at least as important as direct oral communication in bind-ing the sectarians together; they are united more by their theoretical interests than by any shared ritual practices, which fade into the background under these conditions. These features justify the introduction of the concept of *bookish* sectarianism into the theory of atheism.

The interpretation of neo-sectarian texts is complicated by their unexpectedly *parodic* quality. It is not always possible to determine whether a word is being used in its plain sense or as some sort of prank or wisecrack. Some incongruity is always slipping in between the plain sense of a word and its religious sense. Can one take seriously, for example, an "Instruction on the Exchange of Glances"? Is it supposed to be put into practice, or is it a parody of a description of a ritual? Or again: "The ingestion of food is an act of resignation and obeisance before destiny." Should this be taken as a precept or a joke?

It is impossible to answer these questions categorically. Elements of self-parody and grotesquerie are constantly being introduced by neo-sectarians into the very substance of their religious worldview, as evidenced by, among other things, their widely used "citatory" style of preaching. Where a preacher would normally use citations from the Holy Scriptures or other venerable sources, neo-sectarian preachers often use citations from their own compositions, attributing them to someone else in order to make them "authoritative." "Everything spoken," they say, "is only a citation, while the authentic, original 'I' is present only in silence." This motif of citatority and parody is all the more salient in their literary texts, since "the text continues speaking while its author has already fallen silent or is saying something else" (V. Z., "The Silent Word"). For the neo-sectarians, this citatority and parody is a method of exposing the presence of another, a silent "Subject," i.e., the "Creator" himself, who "is silent on our lips" and puts all words about himself into quotation marks. Thus Christ, while not denying the words of Pilate, merely added, "Those are your words," thus transforming a speech about himself, that is, about "God," into a citation.

Thus, in neo-sectarianism we find the novel phenomenon of *religious humor,* never before included in this field of research. Indeed, traditional sectarianism is dead serious and gives an extremely solemn and exalted character to all its expressions. It is precisely the novel parodical quality of many neo-sectarian texts that has delayed recognition of the complete seriousness and peculiar danger of its religious content. "Religion as object is parodied, so that the Subject of religion Itself may reveal Itself. The sermon is parodied and turned into an object so that the Subject of the sermon may Itself be expressed. . . . For false seriousness is killed by parody, false subjectivity by citation. Every word is but a parody of the Word. Every citation is but a parody of the original authoritative source. . . . Every word leads us to the Word, while simultaneously distancing us from it. Thus arises the tension between seriousness and parody in the new theology." This is the explanation of the nature of religious humor given by one of its adepts and theoreticians, V. N., in his work "The Mystery of Laughter."

It is this element of seriousness in parody that was so profoundly underestimated by the first observers of this phenomenon, who noticed, but could not account for, a certain strange style in wide use especially among sectarians of the younger generation—a habit of sanctifying everyday things while profaning and mocking sanctity itself. Scientific atheism, in its current state of development, must considerably deepen its awareness of this contradictory, ambiguous feature of neo-sectarianism and master its double, "playful" style, based on the polysemous character of words, the "flickering" of plain and metaphorical meanings, and a jocular coarseness in the choice of symbols and similes.[1]

One must note that the new sectarianism, while sharply opposed to the "traditional religions," is on the whole fairly "tolerant" toward atheism, sometimes even characterizing itself as "creative atheism." Scientific atheism, according to the new sectarians, simply denies the existence of God, while creative atheism goes much further, asserting and sanctifying the positive values of being. In this sense, creative atheism is closer, as it were, to the original revelation of the creator-God than are the traditional religions, which turn it into a petrified image and thus fall into idol-worship. According to the new sectarians, "God" is much higher than any image of, or belief in, God—He explodes them all from within, as if demanding from true believers a constant creative denial of their own faith, an "atheism in the name of God."

There are many paradoxes in the sectarian ideology that would amaze an old-fashioned religious believer, but these paradoxes should come as no surprise to atheists. They are simply the paradoxes of religion in a godless age, of religion forced to adapt to scientific materialism, to which it remains hostile even when trying to speak its language. The sectarians are constantly claiming that their religion acknowledges the validity of materialism, that it is far closer to materialism than to idealism or spiritualism—since, as they put it, God sanctified the flesh by creating man in the flesh. The language in which the sectarians speak and write actually has little in common with the idealistic, abstract, high-flown, grandiloquent language used by the mystics and spiritualists of former ages. The neo-sectarians often speak of "low" matters, using as "theological" terms such concepts as "thing," "blood," "earth," "liquid," "solid," "surface," "roughness," etc. (By their definition, for example, "roughness" is "the secret Logos of a thing, transformed into a rustling that is transmitted to us by touch.")

According to the sectarians, "only materialistic language can reveal religious truth, only in the language of the world can we speak of God" (N. V., "Language in Search of the Word"). If the world was created by God, this means that its whole order—the sky, separated from the earth; the dry land, separated from the water; everything, separated from everything else—all this not only speaks of God, but is itself spoken by Him: all things in the world are "words of God," and to theologize means to speak the language of things. Accordingly, atheism too, by speaking about things without any mention of God, expresses God's own will to "self-revelation," since He never wanted to present Himself to the world as a separate and alien being, but appeared from the beginning in the Logos of created things and thus in the Logos of the begotten flesh (the "creature world" and the "Son of Man"). In the sectarians' view, atheism is the rejection of faith for the sake of Faith, of god for the sake of God: while the atheists themselves see only the "negative" moment of their "idol-smashing," the business of the sectarians is to bring to light the subsequent, "positive" moment: to find the "Living God" through the rejection of dead, fictitious, otherworldly gods.

In the course of confidential interviews, the sectarians often tried to assure us that the atheism which we openly profess is itself a kind of faith, and in a certain sense even better than the Orthodox Church confession, more fully purified of naturalistic notions of a "particular divine being." To such sectarians, who reject the age-old religious dogmas in order to hide behind atheism, which is by nature foreign and hostile to them, one would like to say straight out: open churchgoers are more honest than you are. As Lenin put it, "A Catholic priest who seduces girls . . . is much less dangerous . . . than a priest without a cassock, a priest without crude religion, a priest of ideas and democracy who preaches the creation and establishment of a godlet."[2]

As for Marxist-Leninist atheism, to its great credit it has never followed the example of Voltairean and Feuerbachian atheism by clutching at religion or trying to pass itself off as a better religion than the former ones. The sectarians, on the other hand, have long been clutching at atheism, trying to present it as a kind of new faith. Engels wrote bitingly of such priests without cassocks: "Merely to save the word 're-ligion,' so dear to idealistic nostalgia, from vanishing from the language altogether, they include sexual love and the relations between the sexes under the rubric of 'religion.'"[3] In this same way, the sectarians, while discussing this or that concrete subject fully accessible to scientific understanding and even to ordinary consciousness, such as "cabbage soup," are constantly trying to drag their beloved notion of religion into it. Parisian reformers of the Louis Blanc stripe said to the communist followers of Marx and Engels: "So, atheism is your religion!"[4] Today's sectarians, parroting social-reformism, tell us more or less the same thing; to which we respond: "No, it's you who take a man without religion for some sort of monster; but to us it is obvious that you are prepared to give your blessing even to the consistent atheism that rejects you." Indeed, the more completely religion is defeated, the more desperately it tries to "hitch up" with atheism, to present atheism's conscious rejection of God as the unconscious suggestion of a new and purified faith.

An important feature of the new sectarianism is its orientation to everyday reality. Whereas the religious and mystical doctrines of the past emphasized in every way their rejection of "worldly" life, the sectarianism of our time, adapting itself to today's needs, asserts that there is in principle no line of demarcation between religious experience and everyday experience. Their subjects coincide: home, work, children, nature—the only difference is the degree of "intensity." Religious experience ascribes an absolute dimension to every concrete thing in everyday experience; it relates every one to the One. If only we go about it with enough intensity, even while living in ordinary conditions and occupied with everyday matters, we are realizing the entire fullness of "religious service."

This position is expedient for the sectarians because it allows them to attract many people who have no interest in changing their habitual way of life. The sectarians say to them: "Bring religion into your home, let it sanctify your daily life, your relations with near and dear ones. You don't have to change anything—just deepen your existence down to its foundations." And so it comes about that someone frying fish in the kitchen or staring out the window from pure boredom suddenly begins to feel the "significance" of his own existence. He becomes a "Foodnik" or some sort of "Fenestrian"—indeed, the latest sects are perfectly capable of taking anything imaginable for a newly discovered "Absolute" or the revelation of a new faith. This is the source of all those numerous "Domesticans," "Sacripathologists," "Thingwrights" —each of them finds its own narrow sector of reality and immediately sets up its own little sect. Thus the world becomes "sectified," split up into sects, instead of being lived in all its fullness, in the consciousness of one's own personal participation in the world as a whole.

Indeed, the very term "sect" is not always appropriate to the religious groups in question. Only occasionally do they establish a definite rule of religious life in common or reach that point of organizational cohesion that would permit one to define them unambiguously as sects. The sectarians themselves, incidentally, almost never use this term; they prefer to speak of a "doctrine," a "faith," a "direction," an "agreement," a "position," or a "version." And from the whole varie-gated scene of contemporary beliefs, it is indeed worth highlighting precisely those that could be called versions, in contradistinction to ac-tual sects. A version is a much vaguer, more indefinite grouping of be-lievers than a sect. It is a unique religious model constructed by its own theorist or propagandist, less a real than an ideal community of believers, who may not even be aware of it.

The Helping Hands are a good example of a "versionary," as op-posed to a properly sectarian, movement. They are not united by any organization; on the contrary, they prefer an isolated and "accidental" kind of activity. But the Helping Hands have their own "doctrine" and their own theoreticians, who note in certain people such general signs of religio-moral self-consciousness as the striving to bring unobtrusive aid to one's neighbors, to facilitate or hasten certain natural or social processes while keeping their own activity invisible, "to do good on the sly" (they are also known as "reverse thieves," with a view to the secret, anonymous manner in which they perform their good deeds). These features permit us to identify the Helping Hands as a version, a sectarian direction without the marks of an actual sect in the sense of a religious community with special, established rituals.

It must be noted that a significant part of the contemporary sectar-ian movement consists not of sects in the strict sense but of versions, where the believers are united not so much by horizontal social con-nections as "by the vertical"—by a type of religious worldview directed "above," to "heaven." These are not actually functioning organizations or collectives, but intellectual-spiritual communities consisting of soli-tary individuals. Nonetheless, in the name of these "many solitaries," all sorts of "thinkers" and "spokesmen" come forth, creating the illu-sion of a closer cohesion among believers than is really the case. This is a sort of "fictive sectarianism," an ideal construction, to which in re-ality there corresponds a certain number of individuals holding simi-lar religious convictions. But experience shows that "no sacred space remains empty": wherever we find certain worldviews in embryonic form today, tomorrow we may find genuine sectarian groups—unless the necessary battle of ideas is waged against them from the very beginning.

It is important to realize that ideas have just as objective an existence in a given society as social roles. One and the same person can appear not only in various social roles ("father," "husband," "shopper," "professor," "deputy") but also as the holder of various ideas. A scholar devoted to the principles of objective research may turn out to be a believer. In a strange way, scientific materialism can consort with mysticism, membership in one sect with participation in another. Such "polyvalency" is characteristic of the worldview of some representatives of the contemporary intelligentsia, including the neo-sectarians. For instance, there is nothing incredible about one and the same person being both a "Foodnik" and an "Arkist": such cases of double and even triple sect membership occur quite often.

In order to determine the reliability of statistics on the numbers of people involved in the various sects and quasi-sects or versions, we need concrete sociological and demographic research. However, it is also possible to carry out a non-sociological description of the sects, describing them instead as elements of the ideological situation or particles of the mental or spiritual field. Sociologically, it matters whether a given position is represented by a single person or by a million; but ideological description neutralizes this difference.

A position taken by a solitary individual is a caprice, a fantasy, an impulse of genius or lunacy; a position taken by millions is a class, a party, a front, a union. But the "form of the worldview" exists in itself, so that in different ages or in different countries one and the same position can belong either to the masses or to individuals. In the same way, one person may be affiliated with only one position or with many at once; at its extremes, this distinction gives rise to the personalities of the fanatic and the eclectic. All these distinctions, however, do not go to the ideological core of the positions themselves but only to their projections onto actuality. The relation of a position to the multiplicity of people is the social plane of ideology; the relation of a person to the multiplicity of positions, its psychological plane. The relation of the positions to one another is brought to light by ideological science proper, of which scientific atheism is a part. Since the term "ideology," meaning literally the "science of ideas," is at present applied to a particular system of ideas which can itself be an object of study, we might coin for the description of ideological positions, i.e. for the science of ideologies, a different term, e.g., ideography. It is precisely this ideography that forms the subject matter of the present manual: these ideological positions must be articulated and described before their social-demographic dimensions can be measured.

This is why it is so important to introduce into Marxist religiology, into the theory of scientific atheism, the concept of the version, i.e., a religious formation which is not yet a sect but is no longer just an abstract idea. The version is an element of the ideographical description of society, a religious position whose social dimension cannot yet be fixed, or is unstable in and of itself. A version has a social body, but in an amorphous condition—like an "embryo" or "larva"; the measurement of its quantitative parameters and organizational structure is superfluous within the framework of an ideographical study. A version, to repeat, is a collection of persons holding, independently of one another, certain common principles of religious behavior and self-consciousness. Among its members there are not necessarily any actual contacts, just a typological likeness.

One could say that a version is a special type of religious formation peculiar to socialist society, where the very atmosphere presents obstacles to the socialization of religious ties or the establishment of lasting contacts among believers. A version is an unstructured religious community based on a typological likeness of beliefs and doctrines. One of the great virtues of the socialist way of life is that it offers an environment hostile to sectarianism and thus prevents religion from becoming a social institution. From this situation emerges the complex task now confronting our propagandists: to react in a timely manner to attempts at an ideological foundation of religion, which in our time often replaces the actual practice of religion. The fact that religion now occurs principally in the ideological rather than the social sphere, in the form of religious doctrine rather than of ritual communities, puts the work of the propagandist and agitator in the vanguard of the struggle against religion.

Unfortunately, even in our times we must still heed the words of V. D. Bonch-Bruyevich, the brilliant early-twentieth-century student and critic of Russian sectarianism. In his report to the Second Congress of the RSDRP, entitled "Schism and Sectarianism in Russia," he wrote: "Even in the specialized literature on this question we continue to find a vast jumble of terms for the distinguishing marks of the sects, their doctrines, and even their very names."[5] Bonch-Bruyevich himself, under the guidance of V. I. Lenin, achieved extraordinary advances in the scientific classification of sects and the identification of their distinguishing marks in his *Materials for the History and Study of Russian Sectarianism.*[6] Although the historical conditions for the existence of sects in our country have undergone radical changes since his time, the methodological principles of Marxist religiology developed by Bonch-Bruyevich remain fundamental in contemporary atheistic work as well. In the first stage of research, special emphasis must be placed on the selection and organization of the material, as exemplified by Bonch-Bruyevich in his annotated collection of literary documents of the Dukhobor religious tradition.[7]

The goal of the present manual is to supply the materials needed by specialists in contemporary sectarianism. For this reason, it presents far more material from unpublished sources than is usually found in an ordinary manual. The most valuable of the archival documents are manuscript works whose authors are religious leaders and preachers. It is left to the reader to reach his own critical conclusions about the samples of sectarian thought and preaching presented here.

This manual presents information on seventeen sectarian groups never before described in the atheistic literature. The material is divided into six thematic sections, classified according to the common "substratum" (national-historical, lifestyle, literary, etc.) of the religious views of each group of sects. Each section is preceded by a short introductory essay that surveys the particular group of sects and offers methodological recommendations for their further analysis and critique.[8]

PART ONE
EVERYDAY SECTS

PREFACE

One of the peculiarities of the new sectarianism is its attempt to bring religion into everyday life, directly into the conduct of ordinary affairs. With the weakening influence of the Church and its traditional rites, believers have transferred their ritual needs to the mundane objects and processes of domestic life: the preparation of food, housekeeping chores, relations with family and friends. Having transferred their sense of the sacred to this sphere, they find in it something like a church. From the Church's point of view, of course, such creeds must be characterized as heresies, but from the point of view of scientific atheism, they are relatively innocuous varieties of the new sectarianism.

These people attribute an extraordinary significance, for example, to food preparation, practicing something like a division of the clean from the unclean, i.e., a certain kind of ritual purification. Indeed, they view eating itself as a religious act, a humble acceptance of food "from the Giver"—although it is evident to us that they are actually "giving" this food to themselves. Such people develop an altogether inappropriate solemn-pathetic attitude toward the most trivial things. They come to imagine that even a grain of sand contains something divine, something around which they can construct a whole ritual of praise, reverence, and sanctification. Or, in order to be "at one with their own creative being," they will spend months fashioning some mundane item that they could have easily bought in a store. Finally, they come to think of their homes not just as places of residence, but also as "spontaneous and unpremeditated shrines" in which the mystery of everyday life is celebrated. Every home is, as it were, an abode of "the joyful Divine Wisdom," an "inner sanctum, into which God distills the whole external world"—i.e., an image of the heavenly life beyond the grave.

It is easy to see that all these "theological" constructions are simply false and fly in the face of common sense. Among these sects, everything natural in human life is assigned a supernatural meaning that is entirely superfluous and can be disposed of quite easily. The most effective way of refuting the "Foodniks," "Domesticans," and "Thingwrights" is simply to demonstrate how unnecessary and unrealistic their theories are. Food is no more nourishing when eaten with "reverence." Wisdom lies not in attributing some sort of holiness to one's particular place of residence, but in dwelling in any residence with dignity and a good conscience, in a manner that is useful and brings joy to other people. Of course, the only way of releasing these "Everyday" sectarians from the narrow, isolated shell of their existence is to integrate them into the general circle of our community's concerns, into the accelerating pace of our social life.

FOODNIKS

Foodniks sanctify the very act of consuming food, and conduct theological inquiries into the usage patterns of various foodstuffs. For Foodniks, the whole sphere of food and drink is full of sacral significance; they exalt it into a ritual whose elements vary with the particulars of various dietary regimens.

When we eat, we display through the sheer materiality of this act the supreme ethical faculty of humility. All living beings require food, thus *ipso facto* acknowledging their dependence on the Provider, their own defectiveness and incompleteness. No one can exist on his own; everyone needs something more, something besides his own flesh; and this carnal need, strange as it may seem, is profoundly spiritual, drawing us beyond the limits of the flesh as such, in which we would be irretrievably mired if not for hunger. Hunger is the origin of spirituality, the primordial vulnerability of life, and the belly is the innate wound that teaches through suffering and prepares us for salvation, like a prototype of the cross. Hunger is the cross in the pit of our belly, crucified together with Him Who thirsted.

The expression of thirst and hunger in a living being can sometimes be repulsive, but even more repulsive is perfect, indifferent repletion. Man and beast alike are compelled to bow their heads in order to lift a morsel of food to their lips, to graze on a clump of grass—they are compelled by a natural inclination to bow at this moment before the Lord. (I. Z., "The Theology of Food")

Hunger is not just a physiological condition; it is an existential emptiness. Non-being has crept up on a man. He is free because he is hungry. He can nestle up to the source of Being—not by eating to satiety, but by acknowledging his insatiability. Hunger is a moral imperative: Humble yourself, for you are not your own; you are but a piece of a part, always longing for a bite from another piece, and never capable of repletion in this life. That is why we are enslaved by hunger: it forces us into dependence on earthly food. And that is why we are liberated by hunger: in its insatiability, it sharpens our thirst for the celestial food that truly satisfies.

Humility is nowhere more manifest than in the very posture of eating—with bowed head, as if in token of humiliation and gratitude. Note that Western people, better bred than we are, eat with erect posture, raising their spoons up high to their mouths—it's as if they stand above their food and condescend to its level, or rather, deign to permit it to ascend to their level. Here in Russia people eat like slaves, bending low over their plates, as if grovelling before their food. But the question is, *whose* slaves—the food's or the Foodgiver's? One cannot judge these people without grasping this point.

After eating, the warmth of grace spreads through the body —not just because it has been filled, but because it has received mercy, it has fulfilled the commandment of humility, it has prayed through each life-giving particle it has ingested. Prayer is the direct disposition of oneself before the Lord to receive His gifts into one's soul and body: "I am at your mercy, I take you. . . ."

This is how gluttony becomes transformed into supplication and prayer. "Give us this day our daily bread," cries every creature, acknowledging its inability to feed itself and bowing before the beneficence of its Creator. (A. Kh., "The Wisdom of Hunger")

Receiving hospitality is almost the same thing as receiving alms. That is why, when you are seated at a table where guests are being served by their host, you feel as if you are at the gates of a church. . . . It does not matter who is offering the bread to whom, who is richer and who poorer: the offering itself is blessed both in the giving and in the receiving. Blessed is the wealth of the host who feeds, blessed the poverty of the guest who is fed. . . .

Honor your host, for he is in the image of your Father, who shared His flesh with you. Honor your guest, for he is in the image of your Son, who feeds on your flesh. There is equal grace in being a guest and being a host. It is holy to give food and holy to receive it; the giver is the brother of the receiver. . . . He who offers food takes upon himself the spirit of the Father; he who receives it, the spirit of the Son; and between them is the Holy Spirit, breaking bread in the unity of the Trinity. . . . (B. Ts., "The Sacrament of Hospitality")

Any act of eating, and not only the eating of holy bread, is itself holy, for when we eat, we are relying on the mercy of the giver and on Him Who gives to the giver himself. In the act of eating, everyone shows his neighbor his weakness; that is why this act is considered shameful in certain non-Christian communities. The custom requiring that eating be done in solitude allows people to turn away from each other in repugnance at their dependence on food. But we are called to share our weakness and shame with our neighbors. Those who eat together are united by the weakness they involuntarily display. From this arises the current of spiritual warmth at table, the brotherhood of those who kneel at the same fount in sharing their food, and the gratitude of all in response to the mercy of the One.

This is the gift of bread, the most vital need. At table it is clearly revealed to a man that his own flesh is itself a gift: his soul hungered after incarnation, and Someone has fed his soul flesh. Bread, taken as hospitality, is the image of the breath of life, received as a gift from the Lord. (Yu. A., "Spiritual Rules for Behavior at Table")

The Foodniks claim that the most important events of human religious history took place through food.

It was through food that sin arose—from the tree of the knowledge of good and evil. And it is through food that redemption comes—from the tree of the cross, through the blood and flesh of Christ. The promise by which Satan deceived Adam, "Eat and you shall not die," was fulfilled in the Son of God, whose flesh we eat and whose blood we drink. . . .

Yet again in our own time, mankind has fallen into sin through the temptation of food, sating himself on it so as to forget its Creator. . . . It was no accident that a high priest of the pagan Temple of Food instituted the rite of cannibalism among men. This was a blow directed against the Foodgiver, in order to seize this gift from God's hands. Food itself was proclaimed to be the God before whom man bows and serves. Hunger was proclaimed man's first and holiest need, the need by whose satisfaction man would be liberated from God. All of history came to be regarded as the history of man's procuring of food, the changes in the ways and means of food production. It was said that before he could think and believe, a man must have first eaten and drunk, must have reproduced his own flesh. This theory first arose in Foodnik circles, but later gradually took on the character of pagan food-idol-atry. . . . What we need is a philosophy that, while beginning from hunger, would arrive not at the idolatry of the material, but at the self-sacrificial beneficence of the maternal, the universal womb that conceives the human child from the Father and nurses it at the breast of the earth.

. . . Food is holy not because it satisfies man's flesh but, first and foremost, because it intensifies that spiritual thirst which can be slaked only by the fruits of the Tree of Life; and second, because in eating, man assimilates to his flesh the low, unspiritual plant and animal world and exalts it by transforming it into the nutritive elements of his developing mind and free soul. Through food, man humanizes external nature and simultaneously transcends the human in himself, striving to satisfy his highest needs.

Starting from the fundamental fact of hunger, some arrive at the fetishism of food, while others arrive at the worship of the Foodgiver. Christianity and materialism have a common starting point: "Give us this day our daily bread." But from here, one takes the high road, the other the low road. In food, the risk of the fall coincides with the hope of salvation. . . . Man is vile in his greed, but at the same time he is equipped for this thirst that nothing can satisfy—in his quest for food he both robs his neighbor and offers up his prayers. It is hunger that brings him into this life, proclaiming itself in the cries of the newborn. It is hunger that leads him on toward the other life, for the flesh is sated with the delicacies of this world, while the spirit keeps thirsting for more and more, for eternal life. . . .

If a man did not know hunger, he would not be dependent on the material world, but neither would he strive toward the spiritual world. Without hunger he would be satisfied and self-sufficient; it is hunger that makes him human by dividing his body into flesh and spirit. An animal can also be hungry, but only incompletely: its hunger is satisfiable. Man, in satisfying one hunger, feels the other more sharply. Man is the insatiable animal. (V. R., "On the Sweetest Worlds")

Among the Foodniks are several distinct groups of Dietarians, who sanctify not food in general but those particular varieties of food needed for the spiritual healing of individuals and entire nations. From their point of view, food is a more important factor than the condition of the arts and sciences in defining the health or illness of a society. Or rather, culture and its fundamental categories *are* the system of dietary rules, the elaboration of a society's relation to its food, the method of preparing and consuming it.

Culture, in its primary sense, is the cultivation of the soil for the gratification of the belly; or, according to an old but exact metaphor, it is the "feast of the spirit." While culture has developed in many spiritual directions over the millennia, its essence remains what it always was: the gratification of a refined taste, the quest for variety. Culture is the sequence of dishes served and removed at table: sweet following sour, boiled following raw, vegetable following meat. So tragedy is followed by comedy, a bucolic landscape is followed by a technocratic utopia, and predatory imperialism is served with a sauce of peaceful coexistence. . . . At the highest level, dietary preferences turn into the various types of worldview: the aesthetic worldview, honoring (sweet) beauty, or the ethical worldview, honoring (bitter) justice; the ecological (raw) or technocratic (cooked) worldview; the democratic (abundance of food) or the aristocratic (refinement of seasonings); the pacifist (vegetarian) or the activist, ranging all the way to the revolutionary (carnivorous, or even cannibalistic); the religious (fast days) or the secular (meat days); the conservative (canned goods) or the radical (root vegetables). . . . Culture is the table ritual of all mankind. (Yu. A., "Culture and Diet")

The Dietarians are subdivided into several groups, each of which offers its own principles of a healthy diet: we know of fasters, vegetarians, raw-eaters, Yin-eaters, Yang-eaters, salt-freeniks, sugar-freeniks, etc.—more than forty groups in all. Here are some extracts from the preface to *The Philosophy of Food,* an anthology certified by the Inter-confessional Soviet of Dietologists:

It is remarkable that great significance has been attributed to the choice of food in all religious systems: Hinduism, Buddhism, Judaism, Christianity. In the holy codices such as the Pentateuch or the Talmud or the Koran or the rules of Christian monasteries, enormous space is given to questions of the preparation and consumption of food. Clean and unclean food, kosher and tref, fast day and meat day, permitted and forbidden—this is the fundamental opposition separating the sacred world from the profane and defining the whole life of believers in opposition to the "pagans," the "goyim," the "unbelievers," the "uninitiated." Not only were food products classified by their ethico-hygienic qualities, but they also defined the sacred rhythm of human life by their intertwining with the structure of the religious calendar: feasts, fasts, and neutral days were distinguished by the permission or prohibition of one or another kind of food.

What accounts for the significance of the "lower," physiological levels of life for its highest levels, as realized in the religious self-consciousness of society? To bring man into connection with the other world, religion establishes the strictest limitations on his contacts with this earthly world. It selects such foodstuffs as stimulate man's animal energies, contribute to his noble behavior, liberate him from his material inclinations, tame his bestial instincts, avert the sin of murder and the torture of animals. It is precisely for this reason that food of animal origin is most often excluded from the diet. Or if it is used, as among the Jews, then the slaughter itself is conducted by a special method—instantaneous and painless, so that the animal's terror and suffering may not remain in its cells to be transmitted to man.

. . . Thus, there is a certain justification for the trite saying "You are what you eat." This formula is not the exclusive property of reductionist materialists; it could be affirmed, with certain reservations, by the ideologues of many confessions. True, it would sound a little different to say "You are what you don't eat," i.e., you become human through abstinence, through refusing certain kinds of food on the grounds of their being unclean or overstimulating. But in either case—that of extreme materialism or extreme spiritualism—the very being of man is defined through a system of dietary requirements and prohibitions. "Give us this day our daily bread" is the general truth of both Christianity and Marxist materialism. The difference, of course, is crucial: does man live by bread alone, or does he need spiritual "bread" as well? But bread, as the first object of eating, signifies man's original defectiveness, as well as his means of perfecting himself. Bread is the alphabet of human essence, a separate part of man's flesh, which must be gotten by the sweat of his brow from external nature. And if hunger sometimes turns him into a beast, it also distinguishes him from the beasts; for their hunger passes, while his does not.

. . . The primal holiness of food is also confirmed by contemporary mythological research. The language of foodstuffs is mankind's most ancient sign system, and lies at the foundation of all semiotic processes in culture. "Fried," "baked," "boiled," "steamed," "dried," "salted," etc.—the flavors and the methods of food preparation profoundly influenced men's ideas about the place of certain elements ("fire," "water," "air") in universal systems of classification, in differing types of ideologies and aesthetic states. Thus, "sweet" corresponds to the idyllic sense of the world, "bitter" to the tragic, "salty" to the satiric, and "sour" to the elegiac.

. . . All this allows us to assert that "Dietetics"—the combination of dietary prescriptions and the methods of selecting, preparing and consuming food—is the most important and dynamic component of human material and spiritual culture. . . . This is why "Dietology" is one of those disciplines without which it is impossible to give a scientifically exact definition of the phenomenon of man or to study the laws of his historical development.

In recent years, Dietology has come to the fore of the human sciences. Its methods are gaining a general philosophic acceptance and influencing the methodologies of the other sciences.

As sociology was the engine of general ideas in the humanities in the first half of the twentieth century, and linguistics in the second half, so by the beginning of the twenty-first century Dietology will very likely take its place as queen of the liberal arts and sciences. The convertibility between the substance of the world and the flesh of man is the central question, whose solution will have broad implications for both the human and the natural sciences. For food is precisely that in which substance and flesh converge; it is the symbol of their union, their wedding crown. Dietology is destined to become the essential foundation and confirmation of the anthropic principle, the assertion of man's interdependence with the physical parameters of the Universe, which has penetrated so deeply into contemporary science: "the Universe is such as it must be in order that man could arise and exist in it."

But this conclusion, which science has reached so paradoxically in spite of its own naturalistic prejudices, only repeats the divine commandment to the effect that the whole world was created for the use and sustenance of man. For the destiny of the organic world is to be food for man; the highest of the creatures was prefigured by the imprint of food in the very frame of the earth and all that lives in it. "And God said: Behold, I have given you every seed-bearing plant which is upon the face of all the earth, and every tree with seed in its fruit; you shall have them for food" (Gen. 1.29). Dietology is the central discipline linking the natural and the human sciences, uniting the human approach to the Universe with the cosmic approach to man himself. . . . (P. V., A. G., "Dietology: The Science of the Twenty-first Century," preface to the anthology *The Philosophy of Food*)

DOMESTICANS (Houseniks)

This is a religio-cultural order that preaches the values of domestic life and creatively multiplies them. The Order of Domesticians, as it is sometimes called in Western Europe, is widespread in many countries of the world, but the experience of their Russian brethren is generally considered to be particularly edifying because it was they who had to discover how to preserve hearth and home in the Age of Homelessness.

In those days, all life, action, and speech had taken to the streets, to the droning hives of the town squares. A brutal kind of social life brutally pursued a man to his very doorstep, trampling at his threshold and panting at his door. But the poor little apartments did not give up their secrets. They had taken treasuries of knowledge and faith into their safekeeping, transforming themselves over the decades into catacomb churches, museums, and laboratories. In this way they not only fulfilled their mission to the culture of our own country, but gave the whole world a model of the domestication of civilization. . . . Just as the great transition from the primitive era to civilization was marked by the domestication of wild animals, so the transition to the next era will be marked by the domestication of technology, industry, and politics. Once it was the state of nature that was wild and alien to civilized man; now it is the artificial environment, civilization itself, that has become a wilderness, and the next step of human development will be to adapt civilization more closely to man, to house it within the walls of his private life. . . . Nowhere has civilization shown such unbridled and rapacious qualities as in Russia, and nowhere else has domestic life undergone such a cruel test, taking upon itself the task of preserving the authentic values of civilization, which civilization itself had renounced. (L. N., "The Domestication of Animals, Ideas, and Machines")

In the works of the Domesticans, the home is presented as an ideally organized, personified space, adapted to the personality of its owner and reproducing his inner world.

My home is my second "I," a spatial image of my soul. Some souls are simple, open, loving; others are reserved, cold, haughty. Every type of soul has its own peculiar type of household arrangement. The street and the town square are the soul of the masses

. . . there no one is himself, we all get pushed onto the cross-roads of other people's views and opinions, and every "I" acts like "someone else." But the home is a space that has been appropriated, where even outsiders can "belong" to one another. The home is an "I" at the outer limits of its capacity, which can include others as well.

In the biblical Book of Proverbs, the entire world is represented as a House built by Divine Wisdom, the dwelling place of God Himself. "The Lord possessed me in the beginning of His way . . . before He made the earth or the fields, or the first of the dust of the world. . . . Wisdom has builded her house: she has hewn out her seven pillars" (Prov. 8.22, 26; 9.1). The house is prior to earth and fields, for these are already turned outward, flung open, exposed; they have left the house of Wisdom like prodigal daughters. . . . Thus our everyday house is built on the model of that original dwelling of Wisdom, as man himself is made in the image and likeness of God. (M. A., "The House and the Soul")

The proud singers of brilliant peaks and stormy waves—what contempt they pour on the domestic hearth! They jeer at the ordinary householder, absorbed in his daily life, they beat at his windows and proudly point out to him that he came from the street and really belongs to an unwalled world, "wide open to the raging of the winds." And only in a distant corner of our memory do we still preserve an image of the sage who, just like our ordinary householder, quietly keeps house and does not participate in the life of the street, but only contemplates it from his window. Is there any difference between our householder and this sage? Only one: the householder has never left his home, while the sage has returned to his, enriched by his knowledge of the world where he found nothing better than his own home, his own original place. Indeed the world as a whole—if only we stop drifting about its middle reaches and go straight to its ultimate thresholds and doors —the world as a whole is wisely built, cozy and homey. . . .

The householder has no history. The sage's history is departure and return. The home he has returned to is not just a cozy place: it is his lot in life. He has visualized everything in it from afar, with longing, and now everything in it has become a revelation. The householder has never left his home; the sage, by returning to his, has made it coextensive with the whole universe: even in the very arrangement of the furniture one can sense that Thought has been at work here, bringing home the distant times and spaces it has known. Outwardly, though, there is no way of distinguishing the householder from the sage, both bundled in their housecoats, holed up in their domestic fortresses. They have the same armchairs, the same taste in flowers and upholstery. The sage's journey is present in his home, but only the most attentive eye can occasionally catch a glimmer of it as the furniture of his soul slides over the furniture of his house. (V. N., "'I am a Householder . . .': The Wisdom of Homemaking in the Poetry of Pushkin")

In recent times, not only religio-ethical but also socio-technical theories have placed the home at the head of the coming world order. With the development of information systems, the home is taking on not only family life but social and productive functions as well. Those activities of labor, distribution, management, and communication that used to take people far away from home are now being moved into the home itself. Thus, the home is becoming an all-purpose institution: a factory, a library, a movie theatre, a school, an art gallery, a political club, a warehouse, a store. In the advanced countries, the electronic dwelling is already absorbing the entire system of municipal, national, and even planetary and cosmic communications: the walls are becoming more and more permeable, and, while still giving a comfortable sense of privacy, they let in everything one needs, thus providing a domestic model of the universe. In the words of an American Domestican-futurologist, "The extension of the electronic dwelling . . . points to a renaissance of the home as the central institution of the future, which will come to perform more and more economic, medical, educational, and social functions." (O. T., "The Third Wave")

Thus, the world is becoming more and more domestic: in the growth of technical equipment we can observe a higher providence, for it is said that "God will bring the orphans home" (Ps. 68.6). Fragmented humanity, broken up into millions of cocoons, each a martyr of isolation, is now finally being reunited with itself. But not, this time, on crowd-filled streets, but in a domestic seclusion suddenly become celebratory and sociable, populated with friends, thoughts, and books. Through domestic seclusion, God is bringing the orphans into the home of all mankind. (I. K., "The Holes-and-Corners Gospel")

Adam's expulsion from Paradise was the beginning of world history, so stern and unsparing to man. History has produced thorns and thistles in place of spiritual bread. Life on its stony soil has been naked and savage; sweat and blood has been the return on man's labor here. But an image of Eden is preserved in the mystery of the human habitation. Here the householder has built himself a paradise on the model of that paradise from which he was once expelled. Here everything warms and feeds him, indulges and protects him, is kind and merciful to him. The tree of the knowledge of good and evil pokes its twisted branches through windows and doors, pleading and urging: Open up, taste, try. The hiss of the many-headed serpent intrudes from the streets and squares: Come on out, lord of the world, test your riches, make trial of your power, and you will become as God. —No! Stop up your ears and close the shutters! Here in your own home the tree of life, your family tree, is growing, its boughs laden with the fruits of domestic wisdom and love. Love for wife and children, satisfaction with the little that life has given you, because it was given precisely to you. . . . This red fruit will not crumble in your hands into black rot, like the wicked gifts of knowledge and history: freedom, equality, the sweet rights of citizenship all turn, as the poet said, into the bitterness of "poisoned bread and polluted air" (Osip Mandelstam).

How mercifully God has arranged it! Everything you need is here, close by, and everything you don't need is there, far off.

The Devil wants it just the other way: he tries to shove you into the very heart of places where you have no business: the boss's office, a crowded meeting, a busy market. He likes to carry you off as far as he can from your own kith and kin, tearing you from your roots so that you begin to pine away. Your house, according to ancient tradition, is the paradisical tree of life, in whose very heart you live until you cross the threshold into the circles of hell. (G. G., "Theology of the Home")

Domesticans are not just stay-at-home old fogeys who would rather have a few friends over than go to a noisy party, and avoid traveling whenever they can. Domesticans take a constructive approach to domestic affairs—active housekeeping rather than passive staying home. They try to turn their homes into studios, museums, temples—that is, to bring into their own homes the whole complex of practical and artistic pursuits that are usually distributed among several different, narrowly functional buildings. Out there in the theatres and casinos, in the factories and fields, many subjects have one predicate: thousands of people are dancing or playing roulette, turning out machine parts or loading conveyors or following the plow. But here in the home, a single subject has many predicates: master and servant, son and father, worker and teacher, reader and maker. A home is an infinity turned back on itself, a synthesis of all the arts, sciences, trades, and faiths that are scattered abroad to the far corners of civilization. . . .

Domesticans profess the principle of "much in little." They try to squeeze into the small volume of their home as many spheres of knowledge and sociability as possible, centered in books and guests. They have special rites for the reception of guests. They gather around the kitchen table, in the warmth of their cooking, near their peaceful ovens, to celebrate the mystery of universal human brotherhood, inaccessible to the streets and squares. Brotherhood can be perfected only at the hearth of a single home. In ancient times it was the clan that gathered around the fire, while in present-day kitchens Domesticans perform the miracle of uniting guests unrelated by blood.

The warmth of the domestic hearth extends not only in space, where it attracts guests, but also in time, where it unites descendants with their ancestors. Domesticans venerate things that have come down to them by inheritance, and make special niches for them—the so-called penatangles, from the Latin name ("penates") for the household gods who (so unlike the mischievous Russian house-spirits!) were considered faithful guardians of the house. Here one may find an old-fashioned watch, a magnifying glass, a book that grandfather liked to read. . . . Thus the Domesticans have revived the ancient tradition of honoring the household gods—not as allegorical statues, but as actual things that have been of service to the house and can transmit the warmth of love, sincerity, and mutual understanding from one generation to the next. A home, according to the Domesticans, is a nexus of various times and spaces, a meeting place of near and distant ones, of the living and the dead, where all belong to each other.

Domesticans prefer to homeschool their children. They rarely take membership in libraries, preferring to keep all necessary books at hand in their own homes. If conditions permit, they hang pictures, keep a piano, and set aside space for games, an aquarium and a little herbarium. . . . In a word, the home becomes a refuge for that authentic culture which has been expelled from mass society. Such is the law of development of a world civilization that brings together its various professions, interests, and worldviews in the warmth of the domestic hearth. . . . Culture at its height was always created in narrow circles, on noblemen's estates—under the domestic roof and not under a circus tent with hungry crowds panting after bread and spectacles. Culture has come to pine for domesticity. It is weary of the coldness of cosmic space, social alienation and mass solidarity, avant-garde enthusiasm and modernistic tragedy, collectivistic heroics and private irony. It needs a home—not the external, mechanical solidarity of the crowd, but the clan-closeness of the family. The move of culture into kitchen and dacha, apartment and room, signals the era of the Second Domestication. (I. M., "A Course in World Housekeeping")

THINGWRIGHTS

The Thingwrights are a community of people who honor and make things. They preach a "docile" attitude toward the world of everyday objects, claiming that this world has a redemptive meaning for the human soul. They have various names for their doctrine: thing-wisdom, thing-love, thing-sanctification, thing-making.

The teachings of the Thingwrights are quite varied. Some, arguing that things are superior to mere signs, call for a complete renovation of culture, a wholesale replacement of signs by things. In the view of this group, such a thoroughly reified culture would be more whole and perfect. Others note that since the world of things is innocent of malice, passion, or greed, it is like a monastery, or heaven itself; these Thingwrights summon mankind to purify itself of the sins of selfishness and violence and draw near to the pure, innocent being of things. A third group are devotees of a special discipline or art of touch, a method of "sensory detox" that begins from the corporeality of things and gradually ascends to their immaterial essence. A fourth group spend all their time making common household objects, in the hope of eventually becoming like God, who created everything. As they put it, they want to live "not in someone else's world, but in a world created by themselves." A fifth group conducts special rites of "sanctification of the things," bowing down to them in prayer and claiming to discern in them the faint outlines of the image and likeness of God. There is no hard and fast line between these various forms of thing-worship, and the same people can participate in several of them; it is just a matter of different "specializations" within a single sectarian school. For clarity of exposition, the following fragments of Thingwright texts are ordered according to the themes outlined above.

OVERCOMING SIGNIFICANCE: All words have always turned out to be lies. The loftiest ideas have always deceived us and reduced us to the level of animals. . . . What could be more solid and dependable than a thing grasped by a human hand? Of

course it's fragile, easy to break . . . like man himself. Everything
authentic is fragile. But it doesn't deceive you. It is what it is. It
doesn't refer to something else, it doesn't point to anything or
conceal anything or simulate anything, it doesn't play any tricks.
A thing is itself and nothing else. There's a saving self-identity
in it. . . .

It is customary to view culture as a semiotic system of signs
all referring to something else. A tree signifies growth. Snow signifies purity. Yellow signifies jealousy and passion; blue signifies
meekness and love. Concepts, terms, symbols, ideas, emblems
. . . Indeed, culture really *is* a system of references and surro-
gates, and that's why there's so much fraud in it. It teases, hood-
winks, and diddles us with a million bogus resemblances. Many
human souls fall into this diabolical trap of signification.

A thing is pure and even holy, for the idea in it is joined to
the matter in it not by some hint or sign, but by the fullness of
mutual interpenetration. A thing is closed upon itself and has
the crystal clarity of self-subsistence: it is what it signifies and it
signifies what it is. Things do not represent one another, but each
occupies its own unique place in time and space. . . . This particular tree growing at your window has fully absorbed the idea
of growth, the idea of life, the idea of the link between heaven
and earth. No abstract ideas are left over; they have all entered
into the very structure of the thing. . . . We are on the verge of
a great transfiguration, a return of significance back to the heart
of things. (V. I., "On the Last Things")

Signification is a form of continuous spiritual anxiety and tur-
moil, an endless relay race in which each thing in its incompleteness designates yet another thing. . . . Ultimately, our entire civilization is a bureaucracy where no one is responsible for
anything, and everyone points to someone else.

Bureaucracy is not a narrowly social but an ontological phenomenon; at its root is semiocracy, the power of signs over the
human soul—a soul that cannot find peace in the hustle and
bustle of intersignifying signs. This is the source of our contem-

porary semiomania: an obsessive search for some clear or even unclear signs, for hints, evidences, clues, conspiracies, webs of intrigue. . . . Contemporary man is poisoned by signification and incapable of accepting life among plain things.

Oh, if only just for once one could say that there is only what there is! It is things that present this long-awaited liberation, this fullness of peace and contemplation. A thing is a being justified in itself, sinless, just as the Lord created it. In the beginning, Adam lived in unity with the things around him, in a state of bethinging, i.e., a union of being with things. Then came separation. Once the being was torn out of things, it took on the emptiness of non-being. As for the things, they turned into mere clumps of matter, obstacles on man's path to himself; they grew deaf and dumb, with their meanings left behind in that mysterious garden behind the fence. . . . Somewhere "over there," in the place from which he was banished, where he longs to return . . .

Signification is the punishment for man's original sin. Man has been cut off from the fullness of things by a veil of apparitions—beckoning and unattainable, inviting and inaccessible. By finding his own self-subsistence, man asserts his inseparability from things. Bethinging means being with things in a single whole, where the thing is no further from a man than his own soul, and where he awaits immortal life together with it. (L. N., "The End of Semiocracy")

HEAVEN: We imagine heaven as some sort of incorporeal realm of spiritual light and so on. But this is just our earthly imagination working by the law of opposites. In reality, heaven is purely corporeal. It is a world without meanings. Everything that was a meaning here becomes a thing there. There everything is at rest in itself, with no urges and impulses, none of this restless straining of ours from nowhere to nowhere. When things are in themselves, they are already in heaven. It's only we who, as Kant showed, cannot know the things-in-themselves. (R. U., "The Heaven of Things")

It is a mistake to think that the real world, or the kingdom beyond the grave, consists of incorporeal beings. No, it consists of things—those very things that appear in this world as conventional signs or handy tools. When a thing is only partially visible, it is mistaken for a sign of something absent. But as soon as it comes into full sight, the significance goes out of it. Smoke coming from the chimney, or a fire seen through the window, is taken as a sign that someone is home. But when we ourselves are sitting in the house, warming ourselves and talking at the fireplace, the smoke and fire are no longer signs; they are just what they are, an aroma and a warmth, the real medium of existence. But we have not yet entered into the fullness of being, and that is why we are surrounded by signs on all sides. Signs are incomplete things protruding into our dimension as mere points, linear fragments, plane projections. But when a sign is wholly situated in the ideal space proper to it, it becomes a thing once more. In the truth of being, a picture becomes one with what it represents. In a sign, being is split up into the material and the ideal, the signifying and the signified; but in a thing it comes into harmony with itself. The archetype of the higher worlds is not ideas, thoughts, dreams, fantasies, but just plain things, which enable us to conceive the extent of those other worlds, their tranquil fullness of meaning. (M. N., "Prophetic Things")

THE ART OF TOUCH: Things ought to be made by hand, to bear the stamp of man, to absorb his warmth. This is the only way they can join the ranks of the integral things of which signs are merely one-dimensional projections. A thing ought to exude its meaning not abstractly but palpably, just as it exudes warmth or an aroma. The feel of a thing in the hand should be like a friendly squeeze. . . . It's no accident that our times have seen the birth of a new kind of art that addresses the sense of touch. The works of this art are specially made to be enjoyed by touch alone, in darkness and silence; for the "toucher" (cf. "spectator," "listener"), the surface of a thing becomes an object of the most subtle experiences, the arena of an artistic quest. "Oh if we could recover the shame of sighted fingers / and the bulging joy of recognition" (O. Mandelstam).[9] Our tactile art is a response to this poetic yearning. . . .

Whereas the spectator and the listener are dealing with projections or symbols of things, the toucher is dealing with the thing itself, a continuation, as it were, of his own hand and body. The visual and auditory senses are overly concerned with signs; they are too intellectual and ideological, always looking for the truth somewhere beyond the things, rather than in the things themselves. Sight and hearing are subject to illusions—it's common enough to "have visions" or "hear voices"—but the tactile sense doesn't lie; it touches the very reality of things. After all, touch is not the perception of a conventional signal far from its source, like light rays or sound waves; touch is "direct access" and even assimilation: flesh with flesh, like with like. The apostle Thomas didn't trust his own eyes and ears, but insisted on touching the flesh of the risen Christ with his fingers—for which he received the Teacher's blessing. Faith is like the sense of touch, groping for what can really be trusted. . . .

This is why we are learning to sense things in the dark, like blind men developing their capacity for spiritual sight. A thing submerged in darkness begins emitting a spiritual light that can be sensed by touch. This is the basis of the Thingwrights' new art form, "sculpture-in-the-dark," or tactile sculpture. No one has ever seen these sculptures, which are submerged in the permanent darkness of underground exhibition halls. Only the sculptor, perhaps, in a moment of weakness or spiritual exhaustion, may have allowed himself a peek at the work of his own hands, a work designed to be sensed by touch alone. For all we know, the visible form of these statues may be ugly, even hideous. But how much they express to sensitive fingers ranging over their delicate tendrils and subtle ligatures, probing all their poetry of invisible and undissembling beauty, the immediacy of their continuity with our own hands, our own bodies! Sculpture-in-the-dark summons forth the deepest artistic attention not to the mere signs of being, but to being as such, in all the purity of its presence. (R. A., "The Twelfth Muse: On the Art of Touch")

We have visual and auditory arts, as well as applied arts of taste and smell (gastronomy, perfumery). But the foundations of the tactile arts have not yet been laid. Only in the single sphere of the amatory caress have the laws of touch been worked out, in ancient treatises like the *Kama Sutra*. But why does touch have to be connected only with lust, with passion? Couldn't it just as well be an instrument of sobriety, of sensing the pure form of things? Sobriety is the perception of a boundary, the capacity of distinguishing one thing from another. The mind gets drunk when it plunges into the dark, deceptive depth of things; touch sobers it up by adhering strictly to the surface, probing the boundaries of things, ascertaining their separateness and impermeability.

Religious texts speak of touch as contact with something sacred, the body or clothing of another person. But human beings are too weak to touch someone else's body without falling into the temptation of sinful thoughts. Such contact evokes either undue revulsion and disgust or undue attraction and lust. This is why people who are not yet spiritually tempered must cultivate the art of sobriety by touching inanimate things.

After long practice in perfecting the sense of touch, one begins to feel on the surface of things everything that is inside them. Eventually, one comes to feel completely intangible things, and in the darkness where this occurs, an immaterial light begins to glimmer through the heat. It is precisely through the sense of touch, the most sensitive of the senses, that sensation itself dissolves. It is precisely through things, the most corporeal of phenomena, that corporeality itself dissolves. This is why perfect sobriety can be achieved only through the art of touch. (N. I., "The Fifth Way")

THING-MAKING: Making things with one's own hands is one of the paths to holiness, to knowledge of God. It was the path of many Egyptian monks, who practiced such crafts as basket weaving. This path leads to the experience of bethinging, where the making of a thing becomes an act of internal making. . . . A thing is our nearest "it"; it unites my "I" with the divine "Thou." This is the clearest way of grasping the mystery of the Three that are One: man—thing—God. Without the thing, we would be missing the essential third link, equidistant from God and man. . . .

A thing into which I have put my labor becomes my future "I," a particle of that new flesh in which I am to be resurrected. Thing-making is the pathway to eternity. I enter into a thing and become lost in it until I finish it. Then I find myself in it yet again, but transformed: I see a glow of meaning that came from me, or rather, came through me and was incarnated in the thing. My will, my design is now within it, and it now gives me a holy joy, a triumphant feeling—something incomparably greater than what I put into it. (G. R., "Images of Things in the Lives of the Saints")

There are three main divisions of the study of things. First, things as material objects are studied in the natural sciences—physics, chemistry, etc. Next, things as signs or symbols, bearers of conventional meanings, are studied in semiotics and aesthetics. Finally, things as beings valued for themselves, as singularities that cannot be reduced either to matter or to ideas, are studied in Realogy. Realogy grasps a thing by ascending from its abstract definition to its concrete being, as to the crown of creation—to *this* unique, unrepeatable thing, as singular as the Creator Himself. . . . Alongside this theoretical discipline, there is also Reapraxis —the experience of spiritual thing-making, or spiritual development through things. . . .

Thing-making is by no means the same as artistic creation. A made thing is intended not for contemplation but for use. Thing-makers use the things they make. When they go on a trip, they take handmade leather briefcases, cardboard folders, ceramic cups, knives in wooden holders. These things need not be especially elegant or aesthetically refined; the point of them is to be their owner's property in the most intimate possible way. The owner owns such a thing not as something alien, something impersonally available, but as something in which he himself abides and has his being. When you touch such a thing, it is like touching the warm hand of the owner himself.

Unlike artists, Thingwrights never sell their things; they only give them as gifts, "hitch them to another's being." Since a thing made as a work of art is to some degree a sign, it can be exchanged for monetary signs. Its being is conventional; its exhibition to spectators displaces it from being itself. But a thing made as a thing is in principle not exchangeable. (M. N., "From Thing-knowing to Thing-making")

Thingwrights are wise: they learn not from books but from things. Thingwrights are laconic because they communicate not with people but with things. On the other hand, the things they make sound like words and read like books. (L. Y., "On Thing-Wisdom")

EXPERIMENTAL CONSECRATIONS

Thing-blessers conduct prayer meetings devoted to selected things. These strange rites are called "experimental consecrations." An "experimental consecration" can be carried out on any concrete object: a grain of sand, a toy, a twig, a forest path, or a park bench—anything that can be seen and named. Depending on the nature of the thing selected, the meeting may be held either in a home or outdoors in the open air. At the meeting, all the thing's attributes are detailed, and each of them is assigned a counterpart among the attributes of God, so that

an image of the One is discovered in a singular thing. It is not true that God is in everything that exists; this is the false doctrine of pantheism. God is not in everything, but in *each* thing, in the separateness and singularity of each thing. God is the One and Only, and every thing in its singularity is made in the image of God. (I. K., "The Thing as an Object of Divine Knowledge")

Here follows an abridged record of this ritual of "experimental consecration" as performed on a grain of sand:

Tiny and meek like all her sisters, blown about by the wind, scorched by the sun, poor speck, ragged mite. . . . We pity this poor bit of stuff to the point of tears. We caress her every nick and pimple. Can you feel the spirit of God in this grain of sand? Feel your way into her forsakenness, into her orphaned state: how she trembles in the wind and drifts about the world, a submissive vagabond, a humble waif. . . . The spirit of God is speaking with you from her presence: Answer!

. . . At this point someone will whisper a word of pity, someone else will suddenly feel a tear welling up, a third will begin to stroke the jagged little thing with a finger. And this utter concentration on a tiny piece of matter, this penetration of all the senses into the world of a tiny trembling creature, will go on for a long time. Suddenly the little thing begins to glow with light; it turns white and enters like a needle into the hearts of all. "Holy! Holy!" they cry, circling round it. . . . Finally, when they return the grain of sand to the earth, they are penetrated by the same reverent feeling for the whole earth: composed of just such tiny grains of sand as this one, yet bearing in itself all of God's creation.

. . . Much, much more takes place at these meetings, but in the absence of the grain of sand itself, they would sound unbelievable. But you, brothers in the Almighty Father and in the meek Son—do not doubt that a bit of universal brotherhood is interwoven into every thing, even the tiniest. Take it into your company, consecrate it with your friendship; it in turn will show you its soul, a child of God like you. Whenever you enter into a particle of His wisdom, your mind may

> see the stamp of majesty,
> the trace of wisdom grand
> in a worm, a leaf, an atom-cloud,
> in a tiny grain of sand.
>   (words of the poet Karamzin)[10]

But then—return this little item to its own surroundings. Let your reverence extend to them as well, in a new feeling of brotherhood with one of God's lesser creatures. ("Notes of a Wanderer among Faiths")

THE HOLINESS OF THINGS: Do not confuse Love of Things with materialism, a consumer's attitude to things. Love of Things sees in things not a source of material prosperity but a path of growth toward holiness. We love things not for the wealth they bring but for the poverty in which they abide. A thing can let itself be owned because it itself owns nothing. A thing, in this sense, is not an object that can be appropriated and consumed, but something that simply is, simply exists, and in whose existence we can participate by gazing into it, "feeling" our way into it. Things are currents of that pure being on whose shore we stand, hesitating to take the plunge. That is only for the strongest swimmers, for those who are ready to become as naked as the things themselves. For this one must renounce all that one has and become propertyless, like things. Although many are drawn toward wealth by things, things themselves are images of blessed poverty, the state of having nothing but yourself. . . . This is why we love things; this is what we learn from them: frailty, meekness, poverty of spirit. For some, things are the way to acquisitiveness and death; for others, to humility and hope. Will you choose to own them, or will you choose rather to emulate them by owning nothing? (R. S., "Lust for Things or Love for Things?")

Let yourself feel this tiny heaven in which each thing obeys its creator from beginning to end. A thing never refuses a request, but at the same time it remains true to its calling: a teacup will never refuse anyone a cup of tea, but neither will it allow anyone to dry his hands on it. Man has not yet attained such faithfulness to his calling and such responsiveness to the world around him. He is hard on others and easy on himself, though he ought to be just the opposite: harder on himself and easier on others. From things he could learn the perfect art of combining infinite obedience to everyone who needs him with infinite devotion to the calling assigned him by his Creator. . . .

Things, like saints, freely give us everything they have and keep nothing for themselves. Naked and meek, they literally fulfill the commandment to "give away all that you have." Everything we have is things, while the things themselves have nothing, and give themselves away for nothing. By giving themselves freely into our possession, things teach us to have no possessions. . . .

"I am what I am." Couldn't each and every thing rightly apply to itself these words of God?[11] No one is so humble as things are, no one is so blessed as "these little ones"; for their blessedness, which man cannot attain, is that of selfless, possessionless being. The world of things is like a monastery immersed in patient silence; people pass through it like pilgrims, learning obedience. (M. E., "The Monastery Around Us")

PART TWO
PHILISTINE SECTS

PREFACE

The term "philistine" may be puzzling to believers. Since philistinism is an apathetic, stagnant, profane way of life, how can it be combined with "spirituality," that is, with religious faith? The point is that when religion starts losing ground in contemporary life, it can easily turn into that very "philistinism" that it had once so heatedly denounced. Let's say a man "fools around," cheats on his obligations, lets the fellows down at work; but still he wants to justify himself in his own eyes, and not just somehow-or-other, but in light of the loftiest considerations. So it turns out that he is not a cheat and a parasite but a "Foll"—something like a contemporary version of a Holy Fool. He purposely "plays the fool," making obstacles for the "godless" regime and its rational projects. He turns the usual understanding of things inside out, confuses and distorts information "absent-mindedly," because "the folly of this world is divine wisdom." No, Folls are not wreckers, as they would have been called in the thirties; they are "connivers," giving an opening to chaos everywhere, making not the slightest attempt to curb it.

It wasn't so long ago that the provinces did their best to imitate Moscow; but now Muscovites and other city people are trying to pass for provincials. One might say, "So what if fashion makes these zig-zags, especially among young people!" But here too we observe the same paradox, the same equivocation, as in the case of the Folls: the so-called Provs take it for a virtue to be poor in dress, poor in speech, poor in spirit. Instead of tattered tunics, the Holy Fools of our times appear in the streets in outsize caps, fishermen's boots, the whole getup of the provincial general store. And their behavior is not without a certain provocativeness: it's as if they are saying, "Our clothes are a mirror of your soul. Look upon your own drabness!" In the words of the proverb, it's hard to say where, in all this, humility crosses over into pride.

And now, into the arena (of history, no less!) file the "Greys." Yes, the Greys. In the past we've had plenty of whites, greens, browns, blacks . . . But apparently these are the first Greys. Without the least bit of shame, they declare that their own poverty of spirit, their passivity, their compliance, is the "sacrificial cup of redemption" that history must drink to the dregs before "history comes to an end." It's as if all history were one continuous liturgy in which they, the "passivists," take upon themselves the role of suffering for the sins of humanity and are "crucified together with Christ." By the logic of the Greys, it is not the heroes and champions but the drab philistines who express the spirit of history and raise it "to the rank of mystery," since "he who is defeated is always right." Such is this unprecedentedly frank theology of defeatism.

The Philistine sects must be distinguished from the Everyday sects. The latter profess values that can be acknowledged as universally human, although on such a low, material level (food, home, things) that it's only by a considerable stretch that they can be taken for "religious." "Philistines," on the other hand, profess anti-values, turning inside out everything that goes under the name of "plain human morality" (Marx). Therefore, the best critique of this "spiritualized" Philistinism is the appeal to those authentic values that are immediate and meaningful for all men: reason, courage, beauty, justice.

FOLLS

This is one of the most widespread sects. Its doctrine is generally known but little studied. In what follows, we will adduce extracts from the most reliable sources.

Folls are the Holy Fools of our time. Their "folly," however, consists not in breaking the conventional rules of behavior, but in following these rules with blissful nonchalance, since society has already turned them upside down. Folls differ from ordinary citizens only in their consciousness of the fatuity of the existing order and . . . their painstaking compliance with it. Unlike civic-minded citizens, Folls do not raise objections, do not take evasive action, do not struggle; instead, their suffocated spirit finds its release in stupidity—Folls fool around by the rules established by the fools. The system is so harsh and inhuman that only stupidity can give it a certain warmth, a semblance, at least, of humanity. . . . Still, stupidity is a gift of nature, and however society may try to argue it to its senses, it still retains its holy truth and purity. Any bit of consistency or method that tries to give stupid nature the slip eventually takes on the form of stupidity itself, thereby returning to its first principle. And in this form it gains admission to the human spirit, however utterly inadmissible it may be to reason. (P. Ya., "Methodology of Folly")

What are Folls, and how do they differ from fools? Folls are fools in fun. They find it convenient to play the role of fools, but they are not fools by nature.

Following the example of the Danish Prince Hamlet, Folls play the fool so as to bear more easily the yoke of being and to avoid, in part at least, being what they are obliged to be. You find such people in every office, every bureau, and every institution: dilettantes of their profession and professionals of stupidity, they are everywhere. Yet they are not fools; on the contrary, they are very much in their right minds. It's just that they have grasped the fundamental law of the upside-down world, which the upper classes have long refused to understand, while the lower classes simply cannot. Folls are people who have chosen folly as their specialty, and, along with it, such qualities as innocence and irresponsibility. Folls are the only people who can enter the System without coming unhinged from terror or going numb from boredom. For Folls everything is possible, because they are slightly out of control—just a jot, but of course this very "jot" is the key point in every art. At the proper moment a certain screw comes loose in these people, and the motor simply disengages. Thus they cannot be counted on, though there is no one else to count on. In certain historical periods the entire nation, in order to save itself, turns itself into just such a Foll. This is not because it is a foolish nation, but because it is a wise one. It doesn't want to be played like a flute. . . . (G. M., "On the Role of Foolheadedness in Our History")

The Folls have long been acting in concert, but their activity goes unnoticed because, first of all, there are so many of them, and secondly, their power lies precisely in the absence of any coordination in their actions. Thanks to their indefatigable activity, every reality turns into a phantom, and even the authoritarian regime turns into a sort of amusing joke. A Foll will generally do everything required by his job, but will leave something just a little underdone. He won't quite finish copying out the last figure, he won't quite take into account some chance circumstance, he won't quite report some ticklish fact. . . . None of his superiors can quite explain everything to him in full, and thus he himself just slightly underexplains things to his own subordinates. Thus a slight underintelligibility actually becomes the basis of the collective activities that gradually destroy the despotic reason of the collective itself.

Since the purpose of any particular activity is not entirely clear, it is carried out with a light spirit and a luminous smile. This luminosity of the obscure is communicated from one person to the next as the all-uniting warmth of mystery. Folls enjoy that atmosphere of slight absurdity in which activity is almost indistinguishable from inactivity or counteractivity. At every step there is some tiny muddle, some pleasant fuss. The accountant didn't explain something fully enough to the planner, the planner didn't lean hard enough on the supplier, and now, instead of the not-quite-necessary "motors," some not-quite-unnecessary "rotors" have been shipped to the warehouse. Still, everyone is trundling in the right direction, strictly by the hand of the clock, which is already showing five to five, which means—closing time, guys! Scandal arises only when clever people try to impose complete lucidity; but then they turn out to be outnumbered by the Folls, who, with their combined (though separate) powers (or rather, weaknesses), almost always win the day without anybody noticing it. Their life is somewhat dreamlike, for it flows according to the laws of sweet absurdity. . . . A Foll strives not to cross the boundary of the lightweight absurd, since the heavyweight absurd threatens to wake him up with a jolt. The difference between the lightweight absurd and the heavyweight absurd is quantitative: responsibility for the lightweight absurd is shared by many, while the heavyweight absurd falls on the shoulders of a single individual. . . .

A Foll, while following the rules of folly, nevertheless must not be foolish about it. One of the rules says: The quantity of folly increases from one Foll to the next by equal and modest increments. A Foll is not obliged to be smarter than others, but no more should he run to the opposite extreme: he should be just a jot stupider. If you are too stupid, the next fellow will seem almost clever—and that amounts to leaving your comrade in the lurch. (Z. Z., "The New Praise of Folly")

When reason is inhuman, stupidity comes to the defense of humanity. Folls are people who, because of their guileless and invincible simpleheartedness, are stupid with all their heart.

From this defect springs their indulgence toward the weak of this world. Folls exasperate the uninitiated, all those clients and petitioners who get annoyed by their disarray. Dissatisfied customers object that the bookkeeper didn't figure the sum right, the cashier didn't count it right, and the boss wasn't at his post. . . . But if one were to unleash on these grumblers a few more eager beavers who would always be at their post, always figuring accurately and counting down to the last penny, they would suffer even worse. The only salvation from the perfection of the system is the imperfection of its operators. The spirit of cleverness is a temptation in the wilderness; if it were a little stupider, maybe some life would force its way up through the dead sand, maybe all sorts of dewdrops and grass blades would start twinkling. . . . That's why Folls are so bewitching—they don't hide their own weaknesses and they forgive the weaknesses of others. (V. N., "The Dream of Reason")

Every weak spot in reason offers a foothold for faith. Thus these softhearted persons, who greet every absurdity with a warm smile, acknowledge their own blunders and indulge those of others. . . . No, they do not consciously believe in God. But then, consciousness is not required by faith. "I believe because it is absurd," cried one religious thinker. The Folls are a sect of absurdists, that is, believers. A steadfast abiding within the absurd, a willingness to be reconciled with it—is this not how the best religious qualities of the soul are formed? (G. S., "On the Psychological Roots of Religion")

PROVS

The Provs represent a "new lifestyle" based on deliberate provincialism. They claim that the Soviet way of life is deeply provincial in comparison with both the West and the East.

Our whole country is one big province. No matter how you look at it, we're just a huge backwoods. The European part is the backwoods of Europe, and the Siberian part is the backwoods of Asia. This is where everything cheap, lackluster, and dated trickles down and accumulates. The only thing we have given the world is the provincial worldview. (P. A., "Far from Paris")

The paradox of this philosophy of provincialism is that it was founded in the capital. The name of the group is based on an oxymoron: *The Moscow Provincials.* They preach a particular style of dress and behavior, called, in their characteristically modest-gaudy manner, "faded sparkle." They make special shopping expeditions to the provinces to buy their clothes directly in village general stores—felt clodhoppers, winter hats with protruding earflaps, side-fastening peasant shirts. . . .

It's not always easy to distinguish prov style from retro style, but as a general rule, "retro" is based on European models of past decades, while "prov" is based on contemporary domestic models. Provs wear only brand-new clothes, whose "fresh-off-the-needle" stiffness is supposed to call attention to the clunky design and unwieldy cut of these out-of-the-way styles. A broad-checked oatmeal-colored jacket of "Sunbeam" cloth, heavily scented with "Sparkle" cologne, is the height of prov chic. While the youth culture of the seventies was ruled by the principle of "extravagant penury"—expensive but threadbare clothes, rigged out with conspicuous patches and other signs of destitution—the Provs of the eighties have promoted exactly the opposite principle: "bargain-basement chic," marks of conventional prosperity that underline its vulgarity and tawdriness. . . .

In conversation, Provs employ ready-made bookish constructions drawn from the *Farmer's Almanac* and old numbers of the *Village Messenger.* They call attention to their ironic attitude to this literary jargon, but they cannot or will not do without it. (L. B., "Notes on Prov Style")

We really love the provincial life, and though we're ashamed of it, we know perfectly well that we can't escape it. We're surrounded by an ocean of second-rate goods—shapeless, colorless, and meaningless stuff! And just as some species of animals change their color to suit their surroundings, so we too adapt to our en-

vironment. But this is not passive conformism. We want our environment to recognize itself in our faces, perhaps to recoil in
disgust from its own likeness. We are forming a collective image
of the country, a mirror in which everyone can see himself: behind the times, scurrying about in rubber and straw accessories
in a lather to catch up. . . . It'll take generations to get the odor
of provincialism out of us, like the clothes your grandparents
put into mothballs. We are living sculptures fashioned by our
environment; the sight of us is calculated to ignite a blush of
shamed self-recognition.

Of course, we're far behind the times, and the in-crowd on
the Arbat look a lot more up-to-date. But aren't the provinces
always behind the capital? Some people like being the *avant-
garde,* but we are the *arrière-garde* of modernity, its hindmost ar-
mored rump. You can be sure that this many-headed beast will
retreat at the slightest sign of danger. It will shrink back into its
old felt boots and woolen coats. Indeed it has never come out of
them; just take a look at those stooped shoulders and shuffling
feet. . . . Take a sniff of that behind-the-stove smell, something
between cabbage soup and cobwebs. . . .

We used to try with all our might to look like Muscovites, but
this only made us look even more provincial. Now we've found
our style, and the smart set on the Arbat are already taking some
lessons from us. After all, Moscow itself is just a province writ
large, and we Provs remind her of the fact—we're her self-
appointed provincial conscience and consciousness. While the
provincials in the provinces try to look like Muscovites, we Provs
of Moscow try to look like provincials. This is how we wish to
express our affection for the provinces and our gratitude to them.
(P. U., "In the Moscow Backwater")

Beneath its unpretentious surface, prov style still has its mystical
or, if you prefer, religious core. I talked with a twenty-year-old
Prov wearing a corduroy cap and one of those brown jackets
with the forest-green collars. "We don't like the proud," he said.
"In these clothes I'm no better than anyone else. And why should

I stand out? Beauty is something that's 'elsewhere'; here, we've got homeliness to dress up in . . ."

For the Provs, the provinces are the fate of man after the Fall; with his dull face and lackluster clothes, he mimics the complexion of the earth he is condemned to work. This is why earth tones predominate in the aesthetic of prov style: muffled browns and greys, sometimes with a tinge of red or green ("mouldiness"). In the words of one of their songs, "We are the mould of the earth, we are the song of the mole. . . ."

For the Provs, the provinces are not just a collection of particular places; they're a whole world "on the outskirts," the abode of "godforsaken" humanity. In their view, the solar system is a province of our galaxy, and our galaxy is one of the most provincial provinces in the universe. As for Russia, she's on the outskirts of the outskirts. . . . Russia has a universal destiny precisely because of her provinciality.

Indeed humanity as a whole—abandoned by God for the last two thousand years, languishing in darkness and obscurity without revelations from higher worlds—isn't the human race itself out in the provinces of the spiritual world? Somewhere out "there," around God's throne, fires blaze and heavenly music sounds, and spiritual beings rush to meet one another in cascades of divine joy, in the games and songs of a ceremonious banquet. But only dull echoes of that celebration reach our Earth, as if from behind tightly closed doors. . . .

The provinces are the fate of our world. That is why it's here in Russia that we feel most deeply the mystical sense of the provinciality of the human race. (T. P., "The Mystique of the Provinces")

GREYS

The Greys insist on calling their sect a "party" and claim that this unknown party, invisible to the world, has won all the decisive battles of history. The combatants were whites and blacks, reds and greens—

but the victors were always the Greys. Their party has a special strategy that enables it to rule from the so-called open underground. This strategy, known as passivism, distinguishes them from the activists of all other parties.

> Those who seek victory always lose, while the winners are those who remain passive in defeat. Passivism itself is always and everywhere victorious. Our precept is: Don't struggle, don't resist, don't win! . . . Passivism is not entropy—it is not universal leveling, dissipation and heat death. It is the warmth of life. It preserves the energy spent by the activists. It is the eternal battery to which activists turn for energy. (G. L., "Heat Life or Heat Death?")

The Greys attach great importance to their emblem, the color grey, which, they say,

> speaks to the soul as expressively as the color of the sky on an overcast day. Neither pitch darkness nor blinding sunlight, but a monotone smoky greyness hangs over our life. "Well, so be it," we say to ourselves, giving up all hope of a nice day. And so it is. What would become of us if the world were strictly divided up into light and darkness, or broken up into bright, gaudy colors? Fortunately, our beloved color Grey invisibly wafts over everything, giving it a soft, melancholy tinge. It's capable of a slight gleam, a melting glimmer, like mother-of-pearl—but it gets absorbed in itself, preserving its dignified mystery. It soothes us and, like a sudden silence in the midst of a stormy quarrel, gives us the feeling of complete, unutterable truth.
> . . . Look around you, look at all the grey people, the grey, tired faces! Be grateful to them: this is the silence behind your words, the canvas behind your pictures. This is the foundation on which all thoughts and paints are applied. When you scrub down to this substratum, you find an even, gentle luminescence that will last for all eternity. All your flare-ups are momentary, while the luminescence of the grey faces is inextinguishable. If

there is eternal life, it is in these grey faces. At bottom, the world is like a grey day when the sun never comes out and the clouds never gather into a storm. That's why it is eternal. . . .

And since the light nonetheless did come into the darkness, and since the darkness nonetheless did not swallow up the light, what remains to us now except this pearl-grey, ash-grey, earth-grey, cloud-grey shade, in which light is mixed with darkness in such a way that both remain themselves? Sometimes you cannot even notice this color, because it's the element you breathe: it is your secret being. Just as you don't feel the air beating against your hands, so you do not see the greyness that embraces and caresses you. (M. P., "The Light of Our Life")

Other parties paint their banners red, green, blue. . . . But under all these paints there lives and breathes the color Grey. We expose it—simple and vital as bread, the color of the stuff itself. The idea of our grey banner coincides with its material base. Down with paints! A painted banner is a conventional sign; it conceals the truth of the grey stuff, which we expose. There has to be at least one party that speaks in the honest language of the things themselves, incapable of deceit. In the words of our poet, whose blood stains your banner: "Nowhere can you find a ground / Purer than the truth of the untouched canvas."[12] (R. V., "The Bare Banner")

Closely related to the party of the Greys are the Passivists, who take an even more subjectivist view of history and justify their nonactivity by appealing to linguistic and liturgical parallels. We will cite here an excerpt from their manifesto, which they call "The Passive Voice of History":

All active constructions in the course of history turn into passive ones. Those who are acted upon turn out to belong to history, while those who act turn out to be superfluous. Christ was crucified by the Romans. But the Romans were only extras in the sacred history of Christ. The genuine subject of history is not he who does it, but he to whom it is done. The passive is the voice of victory, not only morally but grammatically as well. All historical events revolve around the passive voice. He who was sentenced, crucified, and humiliated continues to act in history, while he who did the sentencing and crucifying turns out to be merely the object of a disdainful or maudlin curiosity. . . .

History is an endless sacrifice, a liturgy in which the bread of laborers and the blood of warriors is consumed. Those who bring the sacrifice make history, while those who consume it—those who imagine themselves the victors—are merely the communicants at this immense mass, where salvation is meted out to the repentant and eternal judgment to the proud. The victor consumes the holy offerings of the defeated and becomes a communicant of the invisible Temple that rises on their blood. Wherever there is suffering there is a place of communion, where the victor obediently accepts someone else's sacrifice. . . .

In this Temple of History an invisible service is getting under way at this very moment. The vanquished will appear on behalf of the victors, redeeming the victors' murdered souls with their own murdered bodies, healing and resurrecting them with their own wounds. When the victors finally confess their guilt, let them not say it was their will that prevailed. No, it was the impotence and vulnerability of their victims. For the strong are only shadows of the Light, which has summoned them to itself in order to suffer the darkness and dispel it. History is a round-the-clock liturgy at which the sacrifice of the Lord's flesh and blood is brought for the salvation of the world. The Passivist is the agent of history, understood as suffering and redemption. (G. P., "The Passive Voice of History")

PART THREE
NATIONALIST SECTS

PREFACE

These sects currently present the greatest dangers to our society. They feed the worst superstitions, promoting one nation at the expense of another, claiming to be the "god-bearing" nation. They summon the faithful either to convert the other nations or to annihilate the "faithless," the "aliens." From among the many nationalist sects, we have selected three typical ones which proclaim, respectively, the supreme messianic mission of the Russian, the Turkic, and the Khazar (Judaist) nations. It is noteworthy that some of the sectarians themselves emphasize the pagan cruelty, terror, and bloodthirstiness of these nations. The Bloodbrothers, for example, revere their native soil not for having raised up great sons—generals and writers, geniuses of art and science —but for having drunk a lot of blood; for "where there is blood," they say, "there is sanctity." They imply darkly that the greatest glory has been brought to our land by those who have poured the most blood on her—the tyrants and monsters of ages past. But this is not how our land has appeared to genuine patriots, even those who believed in the "divine mission" of Russia according to the conventions of their time. To them, our motherland appeared not as a "bloody font" but as a "distant glow" (Gogol).

Among the many peoples inhabiting our motherland are descendants of the troops who once invaded Russia under Khan Baty. Though scholars disagree on the historical role and significance of the Golden Horde in the destiny of our country, there is no place for the claim that the Horde "secretly subjugated Russian blood and Russian destiny." The Red Horde goes so far as to claim that the October Revolution and, in general, the victory of socialism in our country are the triumph of "the Horde, the nomadic spirit of the steppe" over the "peaceful Russian spirit of the immemorial forests." According to the members of the Red Horde, Lenin's facial features reveal him as "a new Genghis Khan, only in a cap rather than a turban." The Red Horde defends the Revolution, but strictly on national as opposed to class grounds. In its view, the Revolution is the triumph of the East over the West, and the Golden Horde, having survived "clandestinely" down to our time, has now simply repainted itself red. This view is reminiscent of the long-vanished notions of "Panmongolism" and "Scythianism," so prevalent among symbolists and populists in the Revolutionary years. But those lofty, romantic movements are a far cry from the religious fanaticism of the present-day Red Horde, which in all seriousness calls for the "Easternization" of Soviet society.

As for the "Khazarists," who claim that in ancient times our country was inhabited by bearers of the Jewish religion, their views are absolutely groundless. It is enough to point out the spurious character of the so-called "Testament of Svyatoslav," which was apparently composed in the late eighteenth or early nineteenth century in nationalistically-minded petit-bourgeois Jewish circles. According to this "testament" —whose authenticity has been refuted by the most competent historians—Prince Svyatoslav, after his invasion of Khazaria and the fall of the kaganate, fell gravely ill and saw a vision in which the kagan whom he had killed summoned him to convert all Russia to Judaism. When Svyatoslav recovered, he dictated his testament, with the stipulation that it be published only in the event of his failure to take Byzantium. As is well known, Svyatoslav never returned from that campaign but was killed on the way by Pecheneg tribesmen. According to one version, Svyatoslav's testament, in violation of his express desire, was hidden away and lay for long centuries under wraps of strictest secrecy.

Not until the era of Peter's oppression of the Orthodox Church was this document "leaked," with a view to weakening the Church's position and suggesting the idea of its "illegality." The very father of the "Christener of all Russia," according to the story, not only never intended to introduce Orthodoxy, but even took up arms against Byzantium after the Khazar kagan inspired him in his "veridical" dream. At present, it can be taken as a fact that this forgery was composed not at the beginning of the eighteenth century but much later, and not in circum-Petrine but in "circum-Hasidic" circles. Concrete historical facts and documentary evidence are the best methods of invalidating the prejudices of the nationalistic sects.

BLOODBROTHERS (Holybloods, Glorybloods)

This movement arose from the ritual of worshiping places where a lot of blood was spilt—great battlefields, mass graves. The Bloodbrotherhood, with its special interest not in the individual merits of the fallen but in the actual place of their burial, has always stood apart from the ordinary practice of honoring the dead. Bloodbrothers think the more blood a place has absorbed, the holier it is. Originally, rituals of this type were carried out within the framework of official functions: special brigades tracking soldiers lost in action, meetings of young communists with war veterans, the founding of military museums, etc.

Some scholars believe that the defining mark of the Bloodbrotherhood is the act of pronouncing a certain oath at places of bloodshed (including not only burial grounds but battlefields and sites of execution, shooting, and torture). The core of this oath is loyalty to the memory of the dead and readiness to shed one's own blood for them. But most scholars see the defining mark as the ritual shedding of one's own blood in confirmation of the oath, or even as a substitute for pronouncing it. The act of mixing a drop of one's own blood into the sea of bloodshed signifies "union with all those who lie in the grave" (N. A., "Our Red Banner").

It is noteworthy that there are no state symbols on the red banners of the Bloodbrothers—not even the hammer and sickle. "Plain blood, without regard to divisions and borders, flows through the world. The most ancient testament of all is the testament of the mingling of bloods" (L. V., "The Myth of Cain and Abel in the Historical Destiny of Mankind"). The Bloodbrothers' banners are plain red fields with a few drops of real blood, which show up as brownish spots. Everyone who enters the Bloodbrotherhood donates a drop of his own blood for a banner; this is the heart of their initiation rite.

The Bloodbrothers explain their symbols as expressions of so-called blood union:

> Whose blood is it on the red banner? The blood of those who carried the banner into battle or the blood of those they slaughtered? The warriors' or their victims'?
>
> Two bloods mix and coagulate into one color—a symbol of the mingling of all the blood on which history stands. One drop crimsons another, and the red cloth is a continuum of bloods, spilt blood crying out to blood still circulating in the heart. (N. A., "Our Red Banner")

> Cain is a sinner. Abel is a righteous man. But if the blood of a victim is to be shed, a priest is needed. Who is right and who is wrong in this world? Only the blood itself is right and holy. Cain and Abel are Bloodbrothers. Is this a coincidence? No—priest and victim are always Bloodbrothers. The one who sheds blood and the one whose blood is shed become brothers through that very blood. Blood is the sign and substance of brotherhood. (L. V., "The Myth of Cain and Abel . . .")

The two main divisions of Bloodbrothers can be roughly characterized as Christian and pagan.

> Who is the founder of the great Bloodbrotherhood? He who says "This is my blood; drink it"? Or he who sheds the other's blood? The crucified or the crucifier?

Sometimes mutual reproaches arise among our brothers. On one side they say, "What kind of Bloodbrothers are you?! You are weak sisters, uncomplaining sheep going to slaughter," while on the other side they say, "What kind of Bloodbrothers are *you*?! You are savages, violent brutes, preying on the blood of our flock." But must we quarrel, brothers? Aren't we united in the principle that everyone who gives blood must also take blood, while everyone who takes it must also give it? Don't you see how our bloods mix on our banners? As blood flows through the veins and arteries of a single man, so it flows through the vessels of all mankind: it is taken from one and given to another, making a single channel of circulating blood that flows through each one of us. The Bloodbrothers' mission is to circulate the blood through the entire human race, for if this circulation were to go off on a tangent, a terrible blood-wasting illness would arise. (V. R., "The New Doctrine of Blood: Toward the Overcoming of Victimhood")

While they consider themselves free of nationalist passions, the Bloodbrothers nevertheless have a special reverence for Russian soil, where blood has been spilled in such abundance. "Our land is glorified in blood, and therefore we are Bloodgloriers" (V. B., "Death and Resurrection of the Russian Land"). It is here in Russia that they expect their most bountiful harvest:

Is it only the corpses that are laid in the earth? No, the souls are buried there as well, and together with the blood they feed the soil, nourishing its shoots and fruits. Don't you feel that heavenly steam rising high above Russia? It is her blood calling to us at every step, on every drop of soil. . . . That ever-thirsting soil with its fevered, cracked lips . . . Who could carry his own vessel of living, seething blood past his mother's parched lips? Spill it! Moisten the lips of the mother who suckled you!
  You dread even the sight of blood and would rather have it rot in your veins than spill it from your overcharged vessels. You are a bloodless generation who know not the soil, seeing in it

only a dry deposit of sand—but this is the red clay, the "adama,"[13] from which, according to tradition, Adam, the first man, was fashioned. Has it occurred to you why it is that this primordial clay is red? And who it was that commanded you to emulate the Creator's great self-sacrifice by spilling your own blood? (I. G., "The Night of Creation")

The Bloodbrothers have a special reverence for Russian blood spilled abroad, hallowing the fraternal union of the lands connected by this "liquid life."

We revere the blood shed in the wars of the past; we kiss this holy, lethal, and immortal soil. It is pulsing with humanity, while we are pallid and anemic. The unrealized lives of our ancestors who died before their time have filled the world with the vital strength that we now draw on. We have lived out their youth, their love, their maturity, their discoveries. We are indeed like vampires. We were suckled in our infancy on the battlefields of the past. Over the decades of our lives we drained dry the energy of our fathers; the earth became depleted and could no longer sustain the weight of the firmament—until finally our own boys went off into battle. They piled into their carrier-convoys and set out for Hindoo Kush, tramped through the deserts of Registan, joined battle in the Salang Gorge. Our generation belongs to a brief interval between the terrible bloodshed of our fathers and our children in war, in that most cruel and bloody business of states. Our children's blood is already moistening the seeds of future generations. (A. P., "Drunk on Your Blood, a New Love Is Ripening . . .")

There are some Christian groups in the Bloodbrotherhood move-ment. They still acknowledge the efficacy of traditional baptism by water, but they distinguish themselves from what they call "water-Christians," and regard blood as the supreme baptism. They justify their point of view by quoting from the First Epistle of John: "This is Jesus Christ, who came with water and blood and the Spirit, not water alone, but water and blood. . . . Three bear witness in heaven: the Father, the Word, and the Holy Spirit . . . and three bear witness on earth: the spirit, the water, and the blood" (5.6–8).

Johannite Christians, who preserve a special spirit of loyalty to that apostle and his preaching of a third baptism by blood, often call themselves "Glorybloods" rather than "Bloodbrothers." They consider themselves enjoined not to sanctify blood—since it was already eternally sanctified by Christ at Golgotha—but only to glorify it before the world. According to their doctrine, the rest of the Christian world has long since fallen away from Christ, since

it avoids suffering and fears blood, and if it sheds any, then it is not in the name of Christ and not for the sake of Christ. . . . The Christians of the first centuries had no need for a special rite, since their whole life passed under threat of torture. They not only drank the blood of Christ in communion, but they watered the earth with their own blood. This was their way of emulating Christ, who descended onto the stony, godforsaken earth to moisten and soften it with his blood, so that it would bring forth not thorns and thistles but seeds of the heavenly kingdom. In later centuries, the lives of most Christians became estranged from Golgotha and the cross, and with these went the mystery of the third witness. But this mystery has come down to our time by paths of millennial tradition and is now incorporated by blood-Christians in the mystery of their baptism.

For them, spilling blood on the earth is just as necessary a part of the mystery as immersion in water. In this way they unite, as it were, the beginning and end of Christ's mission on earth: bathing in the Jordan and crucifixion on Golgotha. Water-Christians only set out on Christ's path, but they do not follow it to the end; they go down into the Jordan, but they do not go up to Golgotha. Christ came to reveal the path of salvation "not by water alone, but by water and blood"—as the apostle admonishes us expressly, to prevent halfway interpretations. (K. L., "On Bloodless Christians—Brothers in the Spirit")

Some blood-Christians, after receiving baptism by water, make a cut on the left palm with a special point called a "Roman nail," and while the blood flows onto the ground they read passages from the New and Old Testaments about the holiness of blood and the redeeming sacrifice of Christ. Others think that baptism by blood is not a one-time act but a "gradual" mystery that unfolds throughout human life as a whole.

Each son of man must find his own Golgotha. Your whole life is a search for your destined place, the site of the future temple of your blood. . . . All of human life is only a search for this invisible altar, the thirsty font of the third baptism. *(Baptism by Blood: History, Doctrine, Ritual)*

Some Bloodbrothers are closely associated with the society of Sinnerists (see 112–123) and accept the Testament of Hell.

THE RED HORDE

The Red Horde is one of the branches of Easternism. While opposing the Westernizers, it also conducts polemics against the Slavophiles, arguing that "Slavdom" is merely one of the outer shells of the Russian spirit, deeper than the Western, but still very far from the Eastern core.

Slavophilism, which once stood confidently in opposition to Westernism, has now lost its self-sufficiency and become merely one of the milder forms of Westernism.

The Slavs themselves are the West—the Eastern part of the West. But Russia is the real East, unswervingly advancing in its social system and self-consciousness further and further eastward—past India, past China, past Japan. . . . The closer Russia comes to completing her historical path, the further she gets from all the Westernizing, Europeanizing, Slavicizing theories, which are left behind to wither and die out. . . .

Russia is not just the East, but the East's last stronghold, its best chance for survival in its struggle against the West. Technology, liberalism, industrialization, market economics, pacifist politics—all this is eating away at the authentic civilizations of the East, flattening them out into the Western style. Japan was the first to yield to the alien influence; her location in the furthest Far East brings her right up to the threshold of the American West. After Japan, half of Korea went that way, and that's where post-Communist China is heading too.

Russia is far from those extremes where the East blurs into both the European and the American West. Russia is the real Middle East, the inner sanctum of its special, spicy aroma. When the steamroller of the information systems has levelled out the primordial depths of the Eastern spirit, Russia will remain its only inexhaustible source. Not for nothing has she resisted the West almost alone for so many centuries, warding off its predatory rationalism and individualism on every front of world culture. Russia is the innermost, most immovable and ungovernable East, in which other Eastern countries see, with bitterness and longing, their own lost chance to stand up against the West, to remain themselves. (V. K., "'The Decline of the West' and the Rise of the East")

The Red Horde occupies a special position among the Easternizers. Members have no affinity for the "White India of the Spirit" or the "Saffron Light of Persia," the treasures of Buddhism, Taoism, Sufism. They rarely refer to the works of N. Fedorov, N. Rerikh, V. Khlebnikov, or N. Klyuev, the revered masters of other Easternizers. In all of Russian history, two colors alone are dear to them—the gold and the red. From their point of view, Muscovy, having become the geopolitical and spiritual heir of the Golden Horde, broadened and extended the legacy. There were some temporary retreats before Western influence, especially under Peter I and Catherine II, but in the final analysis they only served to strengthen the Horde by arming it with new technology. Ethnic mixing speeded up the process after the collapse of Imperial Russia. The Russian people lost its Great Power privileges—and once again Asia started moving into the forefront.

The October Revolution not only smashed the Great Russian state and liberated its Asiatic borderlands. Its significance is incomparably deeper—not just social but metaphysical and geopolitical. Great October brought the victory of Asian over European principles in the spiritual character of the country. "Yes, we are the Scythians! Yes, we are the Asiatics, with slanted and hungry eyes!" cried Blok, the poet of the bloody glowering East, just three months after October. And here is another example of amazing poetic penetration into the spirit of the Horde in the post-October era:

> What a summer! The shiny backs
> of young Tatar workers
> bound in maiden bands,
> enigmatic narrow shoulder blades
> and childish collarbones.
>   Hail, hail,
> mighty unbaptized spines,
> our mates in the age to come. . . .
>   (O. Mandelstam)

In the young workers swarming over the construction trenches of the new Moscow, the poet seems to see a splash of Tatar blood flowing in Russian veins. He greets them in that same tone of inevitability in which Pushkin greets the "young tribe" that will outlive him: "Hail, hail!" An elemental and invincible growth, given by nature herself: a forest of mighty spines, slender as pines, and, of course, unbaptized, pagan—this is the age to come. (As for what will become of Christian Europe, Blok had already prophesied: "Ages, ages—you will yet be cursed by your sick posterity, your degenerate progeny!")

Mandelstam, of course, is a European's European in his spiritual roots, and he cannot help being sickened by the evil forebodings of 1931. But with what predatory expressiveness, with what historical perspicacity he stamped the very perspective of his vision of the new people: from behind, from the rear—the very archetype of the Horde! They have no faces or eyes, only shining backs, shining with sweat under the scorching Asiatic sun. These "Tatar spines" immediately recall Tolstoy's Tatar, running away from a whipping, and, even earlier, the countless Rusichi driven into Tatar captivity and visible to us in history only from the rear. Hordes and hordes, receding into history with bowed spines— proletarians stooping over their shovels or captives cringing under the lash. The very nature of Asianness dictates this perspective: not full face and not profile, but . . . there is no word in the European languages for such a portrait from the rear. But what a vivid, expressive picture it is: the vertebrae, the shoulder blades —all the stony elements of the body. . . . No soft, plow-furrowed earth, no faces furrowed with wrinkles—no, just the bony, stony Asiatic desert. And still one more feature: maiden bands, narrow shoulder blades, childish collarbones—their unsexed state identifies these proletarians with worker-insects. The young workers are marked by girlishness, virginity . . .

Such is the new innocence of a class whose bodily eros has been replaced by social eros—an orgy of labor, the sexlessness of slavery. . . . The innocence of the back, which knows nothing of those tortured grimaces and blushes, that whole gamut of European facial expressions exposing inner feelings of shame, sin, and guilt. Spines, shoulder blades, and collarbones symbolize militant innocence, an innocence that denies sin and crucifixion; they symbolize time itself, soulless and sexless, with its childish cruelty, its bent back and its hidden face. (L. G., "The Horde in Russian Poetry," in *The Red Horde*)

Herzen still saw in the proletariat a yellow-faced menace to Europe, an orientalism of homogenization and compulsion, the death of individuality, the triumph of flat common sense and positivism. Europe fostered its own inner Orient in the socially homogeneous mass of its laboring class. And now—in the "Tatar spines" of the workers, in the slave labor of millions, in the word "slave" itself, which has penetrated into the heart of the "Slavic" languages—now, before our very eyes, in a new historical form, but on the same geographical site, the Golden Horde has pitched its tents once more. It has merely changed its color; it has drunk the blood of its victims and turned Red. The golden color of the hot sun that lights the East has turned into the even hotter crimson of the blood that stains the West.

In the annals of history our times may well go down as the Age of the Red Horde—the nomad herd, reborn on a new reel of the historical spiral. Everything Marx said about the "Asiatic means of production" has been brilliantly confirmed by the Russian Bolsheviks, and it is just in this sense that they can be called Marxists. They have justified Marx's characterization of Asia and the "Asiatic means of production" in opposition to Europe. . . .

The Horde is not dead. Routed by the Muscovite princes, it nonetheless penetrated into Russian blood, where it grew into a terrible destiny for its conqueror and finally subjected him once again to the Tatar-Mongol yoke, the yoke of Asiatic blood and style. Russia could defeat the Horde from without only by becoming a Horde from within—an even mightier and more far-reaching horde. . . . It is not true that battle divides peoples. It unites them, weaves them together more tightly than brothers in the mixing of bloods, in the embrace of a single fate. . . . Such is the tight web of Russia and the Horde.

To return to Blok: what is happening there on his Kulikovsky field? A battle between two camps, or their fraternization? Both at once. The mare of the steppe, the feather grass, the impetuosity of Russian mores—do these not stem from the Tatar camp? What is the meaning of the line "Our path has entered our hearts like the Tatar arrow of ancient freedom"? Tatary entered the Russian's heart and soul and built him a path through the wild steppe. The Horde perished in Russia—as an actor perishes in the role he endows with his own flesh and blood. (B. T., "The Mare of the Steppe: Outlines of the History and Philosophy of the Steppe")

According to the Easternizers, this inner "Horde" has once again become a historical reality, taking command over Russia in the wake of Great October. The return movement of the nations has now begun, with Genghis Khan in their blood and spirit. Asia has resumed the invasion of Russia—and through her, of Europe as well. This move-ment is still partly invisible, more on the level of genetics and psy-chology than of geopolitics—though the former can quickly turn into the latter, of course.

The Slavic world is aging, fading, wearing out, while ancient Asia and the Caucasus are flourishing; their blood is getting hot and frisky with a presentiment of the genetic space opening up before them. At present, the growth rate of the Asiatic part of the population far exceeds that of the European and especially the Russian stocks.

It is easy to foresee the denouement: famine, epidemics, floods, exhausted fields, advancing swamplands, the salinization of the soil, the swallowing up of farmland by the spreading desert, the triumphant invasion of the steppe into the forest, the decline of roads and agriculture, and above all, the crash of messianic hopes. . . . In all this, a combination of apathy from within and barbari-zation from without is eroding the thin layer of cultivation, in its rush to accelerate the death of the overstrained nation that took on a burden beyond its strength. The failure in Afghanistan was a sign of disintegration, like the defeat by Japan in the 1904 war.

. . . And as always, her encounter with the external East stirs up Russia's internal East as well. The Revolution of 1905 was a powerful stimulus—a gush of lava from the worker-peasant core, under the pressure of Europeanism. The geographic margins and the social depths always work together. This inner East, this no-madic mass of incensed lumpen, will soon combine forces with the external Asia that will surge into Europe across the great plain like a raging sea: Tatars, Kazakhs, Uzbeks, Tadjiks, Azer-baijanis will be its first advancing waves. And then, after the stormy Central Asian and Muslim swell, the final tidal wave, the deluge that will submerge the whole plain: the Chinese billions.

. . . The Afghans have already landed their bloodthirsty troops in the Russian soul; they'll land them on Red Square too. The Red Horde will get redder still as the blood rises within it. . . . But that's the future. The daily business of the East is the peace-

ful bearing and raising of children. Rather than shed others'
blood, better mingle it with one's own. . . . (A. P., "From Japan
to Afghanistan: Thoughts on the Eastern Wars and the Russian
Revolutions")

As for religious views, the Red Horde on principle doesn't distinguish them from historical and geopolitical views. It holds that "a people
believes in whatever it accomplishes. Faith is a path, and God is the
end of that path" (D. U., "The Horizon as an Archetype of Religious
Beliefs"). It sanctifies every kind of power and greatness, considering
them gifts from God.

The will of God lies hidden in the power of things. We can have
no direct knowledge of God, but the size of things indicates God's
wishes: greatness speaks of God's grace and smallness of God's
contempt. When a great territory is allotted to a people, this is
a blessing from God; when the muscles swell on the victor's arms,
this shows that his victory was God's will. If you want God's
grace, be strong. If you want God's help, trespass. Seek no evidence but your own superiority. Seek no sign but your own
might. Seek no justification for weakness. Whatever you can do
—that is God's will. (T. P., "Faith is Power")

Little is known of Tatar-Mongol beliefs predating the conversion
to Islam, except that they revered audacity and considered an
intrepid person something like a saint. They didn't seek wisdom
in his speeches or consider the righteousness of his life; indeed
they had no standard of wisdom or righteousness. They had only
one standard: audacity. God Himself preserves the man who does
not fear for his own life. Such a man is not afraid to vault across
an abyss; he is not afraid to challenge a mighty warrior to a duel.
Indeed, he is not afraid to take on a whole division of Bogatyrs
at once—and they scatter in terror at his bewildering reckless-
ness. This shows that the spirit of God lives within him, that his
life is holy and everything about him is holy: his body, his words,
his clothing. People seek out his touch and even his glance like

divine grace. Whereas the Judeo-Christian religion values God-fearingness, the Horde's divine gift is God-fearlessness. . . . It was bravery that raised members of the Horde to leadership positions, and if this people had no saints occupied with teaching the people, that was only because their saints were desperate warriors who had lost all fear. Their heroes did not fast and practice self-abnegation, but performed feats of self-oblivious derring-do. They entered into no covenants with God beforehand; but God Himself protects him who does not protect himself. . . . It would sometimes happen that the chieftain himself would avert his eyes before the contemptuous glance of a new daredevil, a new gallant who outdid him, in contempt for his own life because he felt God behind him even more strongly. (R. S., "What is Heroic?")

The Red Horde holds contests for the strongest in battle, the swiftest in flight, the craftiest in cunning, and the coolest in pain. The victors in these contests are given the rank of prophets; since the power of God is in them, they are the instruments of His will on this earth.

The prophet is not someone who speaks well about God but someone through whom God Himself speaks. The Jews and Christians reduced the meaning of prophecy to empty words fluttering lightly over the gravity of things; but God speaks *through* things. God appears to the strong, and the only sign He gives His prophet is victory: power over land and people. The Golden Horde, and later the Red Horde, have been the mightiest powers on earth. Other countries may have built ever so many churches and written ever so many books, but God is present in the Horde, in the stronghold of this vast, eternal land, in the fearless spirit of its conquering heroes. Churches and holy books are flimsy products of human hands, but the earth was created by God and put by Him at the disposal of the Horde. The holiest book is not worth an inch of land, for the earth was given to men by God: "Fill the earth, and subjugate it, and rule over the submissive." God did not say, "Write wise books." God did not say, "Build beautiful temples." He gave the earth into our possession, and every inch of land is a mark of God's love for whoever stands upon it and owns it. (T. K., "Land: The Holy Testament")

The Horde specially honors the so-called horizontal arts. It holds archery, spear-throwing, and distance-vision contests. In the latter, its members use a special method of squinting: to sharpen the sight, the gaze is narrowed into a slit as if looking down a long, thin section parallel to the horizon.

The wide-cast gaze of Europeans flutters about without ever fixing on the most important thing: that plane surface onto which it is easiest to step. What escapes their notice is the plane on which things are fitted to the land, the plane on which the foot of the sovereign treads. (R. S., "Thoughts on the Golden Mean")

The place accorded to the heavens in the Abrahamic religions (Judaism, Christianity, Islam) is occupied by the horizon according to the Horde:

Toward the horizon stretches the land, the unbounded plane allotted to man. To meet God does not mean to rise from the earth up into the empty heights. It is possible to meet God only in that furthest distance where the land itself is pointing. (D. U., "The Horizon as an Archetype of Religious Beliefs")

The symbolic colors of the Horde are gold and red. Here is an excerpt from "Faces of the Grass," a poem by T. Z. (translated from the Turkish):

We believe only what we see. We see only the endless sky above our heads and the endless earth under our horses' hooves. We believe in the sun-flooded sky and the blood-soaked earth. The gold and the red are in our hearts, mighty as an army, deafening as a herd of horses. Our prayers speed behind our horses, behind the necks of our horses cleaving the horizon. Our faith is the greatest of faiths, the length of our journeys has no match. We take the whole heaven and the whole earth on faith, like God's thieves, parcelling them out to men and beasts and sowing our faces in the grass. . . .

KHAZARISTS

Supporters of a universal religion based on the traditions of the Khazar kaganate, the Khazarists consider themselves bound to preserve the inherited link with Judaism as the basis of all the monotheistic faiths.

The Khazar state was inhabited by representatives of the three revealed religions. The Muslims were the most numerous, followed by the Christians. But the king himself, who took the title of "kagan" (high priest), adhered to Judaism, as did his inner circle. Thus the social structure preserved the historical sequence of the origins of the religions: Judaism, Christianity, Islam. The Jewish original rose to the top, as the peak of the pyramid. Lower down came the socially more prevalent and historically later core: Christianity. At the base lay the Muslim confession, chronologically the latest.

The Khazarists believe that at the very origins of Russian statehood and in the depths of the Russian worldview lies the "mystery of the Jewish spirit," "the treasure of Israel." Historically, it was mediated by the huge Khazar kingdom on the territory of what is now Russia, with constant interaction among the tribes sharing this geographical area. As N. Ya. puts it in his book *On the Religious Foundations of the Russian State*:

At the turning point from paganism to Christianity, the ideology of ancient Russia was suffused with many mysteries. There is every reason to suppose that Russia's acceptance of Christianity was prepared by the Jewish element of this ideology; and although this element was later driven out for a time, it was ultimately reborn in the idea of the "God-bearing nation" and the "sacred history of Russia". . .

From time immemorial, Kiev maintained close commercial and cultural ties with the Khazar kaganate. The original name of the population that later entered history as "Kiev" was "Shabat," i.e., Sabbath. This name derived from the Khazar merchants' custom of holding Saturday bazaars on the banks of the Dnieper for the pagans ("goyim"). Near Kiev flowed the river Izraeka. According to reliable sources, Prince Vladimir's mother and, thus, Svyatoslav's wife (or at any rate his favorite concubine) was a Khazar. And of course Vladimir's very title, "kagan," was borrowed from the Khazars. Svyatoslav and his son, the Christener of Russia, considered themselves the heirs of the Khazar state.

The Khazar kaganate fell to the Kievan Prince Svyatoslav more than a thousand years ago. But according to the Khazarists, in every historic encounter between peoples, the forces of action and reaction are symmetrical: the subordination of conquered peoples to their conquerors is balanced by their influence on the conquerors' spirit and destiny. The military-political predominance of one side is compensated by the spiritual-cultural influence of the other.

A people that is physically conquered leaves its mark on the spiritual makeup of the conquering people. How else can we explain that as soon as Muscovy repulsed the Tatar yoke, it immediately adopted the administrative system of the Golden Horde; that no sooner had the Russian Army won its victory over Napoleon than it became contaminated by French Revolutionary ideas; that after destroying Hitler, Stalin at once appropriated his nationalistic strategy and his hatred of the Jews? (A. V., "On the Laws of Historical Reciprocity")

The fallen Khazar kingdom bequeathed to the still-young pagan nation the principles of its religious worldview which, though maintained unconsciously to this day, require constant conscious renewal as an integral part of the spiritual inheritance of Russia. Traces of the Tatar invasion are indelibly inscribed in the historical memory of our country and continue to this day to have a telling effect—not always beneficial or constructive—on the course of our history. The Khazar influences on Russian culture are not so conspicuous, but that is only because they are inseparable from its very substance, which, in pre-Christian times, was so feeble that it sucked in all surrounding influences as thirstily as a sponge. The contiguity of a state with such a religious foundation and form as the kaganate, where three monotheistic faiths peacefully coexisted under the rule of the king/high priest, could not help but affect the turbid consciousness of Kiev, barely awakened as it was from pagan superstitions and thirsting after divinely revealed truth. The acceptance of Byzantine Christianity in Rus twenty-four years after the fall of the kaganate did not cancel out the earlier religious tendencies of Russian culture; it just pushed them into the background, down into the subconscious depths where they continued to influence the furthest reaches of the course of historical development. . . .

Thus, the well-known religious toleration of the Russians during the epoch of Europe's cruel religious wars derived from the experience of peaceful religious coexistence under the kaganate. Rooted in this experience, too, was the idea of the Russian people's messianic destiny and the international brotherhood of peoples, all proceeding toward a common world-historical goal. Paradoxes that seem insoluble when Russian culture is taken in isolation find their explanation in the spiritual legacy of the Khazars: belief in the chosenness of one's own people, together with a tolerant, partly protective attitude to other peoples and religions. . . . Even the fast and furious spread of communism, which looked so miraculous in a peasant country, had long since been prepared by the Judeo-apocalyptic strain of thought that looked forward to the Messianic Kingdom and the end of history. What appeared in consciousness as Marxism had grown in the unconscious from Khazardom. This is the point of intersection between the Jewish background of Marx's biography and the Khazar background of Russia's history. . . . Finally, as for the aim of uniting different peoples and religions under a single government—which led Russia to the status of a twentieth-century

superpower—here too we find the legacy of Khazaria, transmitted by the young Kievan state that was later to extend so far
beyond its original boundaries. (V. Sh., "The Marxist Concept of
the State and the Khazar Kaganate")

. . . The river-cradle of the Russian people was rocked by the
hand of Khazaria, the first great Volga state. Not without reason
is it said that water is memory and that the inheritance of one
nation is transmitted to another across rivers of space and time.
It was in the bed of a great river that time flowed out of Khazar
into Russian history. From there—from the Volga, from the
ancient Khazar encampments, from the region of their former
capital city Itil' (now Astrakhan)—northward like a whirlwind
flew all the revolutionary movements inspired by that dream of
the Kingdom of God on earth, the union of royal and priestly
power, the restoration of the throne of David and the rebuild-
ing of the Temple—which would have made the Russians into
a nation of priests—the establishment of a state whose strength
would lie in its faith in justice and its fulfillment of the age-old
hopes of God's Chosen People. From there, from the broad-
banked Volga on the steppe, on to Moscow and Petersburg rolled
that primordial Russian chutzpah, the spirit of license and rebellion that gave rise to all the great revolutionaries, from Razin
and Pugachev to Chernyshevsky and Ul'yanov. . . . (L. B., "The
Destiny of the Volga")

The Khazarists base their views on two documents which they prize
not so much for their historical authenticity as for their "true feeling
for history" and "depth of religious testimony." The first document is
the so-called "Testament of Kuzari," known in samizdat copies from
an unidentified source, and the second is the "Vision of Svyatoslav,"
extant only in a single late manuscript. We here cite extracts from the
undoubtedly spurious "Testament of Kuzari" (a Khazar king):

Nothing will quicken this gloomy steppe until the Star of David
shines upon it.

We have brought the faith of Abraham to the ends of the earth, his flocks to graze by the Yellow River. . . .[14]

The Christians claim that their God is the son of our God. We must therefore treat them as our own children, and the Muslims as our own grandchildren. If a man despises the other religions that believe in our God, he will be cut off from his descendants and rooted out of memory as a negligent father and a scatter-brained grandfather.

Let the Jews be judges, as our God is Judge. Let the Muslims be warriors, as their Prophet commands. Let the Christians seek mercy, for they have neither judgment nor warcraft.

Cast not out the men of other faiths; but marry not with them. Be a root bringing forth its own proper shoots.

One year we roamed and saw one thing. Three years we roamed and saw one thing. The one earth must belong to the one God.

Grumble not against your life in the wilderness, seek not the flowery places where other nations swarm about like flies in honey. In the wilderness the Hebrews received the Revelation. Fear not the wilderness—it is full of God. In the wilderness you will be comforted.

Danger will come from the North, as Daniel taught.

Kingdoms pass away, but the King passes not away. The broader the kingdom, the deeper its need for the one King. Be our kingdom never so broad, it is fortified only by faith in Shaddai.

He who destroys this kingdom will establish it in his own heart.

North to Rus, south to Jerusalem: one land, and at its center the Mount of Salvation[15] where the Ark came to rest.

A plain without a mountain is lower than the netherworld.

Whoever follows one path to the end will return to the beginning.

The Khazarists see in this apocryphal Testament a prophecy of the destiny of Russia, which, after suffering through the acceptance and rejection of various faiths, will turn to the purest source of faith, concealed in ancient monotheism. The Star of Solomon is already shining throughout the expanses of Russia—raised over city walls, fluttering on banners, flashing from the Kremlin towers. The Khazarists believe the time is coming for the Star of David to crown this radiance with its sixth point. The ray of mercy will blaze up in the star of omnipotence.

The Khazarists believe that the age of the world religion will begin when the "Mogen David" (the six-pointed star) becomes the state emblem of Russia and the direct historical succession of the Khazar kaganate is restored.

At first, the rationale for introducing the sixth point into the emblem will more or less parallel the popular interpretation of the five-pointed star: it will be said that the time has come to include the sixth continent, now explored and partially settled, in the fraternal union of the peoples of the planet. Only later will the religious meaning of this innovation become clear. The Star of David with its up- and down-turned triangles represented the union of man's striving toward God with God's descent to man; but in the Solomonic age this unity was ruptured, God's mercy no longer met with a reciprocal love and reverence, and one point fell away from the star. In its five-pointed form it became a symbol of polytheism and the multiplicity of religions, and began to serve as a magical instrument of power for the prince of evil spirits. The five-pointed emblem of rule stands for five fingers stretching to infinity and gripping the universe. The restoration of the six-pointed star is a sign of God's renewed covenant with man. (G. Sh., "The New Ray")

As for the "Vision of Svyatoslav," the text was published in the Vienna *Slavonic Annual*. In the commentary it was noted that the original was held in a private collection whose owner wished to remain anonymous. The composition of the manuscript is provisionally dated late in the reign of Peter I, when the choice of Russia's religious path had once more become an urgent question.

The "Vision of Svyatoslav" is, in general, a traditional work in the genre of medieval visions. It describes how an impious prince mocked his mother, Olga, the first Christian princess of Russia, when she appealed to him to accept the religion of the Redeemer, and how later he was mortally wounded in a battle with Pecheneg tribesmen and died after transmitting to one of his fellow warriors the visions of the next life that he had seen. One of these visions deviates sharply from the visionary canon and must be assumed to have been the main reason for the composition of this apocryphon, which was meant to influence the course of Peter's religious reforms (the Czar did not manage to implement them in full: he eliminated the Patriarchate but never successfully consolidated the kingship with the high priesthood in his own person, as called for by his plan).

Before Svyatoslav passed terrible pictures of Hell, where the impious are put to torture. But someone's sweet voice drew him on, and before the prince appeared a bright plain on which the righteous were walking. One of them approached him with downcast head, and Svyatoslav recognized him as the Khazar kagan whom he had slain seven years before.

Svyatoslav trembled when he saw a bloody cut on the kagan's neck. Then the kagan lowered his head still more, and Svyatoslav saw a golden crown in the form of a six-pointed star. Svyatoslav shrank back, fearing revenge, but the kagan, without uttering a word, bowed lower still, took off the crown, and raised it onto Svyatoslav's head, whereupon the Russian prince almost fell down beneath its incredible weight.

The kagan disappeared, and Svyatoslav, still following the same sweet voice, and now bent under the crown and not daring to raise his eyes, proceeded to a place not far from the Lord's throne; then he awakened and, after communicating his vision, promptly expired. The record of his vision was supposedly long held by the monks of the Kiev Cave Monastery in strictest secrecy, as a danger to the foundations of Christian government in Russia, but then transmitted to one of Peter's associates, Feofan Prokopovich, during his rectorship of the Kiev-Mogilyansky Religious Academy.

The Khazarists are not to be confused with Jews: they do not circumcise their sons, and they visit synagogues only slightly more often than churches and mosques. Judaism, for them, is not one particular, separate religion, standing against all the others, but the original mother religion that nursed all of them at her breast. Judaism is the prototype of the future unification of all religions, the ascent to that universal religion which will fully incarnate the truth of monotheism.

G. Sh., one of the leading ideologues of Khazarism, writes:

How will the religions be united before His face, how will their divisions fall away like chains? To unite the religions, is it necessary to invent yet another religion? Or was the seed of their unity already planted in the first origins of humanity's religious strivings, and visibly manifested in its history as the Promise to Abraham and the Revelation at Sinai?

It is not for us to invent a more perfect faith than the ones that already exist, but rather, by penetrating to their common source, to prepare ourselves to enter the very mouth of the river, so as to join the end with the beginning. For us, Judaism is not the religion of the Jewish nation but the religion of a united mankind. Unlike the Jews, we do not oppose the religion of Moses to the religions of Christ or Muhammed; in the religion of Moses we see prefigured the union of all religions and the dissolution of all divisions. . . .

We are proud that history's first experiment with the peaceful unification of Islam and Christianity under the rule of Judaism took place in the territory of our country, in the Khazar kaganate. This poor state, flung upon the steppe, ceaselessly roaming and pressed about on all sides by other nomads, provides us with an example of authentic living-together and thinking-together in faith. By crushing and dispersing the Khazars, Svyatoslav implanted that people invisibly, as it were, into the destiny of our much-suffering country with its many religions—for the sake of the ultimate triumph of that unity of religious spirit which nourished the first of first principles of our history. (G. Sh., "The Faith of the Steppe")

The Khazarists consider it their duty to visit the temples of all three monotheistic religions regularly. Their Sabbaths are Friday, Saturday, and Sunday. When Saturday came to be celebrated along with Sunday throughout the Christian world, they brought this practice to Russia as well, and now they are proposing to establish the same universal observance of Friday—for which they have the support of the growing Muslim forces within the territory of our country. Still, they regard Saturday as the chief Sabbath, the one that comes in the center between the other two and was historically the first to arise, and they observe it particularly by studying the literary antiquities of Khazaria.

The Khazarist doctrine is especially widespread on the Lower Volga and in the Northern Causasus, in the Azov region and the Crimea— all over the territory of the ancient kaganate and in the areas of its capitals, Itil' and Semender. The Moscow Khazarists make summer pilgrimages to these places, where they conduct independent archeological excavations. In one of their Moscow apartments they have founded a public museum called "The Khazar Kaganate at the Crossroads of Religions and Cultures," where they conduct weekly readings and seminars.

The reason for the growing popularity of Khazarism is that it organically unites Russian patriotic and Jewish messianic motifs, putting both of them at the service of the united religion of mankind. ("Program of the Society for Khazar Studies")

PART FOUR
ATHEIST SECTS

PREFACE

The unnaturalness of the term "atheist sects" is a sure sign of our times. Never before has religion tried so hard to turn its sworn enemy into a useful ally by exploiting the achievements of atheism. Things have come to such a pass that atheism is now regarded as the path to the true god (or, as they say, the "God of gods"). It is argued that, since "Religion #1" has become obsolete and turned into idolatry, it must now be replaced by "Religion #2"—atheism—whose whole point is merely to reject the previous religion. So goes the reasoning of the "Atheans," who have turned atheism into the profession of a new, more "subtle," "purified" faith. Their fundamental teaching is: live in God's absence as if God existed. They point out that such a faith does not count on any rewards—not even immortality—and is therefore suited to the consciousness of a "mature" person. In fact, though, Atheanism is nothing but a deceitful compromise between religion and atheism; in other words, a cowardly halfway atheism, an atheism that, instead of resolutely following up its denial of God with a wholesale reconstruction of human life, persists in promoting the virtues of abstract faith—faith without object and without hope.

It is clear how dubious this religious "reinterpretation" of atheism is, as soon as we observe the two completely contradictory conclusions, the two opposing sectarian movements, to which it leads: Good-belief and Sinnerism. Good-believers insist that religion should be emancipated from all forms of systematic doctrine, expressing itself only in accidental, unpremeditated acts of goodness. Authentic goodness seeks no reward, counts on no "bonus dividends" in the form of heavenly blessings or a "pension" beyond the grave. One could perhaps agree with this if the Good-believers had exchanged the idea of a religiously based good for some other, earthly, materialistic good—especially labor, social activity, and human cooperation. But in their doctrine, goodness exists in complete isolation from all the laws of historical development, logic, and reason: it comes "from nowhere," "from elsewhere"—which means that it is still interpreted as "inscrutable divine providence." According to them, there is no point in teaching goodness or undertaking any organized mass action in defense of goodness; all we can do is hope for a miracle. Such is the deeply pessimistic doctrine at the heart of Good-belief and its offshoots, such as the "Clandestine Do-gooders" and the "Helping Hands."

One of the most sinister and monstrous developments in religious thought is Sinnerism, which makes the "highest" moral conceptions into the basis of a right to commit sins, including murder. God, they say, allows men to break all the commandments and commit their souls to the torments of hell—if they do it out of love for humanity. This doctrine has a very complex and murky history, including the notion of a "Third Covenant" (which in fact turns out to have two parts: the "Spiritual Covenant" and the "Infernal Covenant"). Without going into all the details, interesting though they may be for specialists, one must point out how monstrously this doctrine contradicts the simple rules of human morality. And it is futile for the ideologues of Sinnerism—who insist that faith in God can justify and even glorify the most heinous crimes against humanity—to appeal to the code of honor of the Russian revolutionaries: the morality of our society has long since condemned the kind of Nechaevism that justified bloody means of achieving ideal ends.

Such are the paradoxes of religion in the age of atheism: it tries to appropriate the language of atheism and speak in the name of atheism. But the very attempts of contemporary sectarianism to identify itself with atheism, to exploit atheism as an argument in its struggle with traditional religion, are telling evidence of whose side the truth is on, which way the irreversible trend of historical development is headed. In its death throes, religion now tries to give its blessing to its mortal enemy. But we will never accept such a legacy. Atheism has dug religion's grave; all attempts to turn it into religion's dutiful heir are in vain.

ATHEANS

Their name comes from the same root as "atheists": "without God," "having no relation to God." But from the Atheans' point of view, atheists betray their first principle when they deny God and defy faith; this turns them into *antitheists*. True "atheism" does not deny God's existence but allows for the possibility of His nonexistence, and on this foundation it builds the "great temple of its believing unbelief." As opposed to the atheists, who demand that man take the place of the absent God, the Atheans call upon men to act as if God exists, even if He doesn't. Their idea of the highest human virtue is to continue living a godly life after losing faith in God, to continue doing good and justice on earth after losing any expectation of a heavenly reward.

> Act as if God exists and requires you to be merciful; and act as if God does not exist and no one will reward you for your good deeds. God demands everything from you and promises you nothing. Probably you'll simply die and never be resurrected. This is the test you must undergo. No one is watching out for you in heaven or in eternity. You are alone. But be worthy of the Creator even in His absence—don't behave shamelessly in His empty house. When a child is left alone, without his parents' supervision, he begins to act up. An adult carries the image of his parents in his own soul and doesn't need supervision. This is the meaning of coming of age: *To act the same without God as with God*. This is the highest form of maturity. . . .

The world is still divided up into believers—those who are with God—and atheists—those who are without God. The highest task is to be a believing atheist. Such a one is in a position to unite both sides in the new maturity of believing unbelief, which is the future of the world.

Those who are with God hope for salvation in the kingdom of heaven. Those who are without God hope for happiness in this earthly life. An Athean has no happiness and no salvation. Like a believer, he rejects happiness—except that he does it not for the sake of salvation, which he doesn't count on, but for the sake of the divine here and now, for the sake of goodness itself and self-denial itself.

Are Atheans fools who lose both ways, missing out on both joys? No. Actually they are like scheming capitalists, multiplying their profits. Recall Pascal's calculation. If one lives for God, one may lose a finite joy but gain an infinite joy. In exchange for fleeting pleasures, one gets eternal bliss. "Let's weigh your possible gain or loss if you bet on the eagle, that is, on God. . . . You have a chance of winning an infinitely blissful eternal life, as against a finite chance of losing something that in any case is finite. This is the deciding factor: where eternity is at stake, and the possibility of losing is finite, there's no room for doubt: one must stake everything on this horse." This is the argument of Pascal, the great mathematician and believer.

But wouldn't it be better to dispense with accounts altogether? Can faith really be based on probability theory? Will anything be missing from this infinite joy if it overtakes us despite our own expectations and calculations? On the contrary, joy is greatest when it is unexpected. Only one who acts without thinking of reward deserves to be rewarded. The real winner is the one who plays without thought of winning. We must go beyond Pascal's calculation: by calculating further, we get beyond calculation altogether. Do what God requires of you, but don't ask anything of God. Act as if there is no winning or losing but only the game itself, on which one must nonetheless stake one's whole life. Live as if there is no rewarding God, only a demanding God.

Know that you will die and will not be resurrected, but live as if your soul is immortal.

This is the highest stake a man can place in this life: a stake made with no calculation on winning. Life for God without belief in God. By giving the most and expecting the least, by acting like a believer and judging like an unbeliever—in this way a man does not struggle against God but also does not haggle with Him, does not barter the goods of this world for those of the next. (V. K., "Godliness without God")

The Atheans grant that faith was necessary in the past, when men received direct revelations from God. But since God has hidden Himself from men, men must accept His silence and "not persecute God with their faith." Where atheists are "marauders," appropriating the attributes of God to themselves in His absence, believers are "fanatics," chasing after the heels of their idol in defiance of His clear desire to hide. The following is an excerpt from A. B.'s dialogue, "Conversation with an Athean":

"Would you like me to reveal to you the ultimate mystery?" he said, with apparent nonchalance. "God is not only the Creator, the Almighty, the Savior, and so on and so forth" (he emphasized by his intonation that such terms are merely formal honorifics). "The main and most terrible mystery is that God Himself is a God-flouter. No one will ever fully understand or forgive God for smashing the great religions one after another, for constantly and tirelessly struggling against the very *idea* of God. For He doesn't want to be replaced by some idea—a dogma, religion, or theology. He wants to reveal Himself to us with such living, overwhelming certainty that our experience of physical touch would seem like a vague dream by comparison. All revolutions, catastrophes, and atheisms are His rebellion against us, against our pathetic notions of the 'all-good' and 'all-powerful.' All those idiotic titles that would tickle the pride of an Asiatic despot—what does *He* want with them? The living God is to be found only where our idea of God is exploded and comes crashing down. This is why atheism is godly and theology is godless.

"You know," he continued, "authentic faith has no need of God, and the authentic God has no need of faith. It's only through some childish misunderstanding that we've got accustomed to joining the two ideas into the nonsensical cliché 'faith in God.' True faith doesn't need to be justified by the existence of its object; on the contrary, it would thereby lose its character as faith and turn into something like a fact. True faith dares to make the concealed assumption that there is no God, never was and never will be—and, nevertheless, man is the son of God and owes God his filial duty. This is the only kind of faith that is manifestly selfless and does not reward itself with the 'certainty' that its hopes will be realized. You must understand that faith is the opposite of certainty, or, rather, it is the rejection of all assurances and probabilities.

"God's existence is independent of our faith; He has no need of it. Or is He so egoistic as to reward us for believing in Him? Does He need our worship? Doesn't He love even those who don't love Him? Don't skeptical scientists and godless artists also receive revelations about God's world? Are the beneficent miracles of technology and medicine exclusively the work of believers?

"No, God is no feudal lord demanding honors to His person and rewarding His vassals for faithful service. We still imagine God's relation to man on the model of feudalism or even slavery, as if He were to say, 'I brought you out of slavery in Egypt, so now you are my slaves, I am your Pharaoh.' No, if God is a wise master, concerned with the success of His undertaking, then He gives the highest esteem to men who are independent, who are willing to argue, raise objections, go against instructions—those are the ones to whom He entrusts His business. This is why God's business in the world is more and more often to be found in the hands of those who don't believe in Him but have soberly worked out the rules of their trade: good artists, good scientists, good builders—even if they are bad parishioners. A slave waits on his master's orders, but a worker wants his own lathe and figures out how to make one for himself. As for whose labor is more profitable, the Heavenly Master knows that as well as any earthly one. Let's learn to think of God's business 'capitalistically' and not imagine Him as a despot demanding faith and obedience, hymns and masses. If there's anything He wants from us, it's just that we should leave Him alone and take care of business by ourselves. . . .

"Thus, the sort of God who would reward us for our faith, and the sort of faith that would rely on God, are both our own fabrications, our own faint-hearted illusions. In fact, God and faith are destined never to meet. Faith and God are two parallel magnanimities that can never intersect. They are two freedoms that value each other too highly to bind themselves into a single chain. Faith passes God by. God passes faith by. They meet only in the children's tales that constitute our religions. True faith would rather acknowledge the devil's power over this world, and the true God would rather acknowledge the atheist's support of His business. This is no paradox; it's the terrible reality to which all religions keep closing their eyes. You can agree with me or not, but it's true all the same: faith assumes the absence of God and God assumes the absence of faith. They are simply incongruous with one another. There isn't a single point where they could meet without doing violence to each other. God and faith are two freedoms, each of which esteems the other too highly to turn into religion through mutual vows. . . . This is why I am a believer without God; and there is no despair in this, since God Himself doesn't demand any faith of me. This is what it means to be an Athean." (From the collection *Conversations on the New Atheism*)

Atheans occasionally conduct "Riteless Meetings" and "Mutual Confessions," where they proclaim "new spheres of godliness in the godless world." These spheres are constantly shifting—from literature to politics, from politics to science, etc.—and "holy resolution" is needed for figuring out the best way to apply one's force precisely "at the points of hiatus and loss." Atheans try to stay as far as possible from all visible centers of God's presence, in the belief that "God comes to the places from which He is absent": neither to the righteous nor to the sinners, but to "those who are indifferent, inattentive, who have forgotten all about God." Hence the importance of the "middle position": neither belief nor unbelief, but "unbelieving belief," which in some Atheans involves the utmost tension between the two poles, while in others it involves dulling them to the point of complete neutrality and indifference. Among the Atheans there are also many who have "simply forgotten," that is, have no relation whatsoever to God, positive or negative, but live stubbornly in "the pallid in-between." Athean preachers see it as their most important mission to remind these most "remote" brethren that

> the absence of relation is itself a relation, indeed the most responsible relation of all, since it's not under any compulsion. He who is furthest from God, who neither bows down to Him nor resists Him in his heart, comes nearest to the final frontier, the abyss of the question: Is the world divine *apart* from God? If God is only in God—in prayer or in church—then He is not God at all, but just one more substance, like fire or water: if you touch it, it's hot or moist, and if you don't touch it, it's not hot or moist. But God—if He is really God—must be present even where there is no God and no relation to God, must be present as the Being in being, as the All in all. This is why we shun God and turn away from Him, immersing ourselves in the here and now—so as to experience Him as Inevitability and Inexorability. Those who draw away from the manifest God draw near to the concealed God—God as He is when He does not exist. (E. E., "Sermon for Unbelievers")

Atheans for whom unbelief is a path to the "eclipse and end of the world" form a special eschatological movement, the Defectors (q.v.).

GOOD-BELIEVERS

The features of this sect are rather hard to pin down. Good-believers have a lot in common with a number of other sects, some of which merge into it: Atheans and Aritualists, Clandestine Do-gooders and Helping Hands, Rectitudinarians and Conscienceniks, Melancholists and Good-griefers. Good-belief is the point of convergence of many teachings that differ from and even contradict each other at points, and this is why it is so difficult to mark off its actual boundaries. Good-believers believe only in the power of good—or as they would put it, the *weakness* of good.

There is no Good in heaven, on earth, in the sea, in God, in the angels, or in the animals. Only man, who suffers and *is conscious of his suffering*, has developed a concept of Good. Angels don't suffer, and animals aren't conscious; for them, consequently, there is none of that constant inner tension from which sparks of Good can fly. For Good is a sense of another's suffering that arises from the consciousness of one's own. . . . These two experiences, the experience of suffering and the experience of thinking, work upon one another and meet in the creation of Good. (G. Y., "The Anthropology of Good")

We do not believe in any social, political, or philosophic doctrines. All of them elevate some groups—the thinkers, the workers, the rich, or the poor—at the expense of others—the workers, the thinkers, the poor, the rich. By emancipating some, they enslave others. One system stigmatizes believers, another atheists. One proclaims the nation, another the class. One praises power, another obedience. All these systems, while proclaiming the Good, do incomparable evil; for Good cannot be systematized. All systems serve to oppress and divide men. The better the system, the worse the evil. Good can only be done piecemeal, outside of all systems; it flares up feebly in the human heart and is all too easily extinguished when people try to cram it into human minds and destinies by the metric ton and the cubic meter.

Soften your hearts! Do not harden them with righteousness! Pity both the righteous and the unrighteous. Only suffering is right, and righteousness is always wrong, because it is pitiless. . . .

How many philosophic and political systems have been proclaimed in words and in steel! But nowhere can a man find pity. He is pressed about on all sides and reduced to manure for the fertilization of ideas. How then has man survived this pressure cooker in which so many millions have been pulped? Only thanks to the unobtrusive spark of Good flaring up from heart to heart. This is how it's always been: from one to another, bypassing all generalities, associations, alliances, parties, religions, and classes. What system can anticipate the unpredictable, which lies beyond the control of will or reason?—a piece of bread offered to the enemy, a word of pity spoken to the defeated, even a twinge of incongruous shyness at the moment of confident triumph. Systems come and go, but this remains. It's from weakness, the incorrigible weakness of the heart, that such things are done. The heart cannot quite conform to reason, which tells it: Kill! Take! Conquer! The power of Good lies in the weakness of the heart. Good, which is always small—endlessly, immeasurably small—cannot be systematized; it can only reject all systems. . . . (V. G., "The One and Only Faith")

The faces of people who do Good are beautiful, and their eyes glow; for they are doing what is natural, instinctive. Do they think about God? Do they hope for some reward beyond the grave? Do they believe in reincarnation? No, they would be offended by the very idea that they have some reason or purpose for doing Good. ("What?! Did someone order me to do it, is someone going to pay me for it?!") Good is the only thing that is dear for its own sake, regardless of causes or consequences.

By placing Good on the ladder of virtue or in the chain of merits and rewards, religion makes genuine Good impossible. If I know that I will get a reward for doing Good—and not a transient reward but an eternal one—then it's no longer Good; it's just an investment at interest.

Here is the reasoning of an ordinary Baptist who recently converted to Good-belief. Why are there so many believers in the West? It's because they're used to living on interest. No one there ever does anything "just for its own sake"; they give at interest, and their charitable deeds are deposits in a heavenly bank account where they earn interest, privileges, and credits. They've got it all itemized point by point in their contract with God. They've already got themselves a good life here on earth, and now they're making their arrangements for heaven. They put their earnings in a pension fund and their sacrifices in a "hereafter fund." For them, religion is something that gives them a right to the use of posthumous capital. Capitalism has got itself the religion it needs. A banker is a banker; he enters everything into his accounts: profitable deals, good deeds, church attendance.

But all this bookkeeping is not to our Russian taste. We haven't acquired any wealth here on earth and we don't even know how to tally up our assets. As for heaven, we certainly don't have any accounts there. When we do Good, it's from the heart and not for a reward. Charity is greater than faith and hope, as the apostle said. And if the Russian people have lost their faith, that's both a minus and a plus. True, there are fewer good people; but goodness itself has become better, more sincere and unaccountable. We have nothing on this earth—no wealth, no assets. Everything's been distributed to the poor, who have now become richer than we are. The treasures that we had stored up for ourselves in heaven have also all been distributed. Our granaries are empty in this world and the next. This is the meaning of Good without faith: leave nothing for yourself; let the others take it.

It's hard not to agree with this reasoning. (F. D., "Good without Faith")

Religious justification is needed only by weak people, by those who have discovered the greatness of Good but have not yet found the strength to do it selflessly. All the religions of the world were only the prehistory of genuine Love of the Good. Mankind needed illusions to strengthen the habit of Good, to make the Good deed into a spiritual need. When the fruit is ripe, it falls from the tree; just so does Love of the Good fall from the branches of the religions that have nurtured it. . . .

We have few Lives of Saints of the Good, and we haven't yet worked out the fundamentals of the epistemology, psychology, and sophiology of the Good. We know Good only in its most childishly naive, religiously selfish form. The world admires the good deeds in the lives of believers. How much more must it admire the Good done to one's neighbor for no reason at all, out of pure Love of the Good, with no religious aspirations? This is the kind of Good that shines with the brightest light, because its source is within itself. When a person is moved to such Good without the promises of religious rewards and blessings, he renews the world. (L. T., preface to *Universal History of Good in Stories and Traditions*)

Atheists of the past used to prove their point by killing themselves or others, as in Dostoevsky or Camus. Through this "test" they were trying to rival God and prove their mastery of fate, as if to say, "It's my right!" But inevitable retribution was visited upon them, for when a soul has killed a soul, it brings upon itself such torments that there's no need for any further hell.

We say: Do a good deed without cause or purpose, without short-range calculation or long-range plan, without profit or hope—then you will really be starting something new. Good will begin shining out from itself, and the world will be transformed, emitting light from the heart of darkness. Look how many ordinary people know nothing of God but do Good every day and every hour. They are the light of the world—which does not know it as light; for knowledge cancels out what it knows.

According to theology, God has two fundamental attributes: He is almighty and all-good. . . . Until now, atheism has been based on only one of these attributes: God's infinite might, which has been appropriated by man. And now the world is groaning from the mighty men who make war on nature and on each other. No, let God keep His might. We choose all-goodness, with all its weakness intact. . . . Atheism is entering a new phase. Love of the Good has no power and makes no claims. Atheism as a system in which the Good rules, and rules even by force, is obsolete; it turned out to be even more harmful to man than all the religions it replaced. With the might he took from Almighty God, man could only build concentration camps and systems of self-enslavement.

Now the atheism of Might is coming to an end, and the atheism of Good is beginning. Man will no longer usurp the rights of God—to punish or pardon, to give life or death. Man will take from God only divine mercy—always to forgive, always to take pity. He will disown the legacy of might and accept only the legacy of mercy. This is our only comfort and our only hope: to be good to the point of impotence. This is the only way in which the Son is above the Father. He is not God and does not need the service of Satan. Let us take the Father's mercy and leave the Father his might. . . .

A man who returns his ticket to the kingdom beyond the grave leaves himself only one privilege and one imperative: to be a true neighbor to his neighbor. In the Good, a single individual becomes all mankind, self and other. This is human maturity: to enter the era of mankind as a whole. . . .

He who believes in God hopes for salvation. But there is something still more precious than faith and hope: charity. "And so there are these three: faith, hope, and charity: but charity is the greatest of them" (1 Cor. 13.13). Faith may vanish, hope may wither up, but charity, as the apostle Paul says, "will never pass away." And Good too will never pass away, for charity is the source of Good.

Everything else is external to a man: the heavenly powers and the earthly powers, and even his own flesh. Only Good is within him; and it is already immortal, for it is always in itself and for itself. Everything else is for its sake, and only it is for its own sake. Religions, nations, parties, and governments pass away;

all that remains forever is the inextinguishable Love of the Good, abiding forever in itself. So long as someone needs an external support, let him go on believing in recompense, comforting himself with a religion of salvation. When he reaches spiritual adulthood, he will come to the Good for its own sake. (E. B., "Beyond Faith and Hope")

Closely related to Good-belief, indeed almost merging into it, is the teaching of the Helping Hands. The aim of the Helping Hands is to help everything that occurs naturally in the world. If a fire is burning, they throw a dry log on it, so it won't go out. If a seed has dropped from a tree onto a stone, they pick that seed up and move it onto a patch of soil, so that it will sprout. At the height of spring they're often to be seen around playgrounds, gutters, and mounds of melting snow: they're clearing paths for the rivulets, so that the business of spring can get on faster. But they consider it unnecessary and even harmful to do any of this systematically. Only when something comes to their notice accidentally do they put it right and help it along, so that growing things may grow, heating things heat, and flowing things flow. If you offer help *on principle,* you can all too easily disrupt the natural processes and destroy the very thing you're trying to help.

We should strew help around the world with the same generosity and randomness with which the Lord helps us. If He had elevated the Good into a principle, we would be living in bliss, with no knowledge of evil; but then the world itself would be different—without freedom and without chance. The genuine Good that comes from God is effected by a power in the things themselves, with no external interference, with no helping hand extended from the heavens. . . . Let us imitate the Lord and help the Good without changing the natural course of things, without encroaching upon the holy of holies, the Design itself. Help is not something mighty, but just a tiny boost, too feeble and incidental to place any constraint on anyone's freedom. Let us be dilettantes of the Good. (N. I., "On the Randomness of Good")

A typical Helping Hand is Nekrasov's Grandpa Mazay. He helps rabbits out of dangerous spots, without doubting for a moment that another time he'll have to go after them with a gun. Helping Hands are of the opinion that the free essence of the Good is more deeply manifest in such random, "dilettantish" acts than in any consistent, goal-directed program, which is more likely than not to turn into a system of compulsory Good. . . .

Helping Hands rarely offer their help ahead of time, but it's even rarer for them to wait until asked. It's as if their conscience is asleep but suddenly wakes up the minute they sense the near presence of someone in need, someone vulnerable. They don't make any preparations beforehand, they don't stock up on anything, and they don't found charitable institutions; but neither do they wait to be openly asked for help. They develop an intuitive understanding of others' helplessness and respond to it on impulse. At difficult moments of our lives they materialize from God knows where, and then afterwards they dissolve without a trace into the general background of life. We know very little about what makes these people tick. (L. A., "On Moral Dilettantism")

Sometimes the Helping Hands are called "Clandestine Do-gooders," because their doctrine is based on the Gospel precept that all Good should be done in secret—not only in secret from others, but even from oneself: let your left hand not know what your right hand is doing.

Good done openly arouses the doer's pride. For the beneficiary, it's just another instance of someone else's power, for however good the doer's will may be, it's still another's irresistible will. Therefore, even in the case of a very good deed, you should leave open the possibility of the other's declining. Mercy should take the form of the sort of natural phenomena that we can decide to accept by our own free will, though we could just as well pass them by, like coded messages that we for some reason fail to notice. When Good is offered openly, someone is forced either to accept it or to decline it with a sense of constraint that not every

soul can bear, and that can cast some into moral bondage. (N. L.,
" . . . He does mercy in secret")

When people heard of the death of V. T., one of the most active
Helping Hands, some said, "What a shame that such a good man
wasn't Orthodox," and others, "What a pity that he wasn't a
Baptist." Y. K. said to them: "If you're so sorry that he didn't join
you, then why didn't *you* join *him?*" (From *Tiny Lives,* a collection of stories about the Good-believers)

SINNERISTS

This religio-atheistic movement arose in Russia in the 1860s and
formed the shock troops of various revolutionary parties.

In some Christian-populist sects, special respect was given to
"comrades-in-sin," i.e., those who took upon themselves as much
as they could of the sin of mankind. Even of hardened murder-
ers it was said, "They have taken our sin upon themselves, they
will bear Divine retribution for us." This movement, while originally Christian, sometimes reproached Christ for not having
sinned with the sinners: though he deigned to keep company
with tax collectors and prostitutes, he didn't descend all the way
into their darkness. The Russian thirst for universal justice was
so intense that to be among sinners without sinning oneself, to
have compassion for the fallen without falling oneself, was taken
as a betrayal of the brotherhood of mankind. (N. V., "Studies in
Russian Sectarianism")

This view was expressed with special force in the activities of the
"Brethren in Sin," who not only helped to shelter fugitive criminals,
but actually reproduced their crimes—so as not to be "raised up before
one's brethren," so as not to "shame" them but to "share in their sin."

Some among us speak in the name of Christ while wishing to remain pure, as if untouched by Adam's sin of knowledge and Cain's sin of violence. Claiming to be more righteous than others, they say that others will die while they will be reborn to see the kingdom of God. Are these people Christians? No, they are Pharisees, for it is said, Christ came not to the righteous but to sinners. "For Christ died for the ungodly. For scarcely for a righteous man will one die. . . . But God shows His love for us in that while we were still sinners, Christ died for us" (Rom. 5.6–8). Ask yourself, then: Did Christ come for you, to bear your sin? Or are you unsullied by sin, so that Christ will not come for you?

He who wishes to be with Christ must turn away from the righteous and the Pharisees, and go to the sinners. This does not mean abiding in sin. We are summoned by Christ not to sin but to be crucified together with the Savior of sinners. Following Christ, who liberated us from sin, we are to bear the weight of others' sins, to take their sins upon ourselves, so as to be with Him on the cross. We have died for sin, but we have not yet died for our brethren in sin. He who falls into sin through temptation is a sinner, but he who takes another's sin upon his own soul is a Sinnerist. We have a sure sign of this from Christ: whoever he has freed from sin is thereby freed to take on another's sin, as Christ himself did, when he became sin for all men. ("Rules of the Brethren in Sin")

Sinnerists do not sin in the usual sense of the term, provoked by anger, profit, or lust. Indeed they banish from their company those brothers who fall into worldly temptation and are caught in theft or adultery. For the Sinnerists, sin is a religious calling: it harrows and even shatters one's soul, but it saves one's brothers and is thereby justified in Christ. Their sin is committed "out of mercy and grace," not for its own sake but for others', not from low instincts but from the highest considerations—in order to save their brothers from sin. If a brother hates someone who oppresses him, the Sinnerist kills the oppressor in order to deliver him from the sin of oppression and the brother from the sin of hatred. The sin of the oppressor is washed away by his blood, redeemed by his death agony, and passes into the soul of the Sinnerist himself.

> In former days too there were holy men who stooped to associate with sinners and took upon themselves the weight of their sins. Thus, in the life of John the Apostle, it is told how he took upon his own soul the sins of the wicked highwayman, thereby saving him from death and making him into the meekest lamb of God's flock. But even the very holiest men took upon themselves only sins that had already been committed, thus assuming responsibility for them only symbolically, so to speak, and not in the very flesh of the sin. It's as if Jesus had taken the sins of mankind upon himself while remaining all the while beside the Father on the heavenly throne, sparing himself the trouble of coming into the world and taking on human flesh. Thus it is that we too dare to take on the flesh of sin, to commit sins ourselves for the sake of our brothers. It is not just through a verbal vow of the soul that we take the sin upon ourselves, but we commit it with our flesh and blood, so that our brothers' flesh may remain uncorrupted and pure, untouched by sin. . . . For sin, which comes through the flesh, must be expelled through the flesh. (D. N., "The Gates of the Flesh")

There is only one path open to a man who aspires to imitate Christ: Sinnerism. God took the sins of criminal mankind upon himself by becoming a man. A man can take the sins of his criminal brothers upon himself only by becoming a criminal—not out of love for the crime, but out of love for the criminal. But, as God took on human flesh immaculately and sanctified it through Himself, so the Sinnerist must commit his sin immaculately and dispassionately, not so as to add to the sins of the world but rather, by taking them upon himself, to purify the world. Not passion but sobriety, not hate but love, not self-interest but self-denial are the marks of the immaculately Sinnerist soul. (I. G., "The Battle for Men")

According to some scholars, the history of terrorism in Russia began with these "Brethren in Sin" or "Fraternal Sinnerists." Some of the brethren, while keeping their faith in Christ, believed that the Lord himself was a Sinnerist, and that this was the cause of his descent into hell. "As he redeemed humanity by his human incarnation, so by his fellow-sinning he redeemed sin, sanctified his brothers in sin, and destroyed hell, where they had been in torments" (N. V., "Studies in Russian Sectarianism"). This is why all revolutionary parties have had an interest in the sectarian movement, from which they drew not only their human resources but also the moral principles of their struggle.

These hapless people—members of the People's Will, revolutionaries and terrorists of all political persuasions—believed in the redemptive power of sacrifice. They did not stint their own blood for the font in which a new mankind would be washed, ushering in its future brotherhood. "Baptism in blood is more efficacious than the baptism of John,"[16] said a famous revolutionary, one of the Social Revolutionary leaders. He may have had in mind the words of the New Testament: "This is he that came by water and blood, even Jesus Christ, not by water only, but by water and blood" (1 John 5.6). Revolutionaries thus actually supplemented or even replaced the traditional baptism in water with a baptism in blood, both others' and their own, whose convergent stream marked this bloody mystery.

. . . The revolutionary martyrs went further than the Christian martyrs, who joyfully ascended to Golgotha to be crucified with Christ. In the name of a Future Mankind, the revolutionaries took upon *themselves* the mortal sin of murder, descended into hell to suffer the cruelest torments—not the torments of the crucified flesh, but the torments of a soul that has taken upon itself the sin of Cain. The revolutionaries, at least the best of them, had more in common with the saints than with their luke-warm church-going contemporaries. They did not stand guard over their own souls and were not afraid to lose them; as Christ said, "He who loses his soul for my sake will save it" (Matt. 10.39). When they murdered, it was not for personal advantage, riches, power, or revenge; they offered their own souls in sacrifice for their neighbors' salvation, transforming murder from an instru-ment of hatred and endless conflict into an instrument of love and the unification of men. Through each act of tyrannicide they were mitigating both the tyrant's lot in the next life and his vic-tims' lot in this life. Not only did they dare to ascend to Golgotha together with Christ, but also to descend together with him into hell. For he who took upon himself the sins of the world could not fail to take upon himself all the sufferings imposed upon sin-ners. And if he redeemed the living and vanquished death by the torments of Golgotha, he redeemed the dead and vanquished hell by the torments of Sheol. A revolutionary is one who is ready not just to be burned at the stake of the Inquisition but to enter the fire of hell. (B. S., "The Religious Justification of Bolshevism")

Each revolutionary association had within it its own "Hell," a group of people who knew perfectly well what path lay before their souls after death. In 1863, for example, the illegal "Fellow-ship" was founded in Moscow, with a strictly conspiratorial group known as "Hell" operating within it, unbeknownst to the other members. To avert suspicion, the members of "Hell" were advised to become drunks and profligates—sins which they took upon themselves while remaining perfectly chaste and sober. They were posted to all the major cities and provinces to keep abreast of the mood of the people. In appropriate instances, they were to destroy persons whom the peasants hated and to execute any agents of the "Fellowship" who deviated from the revolutionary line in the direction of compromise. But "Hell" considered its chief task the systematic murder of tsars, which was ultimately intended to awaken the people and lead them to revolution.

These people, apparently, had been in hell already and wanted to return to it forever. (L. S., "The Theology of Nechaevism")

A high price! A worthy ordeal! For what is our faith without love? Of love it is said: "Greater love has no man than this, that a man lay down his soul for his friends" (John 15.13). He lays down his soul. . . . But this means: he gives it over to the torments of hell. For how else can one "lay down one's soul," surrender it to torment and destruction, if all ordeals of the flesh only serve to strengthen it? If the flesh follows Christ up to Golgotha, then the soul follows Christ down into hell; this is the meaning of "losing one's soul in the name of Christ." Christ himself, in Paul's words, did not know sin, but he became sin, so that we might become righteousness (2 Cor. 5.21). And St. Augustine repeated: "He is sin, so that we may be righteousness." Did Christ not preach that we should become "sins" for our neighbors, i.e., sacrifices for their sins, suffering for them the torments of the spirit and not of the flesh alone?[17]

True, Christ himself, according to Augustine, did not suffer in hell. "He [Christ], by the power by which he is the Lord, permitted some to be tormented in hell, but he himself, by this same power, could not undergo those torments."[18] It is clear that even in Augustine's day there were heretics who claimed that Christ had suffered the torments of hell together with the sinners: having taken their sins upon himself, could he have failed to take their sufferings as well? But even if Christ did not suffer these torments, his followers who sin out of love for their neighbors must, by their own human nature, suffer in hell; this holds not only for simple sinners but for Sinnerists as well.

Nevertheless, even in connection with Christ, some doubts have arisen on this score. It has been said that Jesus, because of his Divine nature, did not suffer pain even on the cross—that his sufferings were only an illusion and an allegory for men to see. This view has been condemned as the Monophysite heresy. If Christ, while being God, could still truly suffer on the cross by virtue of his human nature, as the Church teaches, why then could he not suffer the genuine torments of hell, that very "pitch darkness and grinding of teeth" that his Father had prepared for all sinners, including the first of the Sinnerists, His own Son, who took upon himself the sins of others? . . .

Moreover, King David, "seeing this before, spake of the resurrection of Christ, that His soul was not left in hell, neither did His flesh see corruption" (Acts 2.31). But this means that his soul *was* in hell; and could it have failed to suffer with all the sufferers there, when even on earth his flesh had suffered the pains of all the mortal sons of man? And if he redeemed men by the torments of his sinless flesh, then he could have overthrown hell only by the torments of his sinless soul. (S. B., "Sinnerism in the Light of the Church's Teaching on Hell")

The account of Christ's descent into hell has not become a subject of Church dogma; it belongs to the darkest, most indecipherable pages of Holy Scripture. The fact that it is hardly mentioned in the New Testament testifies, in the view of certain thinkers, to its archetypal meaning for the Third Covenant, the covenant that mankind will make with God on the eve of the final, apocalyptic phase of world history. Moved by the example of Christ's saving death and the dream of blood brotherhood, all mankind is on the path of sacrificial sin to the gates of hell. They will smash those gates, just as the earthly stronghold of the Bastille was smashed in its day. And at the head of this hell-bound procession of all the nations marches Russia, inspired by her own leaders to accept the baptism of blood. In the words of a well-known poet to the Socialist Revolutionary leader of the February Revolution: "Russia is ready to follow you even into hell itself!" "And the immensity of our sacrifices will shake the very walls of hell," as another poet put it after the October Revolution.

This descent into hell, this fearless surrender of the soul to satanic mutilation, this readiness to pay for the resurrection of the spirit with the death of the soul—this has always marked the Russian. The fate of his poor, despairing country has always led him to the ultimate, the most terrible sacrifice: the sacrifice of Cain, who killed his brother out of love and jealousy of God, out of desire for God's mercy and contempt for his own gifts. Cain offered three sacrifices: first, the fruits of his husbandry; second, the flesh of Abel; and third, his own soul. Our nation too has offered three sacrifices: first, the sacrifice of its age-old poverty, for which it did not win favor; second, the sacrifice of its brother's blood in intestine wars, for which it was cursed: turning her face away, the earth ceased to bear fruit for Russia. And third, the sacrifice of its own sin-racked soul. . . .

And now we await the day when the gates of hell shall part and we, who took up our cross and our torment, following Christ further than Golgotha, deeper than Gehenna, will finally be led forth by Christ. We believe that ineffable mercy awaits those who go to hell for others, suffering the greatest torments for them. To lay down one's soul for one's brothers is the highest stage of love, transcending the fear not only of earthly but of infernal damnation. Such love passes beyond hell; it annihilates hell. (D. M., "The Three Sacrifices of Russia")

. . . On the eve of the Revolution there were two paths of renewal and development for Russian religious consciousness. The first was the missionary path taken by Merezhkovsky, Rozanov, Berdyaev, and the other so-called God-seekers, the prophets and preachers of the Third Testament. They conceived of the Third Testament as the Testament of the Third Hypostasis, through which God's will would be carried out in the contemporary world. This was to be the Testament of the Holy Spirit, pouring forth over all flesh; a Testament uniting the truth of paganism with the truth of Christianity, sanctifying the mystery of sex; the Testament of a new religious community, a Church throwing its gates open to the world and openly dwelling in the world; the Testament of free religious creativity, replacing both the Old Testament of law and obedience and the New Testament of suffering and redemption. . . . These ideas, however beautiful in themselves, appear from our present historical perspective as rather starry-eyed, dreamy, and immature.

The second path of renewal was the revolutionary one taken by the People's Will and the Socialist Revolutionaries; along this path the Bolsheviks went furthest of all. Where the God-seekers appealed to the gifts of the Holy Spirit, the atheists and revolutionaries, who did not believe in the Spirit, offered it the sacrifice of their own flesh and soul. This sacrificial mode, this initiation into the mystery of blood, was unacceptable to the God-seekers, who wanted to sanctify blood without shedding it.

These, then, were the main divisions of the religious quest of the Russian people. Some, the more contemplative ones, looked for the sanctification of the world by the gift of the Holy Spirit. Others, the more practical ones, took the path of sacrifice, laying down their own flesh and soul for their brothers, embracing their own condemnation to the fires of hell. Both camps put their hopes in the Third Testament, each interpreting it in its own way. One side called it the "Testament of the Holy Spirit," the other, the "Testament of the Descent into Hell." One found its archetype in the New Testament narrative of the coming of the Holy Spirit upon the apostles, the other in the descent of Jesus Christ into hell. In the theological tradition, one version was called the "Spiritual Testament"—confirmed by faith without blood—and the other the "Infernal Testament," confirmed by blood without faith.

Apparently, the revolutionary idea has defeated the missionary: blood has drowned out faith and displaced it from the historical being of the people. But experience shows that these ideas can be implemented only in concert, in the unity of the Third Covenant. Can there be a covenant without sacrifice? Can one be resurrected in the spirit without dying in the soul? The long *via crucis* of our nation, on which millions have fallen in torment, is now leading us once more toward the fulfillment of the only prophecies that can justify such a path. The nation that has voluntarily suffered the curse of hell as its own sin-offering is the only nation prepared for the mature and perfect acceptance of the gifts of the Spirit. . . .

Before the Revolution, without the Revolution, when it lived only in the wishes of thinkers and the visions of seers, the Third Testament could not be completed or even begun. Like every Covenant, it had to be confirmed in blood—the blood of the Lamb. But in this case, the sacrifice turned out to be not the Paschal Lamb and not the Son of Man, but an entire nation, a collective image of suffering humanity—for this Covenant is fulfilled not in the Shepherd's salvation of his chosen flock but in the transfiguration of the entire human race, the free out-pouring of its creative spirit. The key point here is that this nation was not sacrificed to someone else's treacherous passions, as a pawn in someone else's game; nor was it simply suffering for its own sins; no, this nation brought itself as a sacrifice, took upon itself both the sin and the punishment for the money-lust and power-lust of all the nations. This is the only nation in history to have been crucified—and that not at the hands of some ex-ternal torturer, but by crucifying itself, destroying the flesh of some of its members, the souls of others.

Such a nation must be called not a sinful nation but a Sinnerist nation. A sinner tries to avoid punishment; a Sinnerist brings it upon himself. The Russian people took upon itself all mankind's sin of violence; and for that sin it sold itself into bondage, into the torments of hell. Tormentor and tormented converged in the grimace of one and the same nation, distorted by malice and il-luminated by suffering. This self-crucifixion was required so that God could make the Third Covenant with mankind—on the blood of the murderer-nation, the sacrificial nation, the savior-nation. . . .

The contemplative theorists of the Holy Spirit erred by omit-ting from their prophetic gaze the whole enormous, bloody epoch needed to prepare their Covenant and make it realizable. In their view a "donative" Covenant was possible without sin, without sacrifice, without death; and thus they missed the meaning of the Russian Revolution. Even more, though, did the active pro-moters of the Russian Revolution miss the ultimate religious and redemptive meaning of their struggle. Now we are turning again to the legacy of those contemplatives who rejected the Revolution, for it is precisely thanks to the Revolution and its countless sacrifices that their highest hopes may now be realized. Such is the bright irony of history. . . . (A. K., "The Third Covenant: The Russian Experience and the World's Hope")

The experience of Russian history has shown that gifts and sacrifices are powerless in themselves. Christ's descent into hell and the Holy Spirit's descent onto earth not only followed in chronological sequence in the sacred history, but the meaning of each was determined by the other. Together they form God's integral motion toward man: in His Second Person He descends to the sinners in hell, while in His Third Person He descends to the redeemed on earth, to His apostles.

The integration of the Infernal Covenant with the Spiritual Covenant in the unity of the Third Covenant—this is the lesson of Russian history; this is the religious task of the Russian people. To gain the Holy Spirit through willingness to sacrifice not only one's flesh but one's soul as well, to accept not only the cross of Golgotha but also the tortures of Gehenna—herein lies the fullness of the Covenant to come. The Spirit cannot be born unless the soul dies. "It is sown in corruption, it is raised in incorruption," says the apostle Paul. Not only human flesh but the human soul as well must undergo corruption, so that the Spirit may be born in immortal flesh and soul. The corruption of the flesh destroyed by suffering and the corruption of the soul destroyed by sin are the work of the Spirit clearing itself a path through the human depths. As it is written: "It is sown a body of soul, it is raised a body of spirit. . . . Howbeit the spirit-body was not first, but the soul-body; and afterward the spirit-body" (1 Cor. 15.44, 46). Each man's earthly lot is given him for the mortification of his soul. Those who choose hell are chosen for salvation. Those who lose their souls for their brothers' sake will be raised in the Spirit of their Father.

. . . Human wisdom will never be able to grasp how it is that a soul stained with violence and murder can appear in white vestments before the Lord. It will never grasp how the gates of hell, shut by sin, are opened by Sinnerism. "But the man of soul receives not the things of the Spirit of God, for they are foolishness unto him. . . . But he that is spiritual judges all things, yet he himself is judged of no man" (1 Cor. 2.14–15). A man who lays down his soul for his brother is foolish. A nation that lays down its soul for mankind is foolish. And a Sinnerist is no different from a sinner, although he liberates the sinner while giving himself into bondage to the sinner's sin. Thus does the man of soul judge the spiritual man, although without the power to judge. . . .

How wondrous it is that in the prophets Hosea and Joel, the Biblical presages of the Infernal and Spiritual Covenants directly follow one another in the same sacred order:

"I shall redeem them from the power of hell, I shall save them from death. Death! where is thy sting? Hell! where is thy victory? I shall not repent of this" (Hos. 13.14).

And on the very next page:

"And it shall come to pass afterwards that I will pour forth My Spirit upon all flesh, and your sons and your daughters shall prophesy" (Joel 2.28).

The Spirit will be poured forth upon the flesh—but for that to happen, the flesh must first prepare itself for the pouring forth of the Spirit. The flesh of the flesh must be given over to death in order to pluck out death's sting; the soul of the soul must be given over to hell in order to pluck out hell's victory. Death destroys the flesh, hell consumes the soul—and only then does the Spirit itself take on incorruptible flesh and an incorruptible soul, having overcome death and hell through Christ. (V. S., "On the Soul and the Spirit")

PART FIVE
DOOMSDAY SECTS

PREFACE

Eschatology is a religious doctrine about the ultimate destiny of mankind and the world, about what will happen at the end of time. It is well known that our troubled age, having mastered the secret of nuclear self-destruction, has often been on the verge of bringing the entire history of the human race to a catastrophic end. The uneasy fears and presentiments that have taken root in this soil have sometimes been given religious interpretations of an eschatological color. It is said that the end of the world is now inevitable, that our nuclear arsenals have become weapons of punishment in the hands of an angry God. Mankind must pay for its sins, for its declaration of independence, for the reckless challenge it has thrown down to God by remaking the world to its own specifications through science and technology.

The sectarian views presented in this section are quite varied. One group, the "Arkists," believe that salvation is possible in the coming catastrophe—though only for the elect, of course, among whom they number themselves. Their model is Noah, the righteous man of the Bible who built an ark, a house of salvation for himself and his family, under the direct instruction of God. The Arkists have tried to follow his example by building themselves the "private refuges" to which they devote the best years of their life. But the catastrophe has not come, the human race has not perished; and this is certainly not because the "elect" have been specially saved; it is because humanity as a whole has found the will and the good sense to hold back from the edge of the nuclear abyss.

There are also sects like the "Skin and Bones," which, instead of seeking to be "saved alive," are preparing for the last days by putting on the trappings of "mourning" in advance: they go about in grief, black crepe and haggard faces. Into this general category fall the "Defectors," who profess atheism as a "sign of the last days," preposterously turning the meaning of faith inside out and proclaiming that everything unclean and desecrated is "holy." The Defectors differ from the atheistic sects mainly by the eschatological tendency of their prophecies: since, at the end of the world, "the first will be last and the last first," they conclude that all religious values and anti-values will have to be reversed: true faith changes places with unbelief, and a heap of trash turns into a sacrificial altar. . . . In a garbled way, the Defectors' movement represents the revaluation of all values actually achieved by contemporary society. The truth of their sectarian eschatology, however, is not some impending historical catastrophe, but the inevitable crisis or "last days" of religious faith itself.

Russia has its own long tradition of eschatological prophecies. Some Russian (and like-minded Western) thinkers have declared that "the end of the world will begin with Russia," where the "abomination of desolation" will ascend the throne. This is in effect the view of the so-called Steppies. What they love about Russia is the emptiness of the steppe. For them it's as if Russia has no need to fear the end, for she herself is already the end of everything—which means, according to them, the site of God's presence. "Prepare ye a way for the Lord in the wilderness," they cry, appealing to the prophet Isaiah in support of their belief in the holiness of the empty steppe. Their rites and rituals are in the literal sense acts of draining off some vacuum into the void, and thus can hardly be subjected to content analysis. The essence of the Steppie doctrine is simply "nothing."

One of the most bizarre sects is the "Glaziers." Their supposed direct or indirect connection with Masonry has not been confirmed by any reliable historical evidence. In the allegorical language they use to spread their doctrine, "glass" is just a metaphor for clear vision and the coming of the last, "transparent" days. The Glaziers may seem like a relatively harmless bunch of cranks and daydreamers, inclined to see in every "unremarkable" fellow a possible savior or a new messiah. But such expectations of a miracle at any moment, a supernatural manifestation of heaven on earth, can prepare the soil for mass religious psychoses. The Glaziers' devotion to "invisible work" or "transparent methods" compels us to pay special attention to them—all the more so since they are always trying to usurp certain symbols of our reality, such as the red stars of the Kremlin.

All in all, it is crucial to identify those genuine problems and anxieties of our times that foster eschatological ideas. Whenever someone says that "the end" has "already" come, or that it is "still" possible to be "saved," we must point out that the life and death of mankind is in our own hands. The only counterweight to the threat of civilization's self-annihilation is its own will to self-preservation.

ARKISTS (Ark-builders, Noahites)

The Arkists appear to be an eschatological offshoot of the Domestican sect (q.v.). According to their doctrine, a home is an ark sailing over the abyss of contemporary civilization, a place of salvation for the righteous, the Church of the Last Testament. The Ark is the eschatological dimension of the home, that is, the realization of its ultimate essence as absolute-space-in-itself. In order to survive a civilization that has acquired the means of self-annihilation, homes must be built on the model of the Ark; they must serve not only life but survival itself.

The Ark is a complete and self-sufficient home, fully equipped to create and sustain life. Ordinary homes are made for half-life and half-death, but if total death is reigning all around us, then we must have total life inside. All life on earth will be gathered into the home as into a kind of refuge. The Ark is God's womb, from which the human race will emerge reborn. (I. T., "Thoughts on the New Flood")

The Arkists claim that the new flood will be a deluge not of water but of fire, according to the words of the apostle Peter: "In the beginning, by the word of God the heavens were formed, and the earth was formed from water and in water: wherefore that world perished in a deluge of water. But the present heavens and earth, sustained by that same Word, are reserved for fire against the day of judgment and the perdition of impious men" (2 Pet. 3.5–7). From this the Arkists draw two conclusions: first, the new ark must go not on water but on land; and second, God summons men to build it independently, by their own design and reasoning, every man for himself.

In the days of Noah, mankind had the power to sin but not the power to punish and destroy itself, and therefore the punishment was sent by God from the heavens, in the element of water. But in our days, mankind has come to consider itself mightier than the Creator and has created a world of self-sufficient energies—that is, fires. Thus has man prepared the weapons of his own self-destruction: for these fires will escape from his prying hands and incinerate him.

But something else follows from this as well: if the weapons of destruction are in human hands now, so are the tools of salvation. It was God who sent the flood from the heavens, and it was God who instructed Noah how to save himself from it. But in our days both the punishment and the mercy must come to man by his own hands. We must not wait for another sign from God but get right down to business. At the very moment when mankind acquired the power to destroy itself, a remnant of mankind acquired the will to save itself. This power and this will are given to man from above, by God's anger and God's mercy. (D. Shch., "Noah and the Noahites," in *Modern Parallels to the Book of Genesis*)

The earth is man's home, given into his possession; and the earth will become his Ark, opening its bowels for him. But just as man worked the earth by the sweat of his brow to feed himself on its fruits, so it will be again by the sweat of his brow that he seeks out a path into the earth's womb, to build himself there an ark of salvation. . . . The Ark is appointed for man as an image of the New Earth, which will bury him in its dust and bear him anew from its womb for eternal life. . . . (V. L., "Fire and Earth in Apocalyptic Narratives")

No one will be saved by his own personal efforts, but only by God's grace; yet only by your own efforts will you be able to recognize this grace. It's not for us to decide which regions will be spared and which will go up in flames, who will perish and who will survive. But those destined for salvation will be chosen from among those working for salvation. Each must preserve in himself, in his seed, in his family, the future of all mankind. Each must do everything in his power and leave the rest to God. . . .

When God summoned Noah to build the ark, He showed him all the details of its design and made a Covenant between Himself and Noah. But in the future flood of fire, a way of salvation must be found not only for one Noah and his family but for the 144,000 righteous ones "redeemed from the earth."[19] To these it will be vouchsafed to know the meaning of those mysterious words, "redeemed from the earth"—not only taken *from* the earth but saved *by* the earth. Why else was the earth given to man as his portion before he committed the original sin? The earth became hard, to resist man's labors and punish him for his sin; but it also became soft, to yield to the labors of the righteous and save them in its bowels from the wrath of God.

God will select the worthy, but they themselves will have to make the decision to design and construct the ark. Doesn't the very capacity to make such a decision presuppose a certain chosenness? For one has to sacrifice everything: wealth, success, glory, peace and quiet—everything that gives earthly life its joy. Resolute Ark-builders have been leaving the cities that are destined to destruction, moving out to Siberian villages, as far as they can get from the nuclear vaults. Taking jobs as village teachers, doctors, or forest wardens, they move their whole families out to the deepest backwoods, places situated, by their calculations, far from the arsenals of humanity-destroying technology. There, out of sight of witnesses who might interfere with them or report them to the authorities, they are building arks in the cavities and gullies of the earth, stocking them with everything needed to sustain life. There are hundreds of government agents hounding these God-fearing men all over the country; their mission is to punish those who dare to appeal to the earth's mercy, those who dare to fear Divine punishment.

Building an ark in such terrible circumstances means staking one's life on survival—that is, the survival of others. Any one of us would a thousand times rather lead an ordinary, easygoing sort of life, and yet we proceed, with prayer and trembling, to build our ark. A cross is set over our life—for the sake of future life.

Who knows when, in what generation, the ark will be called for, and God will summon His seed to salvation! His ways and times are inscrutable. Already the first generation of Arkists— those who started building in the fifties, at the first signs of the fiery apocalypse—is dying out. Those who were then in their forties are now over seventy; some have already passed away, without living to see the crown and seal of their labors. They were gifted scholars, physicians, writers, and engineers, who sacrificed their gifts to the great idea of Salvation. Some died at their task in the ravines of Siberia or on the ridges of Pamir, where there was no one to recognize their self-denying, thankless labors for the future salvation of humanity. But it may be that their children or grandchildren, or those who knew their secret, will be saved in the arks they built. . . .

Our souls grieve for these departed; but their efforts have laid the foundation for a Universal Ark, in which a remnant of humanity may sail the fiery ocean and put in at the shore of the Thousand-year Kingdom. (K. A., "The New Ark: In Memoriam, Thirty Years Later")

DEFECTORS (Garbagemen)

The Defectors are an apocalyptic sect closely related to the Atheans (q.v.). For them, defection from God is the chief sign and watchword of the end of time.

> We must turn our backs on the God of the previous religions so as to meet the rising God face to face. Atheism is our about-face from the first Revelation to the Second Coming. Atheism is the midnight of universal time, when the rays of Christ's First Coming have already faded away, and the dawn of eternal light is still just a glimmer in the hopes of those at the limit of despair. We ourselves must become like the night to share the night's wait for the dawn. For the dawn does not come at noon; it comes only in the dark of night. (A. M., "The Hour after Midnight: Light to All Seekers!")

Whereas pure Atheanism is a fairly intellectual movement, most Defectors are manual laborers with little education, and their preachers are marked by a rather crude rhetorical style. Since the Defectors presently have their densest settlements in Siberia, we quote here from a work by specialists from Ulan-Ude, "Religious Beliefs of the Peoples of Siberia, part 2: Small Socio-ethnic Groups":

> They call themselves Defectors because they abandon God in order to seek God. Holy Scripture, temples, dogmas, sacred utensils, rituals—all these are only the image of God as manifested to the world. But the genuine God of the future will appear only where there is not yet even an image of Him. His Coming will take place in the most profane of places, a place He has never entered. Therefore, the Defectors are waiting for God as far as possible from all the religious centers of civilization. That is why most of them live in Russia. Some immigrated in the twenties and thirties, since they found in Russia the country with the fewest churches, a country that had renounced religion and

trashed its religious monuments. Many Defectors were exiled to Siberia in the Years of Lawlessness, and later the rest followed them there, believing that the Hand of God was drawing them as far as possible from the light, into the heart of darkness. They think that God will appear in glory and triumph, and glory and triumph can nowhere appear more bright and dazzling than in a far-off, godforsaken, unconsecrated and even sacrilegious place. For this reason, most Defectors are to be found where there are fewest signs of holiness. Sometimes they say they have a "reverse mission": where the usual missionary brings the light of faith into darkness and unbelief, the Defectors bring their darkness and unbelief to meet the coming Light.

As a rule, Defectors make their homes on the periphery of a settlement. This is why they are sometimes called Edgeniks. But they are "on the edge" in every other sense as well: they attribute a sacred meaning to the most disgusting objects, the most sordid jobs, even the bodily functions. They offer supplications to God before relieving themselves, hymns of praise when they've finished, and various prayers throughout the whole process, all in the conviction that they are engaged in a sacred act through which their bodies are being made anew from dust and freed from impurity.

Defecation is the holiest of our earthly callings, because it purifies us from inner filth. All kinds of external purifications, including the bathing of the body in various religious cults, are only preliminary stages leading to the mystery of defecation, which turns our insides out and brings to light their bulk and feculence. Is it not in this same way that the Lord will come to relieve us of sin, discharging the whole stinking load from the belly of our soul? Pray to God when you are straining to relieve yourself, for this straining is the prayer of our body, our belly's cry for salvation. Let this cry resound in your soul as well: "Help me, Lord! Lord, I am weak, break the yoke of my belly!" (M. N., "Theology of Defecation")

Defectors penetrate into the most far-off, godforsaken, abandoned corners of being—wherever it is most squalid, poor, and dirty. They usually earn their living as sweepers, trashmen, sewage-system workers, and attendants of the sick. Of those few still remaining in the major western cities of our country, most work as shoe shiners, taking upon themselves the daily duty of bowing down before filth, stooping before the human load of dirt.

> Bow down before human feet, for they are coated with the filth and dust of the earth—bow down to them and stay bowed while you do your cleansing labors. A scholar cleanses human minds, a poet cleanses human souls, but a shoe shiner cleanses the lowest thing man has, and therefore there is more grace in his trade than in any other of man's services to man. The mind flies high and the soul even higher, but man, created from dust, willy-nilly returns to that dust with his every step. A shoe shiner is posted to the struggle with this most elementary form of dust, serving on ordinary human roads. (I. G., "The Despised Profession")

In general, whatever is most unclean evokes the Defectors' greatest reverence. Some raise a floor mop as their banner, others a nose-rag—sacrificial fabrics that receive uncleanness in order to cleanse the inner organs or the external surroundings. Defectors are put into a prayerful mood by slop-buckets, trash bins, and garbage dumps, which they revere as sacrificial places that receive heaps of filth so that other places may be clean.

> The sole purpose of every impurity is to purify you. All dirt, decay, and pollution is a sacrifice made on your behalf. Pray to the Lord to accept this sacrifice, and not to cast you into the sewer, into the fires of Gehenna.[20] (M. R., "On the Sacrificial Aspect of Garbage")

This is the source of another name for the Defectors, "Garbagemen." They try to maintain constant smouldering in garbage dumps in order to prepare the garbage to ignite. In their view, "The spirit of God will descend onto smouldering garbage as onto a sacrificial altar" (ibid.).

In the words of I. V., from his work "Light in Darkness":

> Light will appear from the direction where the darkness is densest. God entrusted the easiest work to men, the illumination of the relatively light places of the earth through art, science, politics, education, etc. But the hardest work—the illumination of the darkest darkness, the cleansing of the filthiest filth—is beyond man's powers: God has taken it upon Himself, and that is why His Last Coming into the world is necessary. In filth and darkness—that is where His light-bringing foot will step onto the earth.

Anyone who has met the Defectors knows their genuine zeal for the "dirtiest" work, the work of cleaning. Many have seen with what religious fervor, with what prayerful ecstasy in their eyes, they go about the garbage dumps, stamping them down and compacting them, painstakingly separating the clean from the unclean, so as finally to light the sacrificial fire,

> an image of the brightest blaze from the rotten core. For fire is nothing but the quickest form of rot; it has long been smouldering in the depths of the world, against the day when it will be lit with tongues of fire. Then that slow rotting called history will become the instantaneous rotting called apocalypse. After its long, slow burn around the edges, the world will suddenly catch fire in the very core. . . . (V. T., "Communion of Fire")

Some Defectors have gone so far as to accept atheism "in its most banal and hopeless form," that is, they have taken up the spiritual position furthest removed from God. They suppose that atheism, i.e., godlessness, is the worldview in which the coming God will reveal Himself first, precisely because it denies God. In fact, the Defectors are one of the few sects that consciously program change and evolution into their doctrines (whereas the majority of sects cling tightly to established dogmas). Theirs is a deliberate forward motion toward the greatest possible atheism, toward "faithlessness as an apocalyptic faith." They don't follow the Sun, i.e., the old Revelation already setting in the past; they go in the opposite direction, to the black East, where they hope to be the first to meet the Sun of the new Revelation. For them, Siberia is "where the deepest darkness is waiting for the Light, where the utmost silence is waiting for the Voice" (I. V., "Light in Darkness").

In their daily life they take special pleasure in doing the laundry, washing the dishes, and mopping the floors, because in these activities they see an image of the divine actions that will purify the world, a presage of the Apocatharsis, the final and universal purification. Some of them prefer purification by fire rather than water, so they sear their food instead of washing it. This is a remnant of the ancient belief that, whereas in the beginning the world was baptized by water, in the end it will be baptized by fire (cf. 2 Pet. 3.5–7). Among the Defectors, trash-burning fires become holiday rites with special "apotropaic" gestures: they remove a piece of their clothing, usually a shoe or a hat, and throw it into the fire, so as to "be like trash and bring upon themselves the fires of purification" (V. T., "Communion of Fire"). They prefer the burial rite of cremation to all others. Some people think they are descended from Persia and Assyria, where the cult of fire was widespread, but the Defectors themselves deny any connection with fire-worshipers. "The God we worship is not fire, but the Lord of the fiery furnace, Who will smelt the world in His fire" (ibid.).

In general, the Defectors or Garbagemen occupy that area on the map of contemporary sects where "atheistic" and apocalyptic doctrines border upon one another.

STEPPIES

This is one of the least-studied faiths. Its representatives are sometimes called Void-Worshipers, Holy-Earthniks, Cosanostrans, Plain

People, and Latitudinarians. These names may refer to various still-unknown divisions within Steppiedom itself. On some points, Steppie doctrine overlaps with the Red Horde or Orientism.

From the Steppies' point of view, the atheism that triumphed in post-Revolutionary Russia is a significant step in the direction of those eastern forms of religiosity that revere Nothing. The collapse of Orthodoxy laid the foundations for a new universal religion occupying an intermediate position between eastern and western or "negative" and "positive" forms of religiosity, between "world negation" and "world affirmation."

> Russian Marxism is akin to Buddhism in its atheistic tendency. . . . But the essential difference is that the Russian nirvana is sought within life itself, and constructed from the materials of nature and society. The site of salvation, where the painted veils of Maia are to be stripped away, is located in physical space and historical time. Yet it is not fused with time but raised above time, as the bright kingdom of Superhistory (or "Authentic History"). Likewise, the earthly nirvana cannot be the sum or juxtaposition of several different places with their individual landscapes and climates; it must be one single, continuous place, geographically accessible and defined, but endowed with the boundlessness of the Absolute in its eternal self-identity. This placement of nirvana within time and space (rejected by Buddhism itself) leads to specifically "plane" or "latitudinal" modes of religious existence. The reign of one deathless leader becomes the Chronos of this "plane" state of the world, and the extension of one endless plain becomes its Topos. ("Buddhomarxism: Research Materials")

The Steppies regard the "innate instinct" of Emptiness as the specific form of Russian religiosity, not yet consciously recognized and only now emerging from beneath the flotsam of alien religions introduced from the West. But they interpret Emptiness not as a simple Nothingness or "idle negation," but as an indiscriminate Allness, where everything is dissolved in everything else and thus ceases to be anything in particular.

Here, incidentally, lies the source of the Steppies' quarrel with the Thingwrights. Thingwrights claim that "nothing can exist without being something," to which the Steppies reply, "nothing can exist without being everything" (I. K., "The Antinomies of Emptiness").

The Steppies use the term "breadth" for a state of being in which nothing is distinguishable from anything else:

> . . . a quiet, healthy existence in the mode of breadth. Breadth
> is God's gift to man. According to an ancient tradition, in the
> beginning the world consisted only of heights and depths,
> mountains and seas. When man appeared, he didn't know where
> to live, so he prayed: "Where are You, Lord? I want to be with
> You." And God answered him: "I shall put My heights before
> you and I shall spread My depths before you, for you are My
> true image and My beloved child; and I will keep no secrets from
> you, just as you will keep no secrets from Me." And behold, God
> made Eden, the first level place on the earth, and there He settled
> the man, who began to rule over the earth, which was com-
> pletely open before him. . . . But when he closed his heart against
> God, the earth became closed to him again; again the depths
> were ruptured and the mountains loomed up. . . .
>
> And yet, when God expelled man from paradise, He left him
> a place for his work on the earth. Although the plain wafts sad-
> ness and melancholy over man, it reminds him of his covenant
> with God: this is the earth he was given to rule over. And the
> greatest plain was given to the greatest people, the people chosen
> to sanctify the breadth of the earth. (G. Ya., "Breadth and Height
> in Early Eschatological Traditions")

Remember: you live on the plain, and lo, the plain lives in you. "Plain" is the name of the condition of a man who has attained the point of *we* in his soul. The greatest wisdom lies in being plane, like the space stretching out all around you. One and the same endless plain—the plane on which we meet each other—

extends through all souls. He who goes higher or lower will never meet his brother. If you raise yourself a mountain, you will block your neighbor's light; if you descend into a canyon, you yourself will be beyond the reach of light. . . . Look at the earth, how it stretches out around you for thousands of miles! Nature herself has given it to you as a model. Make yourself like this plain: ever the same, neither rising up in joy nor sinking down in sadness, neither mounting higher nor falling lower. Truth lies in this breadth where everyone meets everyone else; it is not in the heights and depths to which individuals soar up and crash down. Breadth unites, while height and depth separate. . . . Breadth is the openness of God's heart, which collects us, all His children, into a single *we*. He who hearkens to the Lord and answers "we" to His "I" has attained the spiritual plane in his own heart. . . .

The chief feature of each thing is its breadth. The ideal world has neither depths nor heights; there, nothing is hidden from man. On the plain, every place is visible from every other place; voices carry clearly, each audible to each. This is the highest degree of development, the ultimate point in the evolution of worlds, where everything internal becomes external. Everything now hidden on peaks and in abysses will emerge from the darkness of original sin, cast off the stamp of its shameful secret, return to its full and mighty breadth, and become *steppe*. Everything has its own inner *steppe*; but what strength it takes to traverse it from end to end, to become level with everything! . . . Will you find the steppe-trekker within yourself, will you try out the breadth and measure of things with your stride? . . . ("The Book of Plains and Steppes")

The Steppies believe there is a connection between breadth and the phenomenon of Russian drunkenness. The latter has never yet been adequately studied; no one has yet discovered a form of sobriety comprehensive enough to compete with it.

Drunkenness is the eschatological sickness of the Russian soul, thirsting after a new earth and a new heaven. All around us we see "the Promised Breadth," as the poet put it, "which eclipses even the brightest light" (I. Z.). . . . This nation will be cured of its drunkenness only when it finds something in reality itself to answer its broadest spiritual needs. The European forms of civilization, too narrow, specialized, "particular," offer no answer to these boundless needs; but intoxication somehow satisfies them by washing away all boundaries. Of course, drunkenness is an illness. The problem is to find a kind of health that the soul would still desire after tasting the unfathomable longing of the steppe. . . . What is needed are forms of expansiveness so sober that no room is left for drunkenness. (Yu. K., "The Joy of Rus")

Among possible versions of the future "divined" by the Steppies is a return on the superhistorical level to the nomadic life of prehistoric times.

Speed is one of the few authentic forms of sober expansiveness. In moving from one place to another, a man senses that his own boundlessness lies not somewhere beyond the edge of reality but within reality itself. . . . The Russia of the future will be a society of "runners"; there, no one will be where he was the day before. In Old Russian times there was such a sect, whose members were always on the run—from the authorities, from settled people, from themselves. Of course, in our times only an economically prosperous society can allow its members to be in constant motion. But our civilization's actual lines of development —the accelerating growth of the means of transportation and communication—point to the likelihood of such a future. . . .

A man on the move does not drink; he is already intoxicated by speed itself. The lower, alcoholic form of drunkenness is crowded out by the higher, apocalyptic form. Where the Hindu communes with emptiness through contemplation, stillness, seclusion, the Russian does it through a maximum kick of speed. He believes in the emptiness revealed to him on all sides, for speed is the highest revelation of this emptiness, sucking him in like a tornado but keeping him whole as it carries him further and further away. He burns up space and time in his soul, while hovering about the motionless point of the Always-Here. Speed has no boundaries, nothing beyond. Everything is here, everything is now. A horse or a motorcycle is all you need to burn up this heap of importunate, oppressive corporeality, to fly off into eternity while still remaining in time. In the words of the early Steppie poet V. B.:[21]

> "Are you moving, my stallion, or standing in place?"
> Wordless, he soars into infinite space.
> The answerless silence, the boundless inane
>   Mirror eternity as in a pane.

This poem, entitled "Steppe," expresses the religious experience of a man for whom alcoholic oblivion is as needless as metaphysical transmutation, for he attains the annihilation of space and time in space and time itself, penetrating into the very emptiness of being. The "boundless inane," the "answerless silence" —this is nirvana revealing itself in the reality of the world around us.

. . . A move from fixed settlements to nomadism is a likely prognosis for the distant future. According to the spiral-dialectical theory of development, the future continually repeats the past on new loops and even returns to ever-earlier stages. If, in the social-economic sphere, we are headed for a classless society restoring the virtues of the original commune, then in the cultural-psychological sphere a return to nomadic life is entirely likely. Perhaps the only path to the moral regeneration of a nation reeling about in drunken visions is to give it a taste of real traveling. (M. R., "On Ancient and Modern Nomads")

Steppies have their own initiation rite, known as the "tour of emptiness." While most religious rituals present the newly converted with obstacles to overcome, here, on the contrary, all obstacles are deliberately removed. Preferably, the rite is conducted on level ground, as open as possible in all directions, as in a field or steppe. There are no orienting signs: right and left, forward and back are all the same. The initiate goes in circles, first widening and then narrowing back to the starting point, after which he is considered to have been "received by emptiness." Henceforth, the emptiness he has "toured" will be within him.

The Steppies' desire to attract the attention of an international audience is evident in K. K.'s half-mystical, half-promotional article, "The God-Steppe: The Chalice of Illuminations," from which we present several excerpts:

In earlier times, mystically inclined young people set off for a land of dreams and wonders—to the jungles and caves of Hindustan or the peaks of Tibet; following in the tracks of Madame Blavatsky and Nikolai Rerikh, they sought wisdom in inaccessible ashrams and the mountain haunts of mahatmas. Now they are coming to Russia to pitch their tents on the bare steppe. In the summer months, virtually the whole of the great Eastern European plain becomes a plateau of meditations for Western Europeans and Americans. The very country that, as the German writer Ernst Junger put it, "had managed to escape the slightest hint of the miraculous"—a country as prosaic as prose itself, as commonplace as an overcast day—suddenly got the reputation of a "chalice of illuminations."

We usually connect the idea of mystery with hiddenness, inaccessibility. The most widespread archetypes of mystery are the cave, the thicket, the mountaintop: this is where the wise man lives, cherishing his miraculous revelation. This network of associations derives from initiation rites: to be initiated into a mystery, one must first overcome an elaborate system of obstacles.

Yet there is something more enigmatic still: the openness, the full accessibility of mystery. Precisely on the steppe, on the endless plain, you can get the feeling that the mystery is not "out there" but right here: you can touch it, but that doesn't lessen its mysteriousness. The very greatest mystery comes to view just where there are no secrets. Level earth, everywhere the same, stretching in all directions into the infinite distance. . . . Is not the universe as a whole, in its excess of space over matter, just the same sort of uniform emptiness? And even if tracts of "masking" material do accumulate at certain far-separated points of the universe, this is still only a drop in the ocean of indiscriminate homogeneity. The universe is everywhere the same; the density of matter is no more and no less in one big chunk than in another. And this uniformity is the greatest mystery to man, accustomed as he is to experience himself as a person unlike any other.

When people go out onto the steppe for long nomadic treks, it is not in order to see something new (there is enough of that in the West), but in order to see always one and the same thing, in order to correlate themselves with the Universe. They study the characteristics of emptiness, and the emptiness fills them. This is the condition they call "vacuoplenitude."

"On the steppe," acknowledges one of them after a trek of about 1500 kilometers, "I attained what I had not been able to attain in three years of yoga and transcendental meditation. The world is as empty as the palms of our hands at the moment of our birth. No Savior will come to us from beyond, because God is only the Fullness of this emptiness. To accept this means to become no one, nothing at all. The only thing that matters is the place where you are standing and the place where you are going; but it is one and the same place. All the rest is nonexistent" (cited from the anthology *Pilgrims in the Land of Emptiness: Observations and Meditations on the Road*).

On the steppe there is no difference between "here" and "there," and in general there are no differences at all. . . . If God did not create the steppe, at least He lives on it. The steppe is a negative made from Him Who is called God: its emptiness is the reverse of His fullness. . . . The steppe teaches a clarity which is itself the greatest mystery; no solution is adequate to it. All you can do on the steppe is exist, without expecting any events. Nothing happens to you there and nothing ever will.

There have been many teachings about what a man should do with his soul, his mind, his conscience. But no one has yet taught what to do with the steppe, what to do with this environing space, and why it stretches out all around you. On the steppe you suddenly understand that you are called to tour the emptiness. And you will always find enough emptiness to tour. Every city, every street, even every room has its own little steppe. . . .

The Russian poet and sage Tyutchev said that nature's greatest secret is that she has no secrets. This can be seen most clearly in those hinterlands, as he puts it, "where the celestial vault so dully gazes at the bare earth." This is why Western "pilgrims of emptiness" set forth onto the steppe: they want to see face to face this sphinx who has no secrets. The Egyptian Sphinx, with her simple-minded riddles, the answers to which are written upside down at the bottom of the page, is a child in comparison with the Russian Sphinx, who poses no riddles. You can see right through him as he shakes his lion's mane of wild prairie grass. (K. K., "The God-Steppe: The Chalice of Illuminations")

The Steppies claim that Russia is the "motherland of emptiness" and at the same time the "country of the future" or, more exactly, the "country of the end of time." Russia, they say, is ordained to "complete the creative destiny of the world." By way of proof, they appeal to both physical and aesthetic analogies.

Among our thoughts, as among particles of matter, there must be some emptiness, so that they can generate and replace each other. One who fears emptiness is incapable of anything great. A great human being is one who has fully experienced the emptiness of the world in himself, who knows how to be empty, a nonentity among nonentities. While "genius and evildoing are incompatible," genius and nonentity are fully compatible, and even entail one another. " . . . Among the nonentities of the world, he is perhaps the biggest nonentity of all," said Pushkin of the poet-genius, thus denying him any right to evildoing. To be a nonentity means to be empty, to be no one, neither good nor evil. And how appropriate it is that this poet flies from inner to outer emptiness: "to the shores of desolate waves." In order to create, he must feel the great emptiness of nature beside him. He creates from nothing, and that is why he is "full of sound and fury": he has to be hooked up to some emptiness in order to open the springs of inspiration. . . .

Perhaps the original act, the creation of the world from "nothing," is reproduced time and again in the work of every thinker or artist who conjures up his own unheard-of worlds from that same emptiness, that "dark abyss" over which the Spirit of God hovered before the beginning of days. In other words, this "nothing" is needed for the fullness of the creative act—and this is exactly what we are short of in our contemporary civilization, so full of information and culture. It seems that all the emptiness of the world is already divided up among thousands of sciences, arts, theories, and practices, each squatting on its own little piece of the planet, all tracked up and trampled down. . . .

But there is still in the world a great virgin wilderness—Russia. And everything that touches her gets a spark of inspiration. "Everything must become creative in this Russia and this Russian language," wrote Pushkin. Russia is the virgin soil of knowledge, the virgin soil of being. If there is anything great still happening in the world, that is because it is imperceptibly touching this vacuum and drawing new charges of energy from it.

A country with so much hidden space in it cannot fail to be bewitching. And even now the best contemporary minds are turning this way, peeking behind the edge of Western civilization, gazing into the pure mirror of the great plain, so as to see their own future "nothing" as the possibility of "everything." Perhaps the reason why the first day of creation has not yet dawned over this "formless and void" land is that God is keeping it in reserve for the miraculous revelation of the last day. We believe that Russia will become the first transmundane power of this world, that the Spirit hovering over this hazy abyss will create here a new heaven and a new earth, shining with the light of faith, cleansing with the waters of knowledge, springing with the verdure of hope. In our world, nebulous Russia is the embryo of other worlds. . . .

In the book of Isaiah there is a prophecy about the great plain where the glory of God will be revealed to the whole world. "The voice of him that crieth in the wilderness: Prepare ye the way of the Lord, make straight in the steppe a high way for our God. Every valley shall be exalted, and every mountain and hill shall be made low: and the crooked shall be made straight, and the rough places plain. And the glory of the Lord shall be revealed, and all flesh shall see God's salvation" (Isa. 40.3–5). It is from the heart of Russia that this voice of one crying in the wilderness will be heard. The Lord's Day, the Last Day, will come to the emptiness of Russia, straightening all ways and raising upon them a new man—the man who is to smooth the rough places and traverse all of space, the man whose All is delivered from the moldering Nothing of his motherland into the festival of her Fulfillment. (G. N., "Plain Eschatology")

GLAZIERS (Glassmen, Vitreists, Glassars)

This professional-religious association was founded, according to tradition, in ancient Egypt some 3000 years ago. In recent times, obscure reports have begun to circulate about an international brotherhood of Glaziers, their professional secrets and their religious doctrines. The fraternal order of Freemasons, in spite of its conspiratorial character, has nevertheless "made waves" in history and received wide, sometimes scandalous notoriety, as has the fraternity of Carbonieri; but so far there has been no reliable information about the Glaziers (or Glassars, as they are called in the European countries).

To judge by all appearances, the reason for this lies not in any particular secretiveness on their part but in their very doctrine, known as "pan-transparency."

The Glaziers' materials are too fragile and transparent to be used for building street barricades or erecting temples. Only a subtle eye can appreciate such extremes of transparency as can transmit even the faintest light. And only the sad experience of our time,

which has finally thrown out the magnifying prisms of ideologies—only this negative experience has made us, finally, recep-
tive to the simple transparency of glass, a closely guarded secret
for so many millennia. (E. G., "Contemplation or Speculation?")

Various links between the Glaziers and the Freemasons have been
conjectured. Some consider the Glaziers a special subdivision of the
Masonic organization, with its own separate lodges; others regard the
two groups as age-old rivals. Unlike the Masons, who are building the
universal temple from massive boulders, from actions and events that
have weight in history, the Glaziers propose to build it invisibly, from
glass, so as to purify the tarnished surfaces of the world, which, through
this vitrification, will itself be transformed into a temple. Unlike the
Masons, the Glaziers are absolutely apolitical; they do not strive to en-
list the support and participation of the rulers of this world, and they
include in their ranks completely unknown persons who have no influence in any sphere of life and who try by every possible means to blot
out any trace of their own name and their presence on earth. "That
which transmits light leaves no shadow" (O. O., "Untitled").

The theoretical manifesto of this movement is A. O.'s *Transparent
Man*, which contrasts two modes of historical activity. One is the "constructive" mode, leading to the Tower of Babel: throughout the centuries there have been continually renewed attempts to build from the
"weights of the Earth" an edifice reaching to heaven. The other is the
"contemplative" mode, whose starting point is heaven itself, its light,
which earthly objects must learn to transmit, thus gradually attaining
the purity of glass. Glass, which is smelted from sand, from the substance of the earth, celestializes it, as it were, from within.

Whereas through stone the earth sends its weight up to heaven,
through glass heaven gives its transparency to earth. . . . Not to
petrify heaven, but to vitrify earth: not to raise up a tower, but
to bring down light—this is what the ancient masters taught.
(A. O., "Shining," in *Transparent Man*)

"Raki'a," the ancient Hebrew word for the partition between the waters above and the waters below, which was erected on the second day of Creation and took the form of the visible heaven, was translated by secret sympathizers of the Masons as "firmament" (Gen. 1.7). But the Glaziers believe, with some support from philological research, that "raki'a" originally meant "glassy crystal" or simply "glass." This is not just a matter of different translations from one language to another, but of different channels between earth and heaven.

"Firmament" is the way of stone; "glass" is the way of light. The vitreous barrier between earth and heaven is actually the divine revealedness of the created world, the cosmos as religious revelation, as clarity in the relation of the two worlds. God hid nothing from his beloved human children. . . . The vessel of faith is filled with the invisible—not with the hidden but, on the contrary, with the transparent. God's invisibility is His perfect transparency. . . .

Heaven directs our glance beyond the bounds of everything visible, in order to present the visible image of Unboundedness itself. In antiquity, heaven was understood as a piece of glassware worked by the greatest Master, and this was not a metaphor for heaven but a fact about glass itself, which is nothing but the bowl of heaven, charged in holy hands with pouring forth divine light and illuminating the frame of things. . . . Heaven, mounted in a setting of stone or iron, becomes a magnifying glass, a precious splinter of transparency: it is an aid to weary-eyed readers and an inspiration to bold seers. But every one of us knows that what we are holding in our hands is a visible image of the invisible, which we can observe in our own soul when we turn our pupils inward. The inner heaven is illuminated through the pupil of the eye. . . .

Thus we can say of glass, as of heaven, that it is both the invisible image of everything visible and the visible image of everything invisible. The simplest thing is therefore also the most magical. The glassy heaven is the link between the pupil of the eye and space itself. . . . In glass we are always and only contemplating the other; behind it stands the visibility of something other or the invisibility of the Other. . . . And this is why heaven has been represented from time immemorial as the habitation of God or the gods: it is absolutely transparent, as transparent as the Absolute itself. When God draws near, we do not see God, but we see in Him and through Him, because God himself is transparency. God is invisible so that everything may be visible in Him. . . . (A. O., "Sight," in *Transparent Man*)

A transparent human being is one who has attenuated his earthly being to such a delicate state that it begins to transmit light. . . . You do not even notice such a human being, but in his light you see yourself, you see more deeply into yourself. The highest rank in this impenetrable world is that of invisibility. The invisible does not prevent others from being seen. The soul is a weightless bubble of transparency in the misty, viscid, glyceric medium of existence. . . .

In the presence of such transparencies—transparent people or thoughts or works of art—you get a clearer perception not of them but of yourself. In their presence there seems to be nothing external anymore; everything is within you yourself. . . . There are works like precious stones—they break up the light and enchant the eye. Then there are works like transparent crystals—what shines in them is whatever is behind them, and the air of the soul becomes clearer. . . . Every transparency is a part of my own "I," resurrected and rescued from turbulence and oblivion. . . .

The final Revelation received by us has no special Scripture and occupies no particular place in the world, but coincides with everything real as its depth and transparency. Not a transformed world, not an improved world, but the world flung wide open before us. . . . Our task is to pass through reality without a trace, as light passes through glass. A man becomes a void in the Universe—and then he fills it, as air fills a glistening bubble. A glassblower blows void into solid matter to thin it out until it shines. Let everyone become the glassblower of his own "I"! . . .

The time has come neither to strew stones about nor to col-

lect stones, but to look through stones. . . . There is light everywhere; the time has come to wipe the glass clean. The soul is
cleansed by silence, attentiveness, all-acceptance. The last man,
the one who will bring heaven to us, is enjoined not to explain
the world and not to change it, but to *accept* it. To conquer the
world through acceptance. He is nothing, but at his side everyone feels himself to be more himself: his intellect more intellectual, his heart heartier. The all-hearing ear and the all-receptive
soul, entering the world and making the hidden manifest. . . .
To accept the world means to separate it from evil. For that which
is accepted is thereby separated from evil, as that which is seen
is separated from darkness. (A. O., "Receptivity," in *Transparent
Man*)

Some Glaziers, as a sign of membership in the brotherhood, carry
symbolic objects in their breast pockets: watches, eyeglasses, small
lenses. Sometimes they use these things, but, even more important,
they constantly study their magical property: to be without conceal-
ing being.

Unlike the Masons, most Glaziers believe that a person can belong
to their ranks without even being aware of it, and certainly without
going through any particular ritual initiation rites:

The highest degree of initiation passes through consciousness as
through glass, casting no shadow. In actuality, the pupil of the
eye, if it is clear, is a truer testimony than all the oaths in the
world. . . . Even a person who has no dealings with glass can
learn from his own eye how to transmit light. The iridescent
membrane of the eye is the sheerest incorruptible flesh, in which
our soul sheathes itself at death if it has acquired clear vision
during its life. Everyone must, as far as he is able, assimilate his
existence to vision and his soul to the pupil of the eye, so as to
earn the portion of the sons of light. Observe in the pupil of your
own eye the prototype of the resurrected flesh. (V. O., "The Mirror of the Soul")

According to the Glaziers (who claim, incidentally, that the ancient German word "glass" is etymologically related to the Russian word "glaz" [eye]), the eye is the glassy vessel of divine light. When a man dies, he turns into pure vision, which no longer needs the pupil since it sees with all of itself. The eye, after absorbing light during life, emits it at death, like the setting sun. By learning from our own eyes, we prepare ourselves for a luminous existence in the form of rays that can travel through thousands of worlds as instantaneously as through plain glass. Herein lies the explanation of the lines addressed to death by the poet-Glazier A. K.: "Obliterate me, merge me into earth, but leave me, oh leave me my sight." According to the commentary of L. O. in his "Mythology of Sight," the meaning of these lines is that "for one who was diligent in his contemplation of this world, all worlds will be transparent."

The Glaziers trace their tradition in Russia back to Count Shuvalov, the celebrated patron of the arts who traveled all over Europe and became a Maecenas of our country's arts and sciences. It was to him that Lomonosov addressed his remarkable "Letter on the Usefulness of Glass," whose meaning has yet to be fully deciphered. On the basis of historical-philological analysis, the Glaziers have concluded that this ode is a document in a controversy that arose in Masonic circles over the symbolic meaning and rank of various minerals. Gemstones, whose properties put them in a sort of intermediate position between stone and glass, were a subject of particular controversy, for here lay the point of divergence between the properly Masonic view and the view, so brilliantly expressed by Lomonosov, of the Glaziers. Gemstones differ from ordinary stones in having higher indices of reflection and diffraction, but, as the poet-scholar shows, these are merely imperfect expressions of the property of transparency, which reaches its perfection in glass. At the same time, the fragility of a transparent object only serves to heighten its preciousness, as in the proverbial expression "to guard something like the apple of one's eye."

Gradually, however, the doctrine of the Glaziers passed into the undercurrents of culture, from which it continues to float up to the surface among a few poets and philosophers (including Afanasy Fet and Vladimir Solov'ev). Freemasonry, with its zest for technology and its stone utopia, with its adamant striving to transform the world in history, occupies the foreground. In our time some Glaziers restrict themselves to an ancillary trade: glazing the windows of the temples erected by Freemasons.

But among the Glaziers there are still some who dream not of glass surfaces on stone edifices but of transforming the entire frame of the earth into glass, making a glass city from earth's dark depths and steeps. Widespread among these Glaziers is a tradition about golden glass, the color of the sun itself, in which the new heaven and the new earth are melded together, giving the glass an indestructible hardness and an inextinguishable brilliance.

Glass is the ultimate destiny of earth, the end of the spiritual transfiguration and enlightenment of substance. . . . Everything that undulates, oscillates, and trembles will become a vitreous sea before the Lord's Throne, and upon this transparent glass the righteous will stand, playing their lyres to the glory of God. For this glass is the light of the world, and it will bear them up. . . . And when the Word descends to earth, in its shining light the whole earth will become transparent glass. There will be no temples, for the earth itself will become a temple, and upon it will arise a new Jerusalem, made all of vitreous gold, for the sun and the earth will become one, and the least grain of sand will become a ray of light. Thus speaks John the Theologian in his vision of the heavenly Jerusalem: "The city was pure gold, clear as glass. . . . And the street of the city was pure gold, transparent as glass" (Rev. 21.18, 21). This is your destiny, to this shall you attain. (Ya. O., "The Architecture of the Heavenly City")

PART SIX
LITERARY SECTS

PREFACE

In recent times, various types of mystical orientations have started to blossom even on the soil of the literary arts. The problem we are dealing with here is not just that writers are expressing their religious views in an artistic form—a perfectly well-known and ordinary phenomenon. But when a writer is himself made the object of a sort of religious cult, and a whole religious doctrine is formed around him, we are face to face with a specific feature of the new sectarianism. Cults of this type have grown up around Pushkin, Dostoevsky, Blok, Khlebnikov, Yesenin, Mikhail Bulgakov, and Vysotsky. We will look at the most important among them: Pushkinianism.

Pushkinianism as a religious doctrine must be distinguished from Pushkinistics as a scholarly discipline and from Pushkinism as a literary-aesthetic tendency. Of course, the works of Pushkin are greatly beloved by the people of our country, and his name is surrounded by thrilling legends. But we cannot ignore certain excesses and distortions in the interpretation of Pushkin's image, where unrestrained adulation reaches the point of religious exaltation. Things have crossed the limit of the permissible when a well-known Pushkin scholar, a teacher with a following of ardent students, exclaims in the midst of a lecture: "Pushkin. Pushkin. . . . Pushkin . . . is religion!" Things have crossed the limit of reason when a well-known writer announces in an article, "Pushkin

153

is my God," and proceeds to demonstrate it in reality: "Pushkin is like God. . . . He was destined to become the spiritual principle that would unite the nations. We see the world through Pushkin's eyes; we feel Pushkin's feelings; we think Pushkin's thoughts. Pushkin is the father of our souls."

"The father of our souls." From here it's an easy step to "the Creator," "the heavenly Father," etc. But what has all this to do with our very earthly poet-genius? As an artist he was certainly very great, but he was not the supernatural personality that emerges from the pages of many "Pushkinianist" works. The result is that, instead of an understanding of Pushkin, we get yet another God-seeking construct, as alien to literary science as to the worldly, earthly genius of Pushkin himself, who had no patience with mystical obscurities and metaphysical enigmas, who from youth onwards took "lessons in pure atheism."

Our press has published some sharp and justified criticism of V. S. Severtsev's book *The Fate of Genius*, in which many facts of Pushkin's biography are cast in a mystical light; even his name—"soldierly as a cannon *[pushka]*, and light as goose-down *[pukh]*"—is read as "the Word in whose image and likeness Russia was created." What attitude can one possibly take toward the same author's pronouncement that "Pushkin is the self-knowledge of life, which neither thought nor deed can exhaust"? The idealist Hegel would probably envy the capaciousness of this definition and apply it to his own Absolute Idea.

There is a group of authors for whom Pushkin's significance altogether escapes the bounds of culture and enters the sphere of cult. We meet here the typical marks of all religious cults: the idea of suffering and sacrifice, sin and redemption, with the addition of such "pagan" motifs as life, creativity, and beauty in their fateful interrelations. Pushkin's oeuvre, so optimistic and life-loving, harmonious in form and revolutionary in content, is dissolved in abstract moralistic concepts: "melancholy," "hope," "wisdom," "incantation," "pan-humanity," etc. Shrouded in a mist of stoic and skeptic philosophy, Pushkin is finally crowned with the gleaming halo of a Christian saint, as if to say that Christianity had triumphed at the end of his "path on earth" (an expression reeking of incense—after all, there cannot be any other path than the path on earth).

Things have come to the point where one of our "well-wishers" from abroad suggests the following interpretation:

> Pushkinianism, with its apologetics of "autumn," "clarity," "melancholy," is undoubtedly a pagan doctrine, but it is closely akin to the pre-Christian attitude of the Stoics. . . . Under the conditions of Soviet atheism, Pushkinianism presents itself as one of the "recursive" approaches to the lost Christian faith, a sort of substitute enjoying official support, though without those extremes of exaltation into which other idolators sometimes fall. For these people, Pushkin is the national Christ.

This passage is from George Stein's article "The New Russian Religion." And this is a dangerous sign: Pushkinianism is already beginning to be regarded abroad as a symptom of the "crash" of our scientific-materialistic worldview. The task of authentic literary criticism and of all scholarship in the humanities, which coincides with the aims of scientific atheism, is to return Pushkin fully to our artistic culture with its glorious humanistic traditions.

PUSHKINIANS

Pushkinians believe in the bright solar god born in the north country and slain amid the snows. In this combination of the bright light with the snowy element lies

> the mystery of Pushkin's gift—the transformation of heat into light, of midnight blizzard into midday clarity. . . . One of Pushkin's ancestors was born beneath the blazing sky of Africa, the rest beneath the lowering sky of Russia. It was his destiny to unite these two natures creatively, transforming each of them so as to make them glow together with a spiritual light. . . .

The followers of Pushkin often meet on sunny winter days in snowy glades where they fill their eyes to overflowing with visions of Pushkin's Muse: the solar flame sparkling in the cold snowflakes. This is the meaning prefigured by the snow cover, which pre-Pushkinian poets and prophets had identified with the gloomy savannah—the shroud of the dead. Pushkin was the first to grasp that snow is the garment of the regenerative body of the earth, a garment which absorbs and multiplies the rays of the sun. In Russia, cold is akin to light . . . hence Pushkin's vision of harsh Russian nature drawing in the fullness of heavenly light. "Frost and sun: wondrous day!" On that day the sleeping beauty of Russia will be awakened and revealed to an astonished world. "The time has come, my beauty, to awaken / Open your bliss-fully sleeping eyes / to meet the Northern Dawn, / Show yourself like the North Star!"

"Beauty will save the world," said Dostoevsky, doubtless having in mind the worldwide significance of Pushkin's work, which displays the northern beauty of Russia as a spiritual radiance for all mankind. On that day of universal transfiguration, the Sun will be reflected in every snowflake, glittering like a diamond crystal. "Frost and sun"—the mystery of this combination prefigures the miracle of the Last Day. . . . (A. B., "Transformation: An Attempt at a Pushkinian Eschatology")

The rituals of Pushkin-veneration include a continuous year-round cycle of readings from his poetry, which thus takes the form of a sort of modern Holy Scripture, authenticated by the blood of its poet-prophet. The cycle of readings begins on 6 June, the day of Pushkin's birth, and concludes on 29 January, the anniversary of his death, strictly following the chronology of Pushkin's oeuvre, in which "the sequence of days had the inexorable logic of the divine gift incarnated in the human word" (S. B., "One Day in the Life of Pushkin"). The period from February to May, from the death of Pushkin to his new birth, merges in the minds of most Pushkinians with the Paschal cycle. It begins with the Great Fast, which is interpreted as a mournful tribute to the memory of the poet, and ends with Pentecost, when the Holy Ghost descended onto the apostles and they began to speak in unknown tongues, glorifying the coming Feast of the Word. In the course of the Paschal cycle, verses from various periods of Pushkin's lifework are read together with the canonic prayers. The identification of Pushkin with the dying and resurrected Word occupies a very important place in this unique cult, which numbers among its adherents many sincere Christian believers for whom Pushkin the poet is, as it were, the artistic hypostasis of the Christ, the anointed of God.

> Goodness came into the world through the Word, and the world crucified Him on the cross. Beauty came into the world through the Word, and the world trampled it in the snow, plunged it into the ice of the Black River. But at the final point of all time, Goodness and Beauty, merging into the one Word, will conquer and save the world. (A. B., "Transformation . . .")

While the winter motifs of Pushkin's poetry predominate in the eschatology of the Pushkinians, no less significant are the spring and fall motifs, according to which the devotees are divided into "Intoxicates" and "Sobriates." The Intoxicates specially venerate the poetry of Pushkin's youth, full of romantic longings and revolutionary impulses. Their gatherings always feature a cup of wine which they pass around while reading the "Bacchanalian Songs"; indeed, it is thanks to them that Russia has enjoyed a rebirth of the tradition of making punch, which "in the fizzing of the foaming goblets" pours the Pushkinian "life-bliss" into his inflamed worshipers. The Intoxicates revere Pushkin almost as a pagan god, patron of waves, winds, and the raging elements, who "through the outburst of his wild passions brought redness into the cheeks of the sleeping beauty, Russia, and awakened her from a centuries-long dozing sleep" (E. E., "Pushkin and the Peruno Legacy").

The Sobriates, on the other hand, look down on the youthful ecstasies of Pushkin's poetry, holding that here he was paying his dues to the human, so that later, in his mature years, the divine would be able to manifest itself in him. He intensified the passions of his heart so as to exhaust them all the sooner. He erected a lofty idol from the aberrations of his youth, so as then to overthrow it. He swilled the liquor of life, so as to drain it to the last drop and thus reach the truth of sobering-up. Pushkin gives us the capacity to see life soberly, without the slightest delusions, through neither rosy nor dark glasses but with the clarity of morning's awakening and autumn's unveiling of nature. (A. N., "In the Clear Air of the Soul")

The Sobriates do not gather in noisy, ecstatic assemblies to celebrate, amid the smoke of burning pipes and the steam of gushing wine, Pushkin's "liquorous intoxication with life." They usually gather when the leaves fall, in the autumn forest, where the boundless heaven opens up behind the thinning treetops, where one can recognize in the interlacing of bare branches the angular script of Pushkin himself, the unforgettable patterns of his drawings. "The pale blue sky appears in the apertures between the black branches, like a subtle autumn graphic that might have been sketched by Pushkin's own delicate pen. . . . Pushkin's handwriting is the perfect incarnation of autumn, its celestial cryptograph" (ibid.). At these gatherings or, as they still call them, "autumnals," they read Pushkin's verses and their own too, while

the resonant depth of the autumn forest gives their words an incantatory tone, a mysterious echo, as if the wind were whispering them or drafting them on leaves blown about by the same gusts that turn the pages of the books. . . . All the books have yellow and crimson covers, as if it were the very spirit of autumn opening and reading the lines of Pushkin. (ibid.)

More recently, we have witnessed a certain convergence between Intoxicates and Sobriates: there is now an influential version according to which the meaning of Pushkin-worship is the *path from intoxication to sobriety*, the transformation of the truth of paganism into the truth of Christianity. "Only after draining the foaming cup of life to the bottom does one perceive its transparent depths" (A. B., "Transformation . . ."). Therefore, one must devote oneself to debauchery and sobriety in turn, so as to feel the spiritual fullness of the gap between them, the wisdom of their fluent crosscurrents. "Refreshed by liquor, we attain the mystery and the intoxication of sobriety itself" (ibid.). This compromising approach is unique to Pushkinianism among all existing cults of both pagan and Christian provenance.

Like Pushkin, the pagan gods of antiquity were glorified for their amorous adventures; but he differs from them in his pensiveness, his frequent bouts of heartache and melancholy, his always-frustrated impulses toward resignation. The votaries of this god give themselves over sometimes to orgies reminiscent of the rites of Dionysus, sometimes to a dolorous sobriety reminiscent of the early days of Christianity. But between these two extremes, they especially value the state they call "brilliant gloom" or "lush desiccation." They find a keen intoxication in the very process of sobering up, an enchantment in the very parting with life. (V. S., "Pushkin: The Path of Life")

Here we adduce an excerpt from a "theological fantasy" of G. R., which offers a sort of synthesis of "intoxicate" and "sobriate" motifs in the cult of Pushkin:

Is this the god of spring, exultantly bringing us cups of foaming, fizzing wine? The cry of naked Bacchantes rings out in the verdant forests—"Eloa! Eloa!"—as they tear the flesh of the young god. He has given himself over to them to the very tips of his toes, sowing wild curly-headed scions. . . . In the high temple of his posthumous grove, beneath the canopy of his tossing curls, we bow before the king of our free oak groves, drinking in his pure breath from the rain-washed skies. . . .

But the wisdom of Pushkin goes deeper than the springtime frolics of these lithe bodies penetrating each other, with moans

of pleasure, on the velvet meadows. For Pushkin is not just Dionysus, miraculously reborn in the glorious pantheon of our father-
land; he is also the "hidden, unknown god" venerated by the
Athenians and preached to them by the apostle. The quiet rustle
of beauty departing from this autumnal world, the gentle drop-
ping of every garment from its naked, trembling soul: for this
insight into the world of transparencies we are wholly indebted
to Pushkin. He is the god of autumn purity—not the kind of
purity that stares through empty space, but the kind that shines
in the very nature of things and is imbibed by the soul in the
bracing autumn air. . . .

The word "windfall" is the key to the Pushkinian faith. This
word combines two senses: "autumn" and "godsend," since it is
precisely the chilling and withering of nature that opens in the
soul a transparent fountain of inspiration. "Windfall" is the
illuminated condition of a soul that takes the dissolution, the
extinction of the world as a support for courage and hope. We
experience "windfall" in the sight of falling leaves, in the anxiety
of long separation—above our heads the earth's canopy disperses
to reveal the boundless canopy of heaven. Through the thinning
treetops, through the pain and melancholy of senescence, the
sound of "the wind and the fresh breath" of our celestial home-
land is wafted to us. . . .

And when, at the end of life, an infinity without consolation
opens up before us, we find revived in this emptiness that feeling of the "hour of farewell," that creative hope. We feel on our
face the breath of the Boldinsky autumn, and our journey beyond space and time is consummated by our long-awaited meeting with Pushkin.

One can go on to ask: dear Pushkin,
Why should I think of inscrutable emptiness
As lying beyond the terrible grave?
Shouldn't I rather think it's wherever you are?

These are the words of the poetess known as "the White Angel
of Pushkin's snowy world."[22] And, indeed, is it not Pushkin whose

poetic breath permeates Russia's endless frozen expanses? Is it not his breath that will blow upon us at the entrance to the infinity of the next world? Is not his spirit—the spirit that first gave form to the boundless chaos of our great country—the first to meet us in our sojourn beyond the grave, as the surest sign of that which has no name and no image? (G. R., "Pushkin and Knowledge of God")

Of course the Pushkinians do not rest content with this "other-worldly" means of communicating with their deity; they look for signs of him in reality itself, for

a poet's presence in the world does not pass without a trace, and the imprint of the world on his word is at the same time the imprint of his word on the world. The world is changed after Pushkin, as if a sculptor's chisel had passed over it; in place of the former confusion of its infantile features, a mature and wise expression has appeared on its face. . . . It is through Pushkin's eyes that we see sharp mountain peaks and furious ocean surf, the glitter of the snowy plain and the towering of the evergreen pines. . . . Pushkin's words forged the world we live in, the one we consider our own. In this sense, everything we perceive is actually something we are reading in the depths of Pushkin's lines. Pushkin is not just a book of verses that one can close and put on the shelf; he is the language spoken by the eternally revealed book of the elements. (E. N., "The Verses and the Elements: Introduction to Pushkin's Cosmogony")

We know almost everything about who Pushkin *was*. But what *is* Pushkin? He has not vanished; he is still present with us—in little things and, through them, in great things. How can we know this? We must work out a special technique for making contact with Pushkin, for communicating with him in the world he has left behind. Of course, his verses offer no small help—but they are only hints, only clues to what Pushkin is in nature, in society, in our nearest surroundings. . . .

Pushkin is a certain property of freshness and contrast in the world. Skates cutting the ice . . . a kiss blazing in the frost . . . a feast in the time of plague . . . rapture at the edge of the abyss. . . . Pushkin is Being, not as given but as revealed: the unforeseen essence suddenly cutting through the veils of being. "You showed yourself before me." "Show yourself like the North Star!" Wherever things are not mixed up and muddled together, but flash with diamond facets, wherever essence is displayed sharp-chiseled, there Pushkin is with us as the spirit of freshness, the spirit of pure and bracing contrast.

This is his religious mission in our Russian world: with the sword of his creative word to cleave the earth, still unformed and void. Was it not for this that Russia, with her interminable folk songs, her endless spaces, her dismal monotony of snowy plains, was sent this genius of contrasts? Pushkin is our first day of creation, the spirit that hovered over our deep, separating the light from the darkness, the dry land from the waters, fire from ice and verse from prose. . . . "First poet" literally means "first creator." Thus it is that in those phenomena that do not simply "exist," that are not simply poured forth in being, but truly *reveal* to us, like a flashing blade, the sharp cutting edge of Creation—in these phenomena we clearly perceive Pushkin himself, his very flesh, as the flesh of the incarnate Word. For the Word of God, in the words of Scripture, is "sharper than a cutting sword"—and such is the creative word of Pushkin. (V. S., "The World as Sword: The Theology of the Pushkinian Word")

One of the most important concepts of Pushkinianism is that of the "All-Man." Pushkin not only combined the wisdom of drunkenness with the wisdom of sobriety; he revealed the whole range of the human, from the mountain peaks of the spirit to the deepest abysses of nothingness.

Unlike the German Over-Man, who is raised up above men, the Russian All-Man embraces and reconciles everything human. He is not superior, but commensurate with everything; he fully incarnates both the wisdom and the folly, the holiness and the sinfulness of mankind. His allure is not in the purity of a higher race but in the symphonic harmony of all the races. All the moral, psychological, and aesthetic elements of the world are represented in Pushkin: he is a microcosm incarnating the image not only of God, but of all powers that have defected from God or are at war with Him. Such an All-Man is more of a God than the one we venerate by the name of "God," whom we distinguish from whatever is earthly, creaturely, human, etc. For everything that God created in the beginning but then rejected and disowned—the world of agonizing aberrations and mysterious degradation, of playful allusions and bits of nonsense—all this also enters into the nature of the All-Man. This All-Man is God in the fullness of His potentiality, before His separation from the reality created by Him, from the fallen world and erring man. (D. M., "The Idea of the All-Man in Russian Culture")

According to the Pushkinians, it is precisely Russians who are most inclined to All-Manhood, whose eternal image is Pushkin. One can see leanings toward such All-Manhood in Gogol, Dostoevsky, Tolstoy, Solov'ev, Rozanov, and Blok, all of whom are as close to the idea of the God-Man as to that of the Man-God; but they all bear the stamp of either an excruciating schism between these ideas or a one-sided conquest of one over the other. Only Pushkin represents their harmonious reconciliation.

After Pushkin begins the suicidal struggle between the divine and the human in Gogol, the palsied human thrust toward the divine in Dostoevsky, the mortification of the human by the divine in Tolstoy, the extension of the divine at the expense of the human in Solov'ev, the extension of the human at the expense of the divine in Rozanov, the solution of the human in the divine and the divine in the anti-divine in Blok. The gauge of all of them is Pushkin. Pushkin's spirituality is the broadest, although not the deepest or the most devout.

. . . Pushkin's All-Manhood extends to the depths of human

ignominy. "Among the base children of the world, he is, perhaps, the basest of them all"—we know from the memoirs of Pushkin's contemporaries that this is not just the poet's coy manner of self-description, but a fact of his everyday existence. Inanity, deceit, laziness, betrayal, callousness . . . But Pushkin's very baseness bears the stamp of commensurability with the lot of all mankind: he suffers as we suffer, he is bored as we are bored, he betrays as we betray. He has certainly clothed his Word not just in human flesh but in the sins and sores of the flesh. The God-Man in him descends all the way to self-crucifixion and self-redemption. In moments of depression, or shamelessness, or loneliness, everyone can identify with Pushkin, falling and rising in the raiment of his incorruptible Word. "And, reading over my life with loathing, I tremble and curse." What other God has sent us so stunning a revelation, what Savior has conversed so openly with the sin in himself? . . .

The life-philosophy that arose afterward in Germany was only a poor shard from the life-philosophy of Pushkin, the most *life-loving* of all who have ever lived on earth. Not only did he love life as the commonest people do, with equal praise for his "pot of cabbage soup" and his "foaming glass," but he was shamelessly, garishly loved by life and destroyed by life's jealousy. Something else, eternal and above life, had already begun to master the poet's soul in his last years. Finally, out of jealousy, life pierced her beloved to the quick in a tragic duel. . . .

But the All-Man brought even his death down to life, remaining for three days in the tomb of his body and then rising in spiritual immortality. Pushkin died on the third day after he was killed. . . . The All-Man closed the circle begun by the God-Man. Three days was the term of the supreme transfiguration. The death of the word is as unbearable as the resurrection of the flesh is incredible. . . .

The Divine Word, resurrected in the flesh, died again in the flesh—so as to be resurrected in the human word. Pushkin is the final and ultimate incarnation of the Word, but this time with a human nature and a human gift. Pushkin's poetic gift is the mystery of the Logos made human. . . . Now they have finally found each other: the Word that was God and the word of the sinful human tongue. (V. S., *The Life and Death of Pushkin*, vol. 2 of *The Religion of the All-Man*)

Pushkin left no literary disciples or successors. And no wonder. The Galilean carpenter also seems to have left no disciples or successors in his useful trade. And the fisherman-apostle who followed him also did not found any fishermen's union. They taught something else. . . . A startling energy of spiritual incandescence issues from every line of Pushkin. Pushkin's literary work has cross-references with our life. It is precisely Pushkin's work that teaches us how to live. . . . Life does not teach us how to live, for this need not be taught; writing does not teach us how to write, for this cannot be taught; but Pushkin's writing teaches us how to live, and Pushkin's life teaches us how to write. It is precisely in this connection between literature and life that we find the figure of the mysterious crossing, the sign of the cross, the suffering and life-creating service of Pushkin. (V. N., "Fateful Configurations: The Cross")

SELECTED REVIEWS OF
THE NEW SECTARIANISM

Reviews of this handbook began to appear as early as 1986, immediately upon publication of the classified edition, copies of which were all too easily smuggled abroad in the new conditions of semi-glasnost. The texts of selected reviews are presented here with some lacunae: discussions of narrowly specialized subjects have been omitted, as have quotes from the texts printed in the handbook itself.

IVAN DEDOV
The Dal of Russian Thought[1]

By my calculations, this book has more than a hundred authors, whose works are presented in brief or extended excerpts. Nevertheless, the reader gets the unmistakable impression of being in the presence of a single author—the Russian people itself, whose spiritual wealth cannot be reduced to the plane of a single idea or the point of a single concept.

Popular thought is like a language: it is an instrument with which one can say true things or false, good things or bad, wise things or foolish ones. Thus, this book presents both true and false speeches in the language of thought. But the main thing is the language itself. In itself, it can't be right or wrong; it can be judged only by the richness, flexibility, and variety of its expressions. . . . Perhaps we find here the reason why Russian professional philosophy of the 1970s had become so impoverished: by that time the initiative had passed to the people itself, to scores and hundreds of the people's nameless representatives. In the work before us, these representatives are designated only by their initials, and nothing more is needed. For the name of the collective author is simply "the people."

Of course, the editors of this book could be criticized for their bureaucratic, atheistic approach to the treasures of the people's creativity. But not for nothing is it said that God's work is carried out even by the hands of the godless. The professionals of godlessness have painstakingly gathered up the crumbs of the people's expressions of faith, which would have been lost forever if not for this stubborn scientific research. . . .

Here another analogy springs to mind. Just as Dal was the first to gather and inventory the treasures of the living Russian language by recording it directly from the lips of its speakers on all the byways of all the hamlets where he collected his sayings, so the compilers of this handbook have turned to the people themselves for direct evidence of today's thought. Not to professional thinkers with their abstract discussions of the "categories of the dialectic" and the "laws of historical materialism" but to ordinary people, not always very well educated, whose thinking deals with everyday subjects of concern to everyone everywhere: home, food, family, intelligence, stupidity, good and evil, sin and redemption, words and things, war and salvation. . . . And it turns out that on every one of these subjects, the people have something to say about its meaning and its place in the world as a whole.

These ideas, to be sure, are not of the loose sort that people exchange in the streets and discuss on park benches. They are thought out and *written* out. This is not an oral but a written folklore, the people's speculative or written religious thought. And just as a bard does not separate his "I" from that of the people but weaves his song from shared motifs, so here too the reader must not expect any particular originality; for the strength of popular speech and thought is not in originality but in wholeness, depth, and comprehensiveness. Here too, as in folktales and legends, common motifs are woven together. This is the thought not of one particular person, an "I" or "you," but of the people in general. It's a secondary matter that one or another individual has expressed one or another thought in a particularly vivid or colorful way.

Of course, a folk bard is not a Leo Tolstoy. . . . But Leo Tolstoy himself admired the simple wisdom of folk songs and folk tales, ranking them much higher than his own works or those of any professional. So too with these A.P.'s, D.G.'s, and S.U.'s: they do not set up philosophical systems like Kant or Hegel, but move straight to their intellectual goal, just as a folk song moves straight to its emotional goal of arousing sadness or joy, sympathy or indignation. Here too the goal is simple: to understand. How is God to be served? Why does this or that object exist in the world? What is the meaning of human life? Perhaps even the initials are dispensable. After all, Dal did not enter into his *Lexicon* the names of those whose words he recorded; it was the language itself that spoke from their lips. So too with this handbook: it was hardly worth the trouble of attributing specifically to "A. T." or "E. G." a discussion of the importance of food or the sanctity of the home, the enigma of the Russian steppe or the idiocy of bureaucratic procedures. What speaks through them is the thought of the people itself, expressing itself through many individuals whether in writing or orally, consciously or unconsciously, aloud or silently. The only real author is the people itself.

As for the transformation of the people from the yarn-spinning chatterbox of traditional folklore into a silent thinker and pencil pusher —this is both its woe and its merit. Its woe, because this people lived for so many decades with a gag in its mouth, training itself not to trust any spoken word, but only the mute page that would never betray itself. Its woe, because a person's voice had no hope of being heard in his lifetime, while the written word lasts longer and might be read, say, by his grandchildren. . . . Writing can be kept in reserve, speaking for the time being only to itself, entrusting its secret thoughts only to itself.

But this is precisely the source of its merit. In the move from conversation to writing, the people's thinking deepens and concentrates on things that are truly serious and permanent. The people's means of salvation in ages past—legends and tales of miracles and heroes— are now mass-produced to order by hired hacks celebrating "the miracle of a transformed earth" and "the doughty deeds of the hero-nation." The people realized that their own ancient images and tales had been adopted to mock them, to trick them into carrying out some master's designs. And the people's soul recoiled from these noisy songs and miracle-tales. The people started thinking their way into real life and gave up their imaginary flights to the ends of the earth, their fantastic rivers of milk and honey; they had already heard their fill of these grandiose invocations and utopian promises from their own "popular" poets, and now started thinking about how to live among ordinary things, in this difficult and only life, so as to answer their vocation and give an account of themselves before God. . . . Not an account of their performance before the boss, but an account before God of the meaning of their life on earth.

In every object, in every act, the people saw a non-arbitrary, self-subsistent meaning, for which, if one really followed it to the end, one would have to answer before God. Even in empty space, on the wind-blown steppe where the people live, there is still something holy, some way to stand before God and pray to Him. Even playing the fool has its own special meaning: without literally going around in rags like the Holy Fools of antiquity, one can still sometimes slightly botch some job or leave it just slightly undone, and—who knows!—maybe if some tiny misunderstanding is thus introduced into the crazy machine, it may suddenly give out some little squeak of sense. And even in un-belief, in the very defection from God, where the people followed in the footsteps of His persecutors, they still found something edifying for the soul, something leading back to God from the opposite direc-tion, since there is no getting away from His omnipresent love. If you circumnavigate the earth, you'll come back to your own house; how, then, could one go away from God without eventually coming back to Him?

Thus we find the "Good-believers" expressing not a cool and sophisticated philosophy, not a made-to-order, high-salaried "athe-ism," but a wise doubt, a heartfelt hesitation, a skeptical faith seeking no reward from God but wishing to serve Him honestly, without pay and without contract. And where but in the people's heart could a place be found for the mournful memory of its own predecessor, the ancestor-people with its several faiths, later driven out by a younger and stronger people that nevertheless still clings to the spiritually ecumenical origins of its native land? Could professional philosophers in academic departments ever have given rise to the Khazarists, votaries of this poor steppe-people forgotten by all the world? The very idea couldn't arise there. Even the authentically God-inspired poet Pushkin spoke of "vengeance against the irrational Khazars." No, only the people itself could so conscientiously memorialize its en-emy-predecessor, carrying its wisdom down through the ages and finally founding a religious worldview in its memory. A separate indi-vidual's memory is shorter, his heart colder. . . .

In the recent film *Repentance*,[2] which shook the whole country, the question is asked: What's the use of a street if it doesn't lead to a church?

The street in question is named after the chief butcher of the country —Lenin, Stalin, whoever—and the idea is that such a street, running in the blood of history, cannot lead to God. But the book under review here, soaked as it is in the experience of three generations under the Leninist-Stalinist regime, proves that there is no other way to church but the way of suffering and sacrifice. The religious destination of our revolutionary path is at hand: it is time to enter the temple built on the blood of the street named for the butcher. It is just this very path of destruction that leads to the Temple; there can be no Via Dolorosa without its persecutors. . . .

Let us be grateful to the compilers of this book—both the anonymous "initials" and the named editors—for jointly carrying out the truly Dalian labor of collecting the people's thoughts and assembling a "dictionary of the *living* Russian consciousness." This consciousness has not withered even on the barren soil of compulsory godlessness, but has proceeded on its own paths to bring forth its own thinkers, as it had earlier brought forth its own bards and poets. The people's creative thought is alive and undiminished. This is the main conclusion of this book, which reveals to us the unplumbed depths of contemporary Russian thought.

PIERRE DANIEL
The First Socialist Philosophy[3]

When you read this book, the first thing you experience is bewilderment, as if you are standing before a cyclopean structure with many entrances and exits but no clue to the point of it. A conglomeration of fantastical sects with as much relation to religion as to anything you care to mention. Scores of novel technical terms incessantly interpreting and refining concepts alien to all the sciences. And above it all, the roar of the atheist loudspeaker announcing that there is no God, repeat, no God. You get the impression of a gigantic mechanical brain grinding out tons of ideas, concepts, systems. But what is it all for, what is it all about? It's like a mound of earth dotted with thousands of openings: when you look at a single ant, you can guess the meaning of its activity, but the thing as a whole is frightful, like the display of an unintelligible but absolutely self-assured extraterrestrial mind.

I experienced something like this in reading the works of ancient Eastern literature, like the Tibetan "Book of the Dead." A different, unfamiliar type of reason started operating in me, as if a third hemisphere had been grafted onto my brain. . . . But still, with those works, centuries of study and mountains of commentaries somewhat cushioned the sensation of an intellectual abyss—its verges had already been smoothed by the footsteps of thousands of pilgrims bowing down to the religious enigma of the East. But in this Russian book, which assembles under one cover a mass of the most incredible beliefs— well, this is a novelty of a different order. This exists at the same time as I do, but as if on another planet. A harsh, unpleasant, exasperating and at the same time bewitching novelty. . . .

And then a thought dawned on me, which I will venture to share with the reader. Although I've read whole mountains of socialist literature in my time, I had never before encountered *real* socialist thought arising on the soil of *real* socialist relations. All those manifestos, proclamations, monographs, reports, lectures, and resolutions, however decisive and uncompromising in their socialist content, had still been constructed within traditional feudal-bourgeois forms of culture. We were always dealing with an "esteemed author" or a "recognized leader" who was "presenting his views," or with a "document" reflecting the "fundamental line of political struggle in contemporary conditions." In all of this there was still the good old definiteness and reasonableness: here is what we mean to say, here is what we are trying to get at. The point was unambiguous. But what lies behind these innumerable I. K.'s, N. A.'s, V. R.'s, D. S.'s, A. M.'s, G. Y.'s, behind these truncated initials swarming about like ants on an anthill? Who wrote all these countless texts, each of which flares up before the reader in a single brief quotation, only to drop away without a trace? Poor Wittgenstein, horrified by idle speech about the unspeakable: his famous aphorism about the use of silence has been stood on its head.[4] Now, whereof one must be silent, thereof one may speak—under the pretext that clever loquacity extends, as it were, the field of the ineffable.

You can't accuse this book of any paucity of thoughts—thoughts are on offer here by the ton, by the kilometer, by the kilowatt, as if in "socialist competition" for the highest output of mental labor. But then again, not a single one of these thoughts has a face, an author answerable for it; they're all being spoken into the air, like some heroic report on something nonexistent. All of them, even if not actually borrowed, are presented as borrowings—everywhere extracts, abstracts, everything adopted from somewhere else, ripped off, "expropriated" into the common stock. Quotation marks, quotation marks . . . This is authentic collective thought such as we never dreamed of before. All that is left of the authors is their initials, and all that is left of their thoughts is quotations. Torn from their names, from their contexts, they are like scraps of bloody flesh interred in a common grave. Each individual is reduced to a minimum, while the quantity of individuals grows to the maximum (by my calculation, more than a hundred authors and about the same number of works are cited). Abstraction from names. Abstraction from ideas. This is the abstractness of genuinely collective thought, where not a single point of view is omitted, but neither is any developed into a line of logical exposition. Dots, ellipses . . .

In essence, this is a method of splitting thoughts into infinitely smaller and smaller units, which keep losing more of their properties with each division. In pursuit of these "atoms" of sense, the very stuff of culture is made senseless: it is overtaken by a cancer, a feverish multiplication of the cells called "sects." Everything becomes a cult, a mystery, a salvation, an absolute. At the same time, these cults become so numerous that they lose all religious meaning: what soul would want to constrict itself to the point of worshiping articles of handicraft or spilt blood? Religion here is collapsed into a sect, which in turn collapses into a mania—a phenomenon no longer of a religious but of a psychopathic or sociopathic order.

Different structures and levels of the social edifice mature at different rates. First the economic foundations of socialism are formed, then the political structure, and only in the final stages does the ideological superstructure, the "cupola," take shape. Only now are we witnessing this majestic phenomenon: out of the depths of the economic basis of socialism, out of the nucleus of its political system, *socialist philosophy* is arising—socialist not only in the content of its ideas but also and especially in its mode of production. This is philosophy collectively produced, like folklore. This is thinking that is socialist in form and religious in content—the final phase of the collectivization of intellectual property. From above it is collectivized by the Absolute; from below, by the Collective. Thus, there is no contradiction between its socialist form and its religious content. Before us stands the first attempt to construct *socialism with a divine face.*

But not Christian socialism; experience has shown us that Christianity is incompatible with socialism. One would like to call the type of socialism in question "sectarian" socialism. Here the divine is not so much humanized as reified: it presents itself as house, blood, food, ark, wilderness, or as particular human qualities and activities: sin, goodness, assistance. Many sacraments and priesthoods, a whole confederation of faiths . . .

Of course, just as with folklore, there is no direct identity between the consciousnesses of I. K., N. A., V. R., etc. This is post-individualistic consciousness, which reproduces some relics of individual differences, but within the framework of an ever-expanding collectivization of consciousnesses. All that remains of individual productions are quotations, which are compounded into a collective work of a new kind, no longer a text expressing individuality but a manual or lexicon, like some congress of thoughts, opinions, turns of speech, trends. Separate voices momentarily drift up from this chorus, only to be drowned out again. The initials, once severed from their names, go to make up the name of the collective author of the lexicon, and this name is Alphabet. Comrade ABCDEFG is the real author of this strange book.

The fact of the matter is that whatever the editors of this manual intended by assembling extracts from scores of compositions, they have made something far greater than a manual—they have made a work of the new philosophy, the new religion. The fragments here collected are to be understood not in connection with the unknown texts from which they were extracted but in connection with each other, as elements of a new text, a Universe of Quotations. What does this Supertext have to say to us? Like all lexicons, it has no opinion of its own. *Everyone* speaks in it, while it itself remains silent.

And this silence is just about the most shattering thing I have ever heard—the silence of thousands of utterances dissolving into one another. This is the way God Himself is silent with us, the way His eternal absence is silent. This is the great silence of a lexiconical society, the silence of the Word emerging through the noise of thousands of words.

GUSTAV SCHNEIDER
From Atheism to Paganism[5]

There is a surprising relation between the spread of unbelief and the increasing number of new theologies in our time. It wasn't so long ago that we saw the birth of "liberation theology," the "theology of hope," "festival theology," and even "God-is-dead theology." But these new Protestant theologies arose at a leisurely pace, one or two a decade, and each of them underwent enough public discussion to strike root, if not in the general consciousness, then at least in the academic world.

And now, suddenly, the lid has come off altogether, and seventeen new theologies have popped out of a hole in the heavens. It's like the situation in art at the turn of the last century, when realism was suddenly replaced not by one or two, but by a dozen new avant-garde tendencies all at once, from symbolism and cubism to fauvism, dadaism, imagism, and surrealism. . . . Now the avant-garde has irrupted into theology, the sphere of culture that had held out the longest, behind its canonical fortifications, against fragmentation and atomization. The logic of this disintegration is obvious: once theology loses the absolute unity of its subject matter and starts to be split up into liberation theology, festival theology, etc., why shouldn't there arise also a theology of sin, a theology of blood, a theology of glass, and a theology of garbage dumps? Scores of so-called alternative theologies, heirs to the majestic Christian doctrine, are busily minting it up into small coin.

It will come as no surprise that this jumble of new theologies has burst forth from that very country where, until so recently, atheism had been raised to the level of state law and was inculcated willy-nilly into the consciousness of every citizen. Now the question arises: are these new theologies a sign of the religious renaissance that many people believe has been taking shape over the last twenty years in the consciousness of the Russian intelligentsia? Or does atheism itself, once it has sunk its roots deeply enough into a society, become a breeding ground of new speculative theologies? In the West, theologians are often persons without the slightest flicker of faith, who for this very reason can coolly edit Holy Scripture by the same methods they would apply to the works of a second-rate poet. In a society that has survived decades of mass atheism, where faith itself no longer exists, it must be all the easier to succumb to the temptation of constructing abstract faiths.

In essence, what the new Russian theologies do is to take those same beliefs that replaced religion in their atheistic society and raise them to the rank of religion. For example: devotion to the power of the nation, to its lofty spiritual mission. Or belief in the spiritual significance of food. Or faith in the purifying and redeeming virtue of garbage. Before us stand the derivatives of atheistic beliefs that are suddenly, as if at the wave of a magic wand, being presented as postulates of a new faith. This kind of theology grows directly out of atheism and sanctifies its foundations. It's as if the same music had merely been transposed into a different register; what used to be played on the drum is now being played on the organ. But the ground of this fantastic worldview remains the same, whether you spread it with manure or sprinkle it with holy water. . . .

Whatever religious coloring it may assume, what we see emerging in this "post-atheistic" society is really nothing but a return to paganism, i.e., to the deification of the natural and social world. Sixty years after the victory of Marxism, remnants of the most primitive superstitions are coming to life in Russia—all the refuse dumped outside the bounds of the universal and national religions, even outside the bounds of Marxism itself. And now that "fringe world" out there in the interstices of religion, philosophy, and science has got into the action. All the pitiful crumbs dropped from the table of civilization have been gathered, and the feast of the philosophic troglodytes has begun. What we have before us is a handbook of every conceivable and inconceivable religious doctrine ever discarded by East or West, scraps of all religious and philosophic systems—a heap of intellectual trash rising on the vast Eurasian plain. . . .

This weird scholastic delirium would be beyond description if not for the fact that the atheists themselves have gone to the trouble of putting it all in order, codifying everything under itemized headings, and presenting it all to the reader in a "watertight" form. The question is—*why*??

Whatever contradictory opinions this work may evoke in Western readers, it compels us to pose one general question: what is the relation between this mélange of religious views and the official ideology? At first glance, the Marxist point of view seems to be unambiguously expressed by Professor Gibaydulina in her introduction to the hand-book. But the very fact of the publication of such heretical ideas forces one to wonder: are they *really* all that heretical? Isn't it rather that the Soviet ideology is preparing a strategic retreat or, rather, shifting onto a new track, where it will be able to keep chugging along in the future? To this end it has been concocting a new system of ideas and indirectly inculcating it into the consciousness of the masses under the pretence of subjecting it to official criticism. The new system is broader and more flexible than "scientific atheism," and more suited to the ultimate goals of the communist strategy.

"What?! Religion—the handmaiden of communism?! After every-thing the classic authors of communism have written about the opiate of the people?!?" But if a society is suffering from a serious—or let's say an incurable—disease, then from a medical point of view opium is by no means ruled out and may even prove the drug of choice.

What is there in the new sects that could possibly present a serious threat to the Moscow atheists? Their "theism"? But the new sectarians take the name of God in vain so freely and frequently that it loses any meaning. It's like punctuating every phrase with a meaningless "For God's sake": the whole theology of the Russian sectarians comes down to mere mechanical swearing, and in their mouths the name of God turns into a casual interjection. For them, belief in God is just a pretext for belief in the divinity of all sorts of outrageous and absurd things. It's like a grotesque contest: who can come up with the most outrageous and absurd things to believe in? One sect deifies blood, another empti-ness, yet others food, glass, grains of sand. . . . What we have before us is a new paganism, deifying literally everything and anything with no particular attention to the distinction between clean and unclean, high and low. Every trifling bit of nonsense gets its own "theological analysis," comparable with psychoanalysis in its manic obsessiveness, except that the object of its quest is not "the sexual" but "the sacred."

The sectarian writers openly assert that now, in the wake of the atheistic age and taking account of its lessons, it has become impos-sible to distinguish the sacred from the secular, God from the world. "God is not in everything, but in *each* thing . . . God is the One and Only, and every thing in its singularity is made in the image of God" (I. K., "The Thing as an Object of Divine Knowledge"). Obviously, such a formulation makes neo-sectarianism indistinguishable from the merest paganism, which is precisely what it is. . . . "God" turns into a formality, a sort of parenthetical convention, while at the same time everything and anything becomes deified.

This new sectarianism has great advantages for the Moscow ideologues, especially in their present posture of denying it any official recognition. First of all, it's useful in the struggle against the two major historical religions that present the greatest dangers to state atheism: Christianity and Islam. By breaking down canonical doctrines into a hodgepodge of interpretations and "versions" with no deep traditions, the new sectarianism makes them that much easier to wipe out. Second, neo-sectarianism fully recognizes the rights of atheism as a special form of belief with greater validity than the petrified forms of dogmatic religious belief. Third, and most important, neo-sectarianism *sanctifies* the actual status quo, gives religious sanction to the modes and orders that, according to Marxism, can have only a social-historical sanction. Historical rationalizations are short-lived by their very nature, and for a society thirsting for permanence, it would be desirable to have in reserve some more reliable, more "absolute" means of justification "from above." . . .

In the end, Marx's atheism has played out its role in Soviet society and now, like the "dear departed," can gracefully accept the ritual honors bestowed upon it. "The Moor has done the deed, the Moor can leave," as Mr. Ridler observed in a jocular allusion to Marx's family nickname.[6] But the task of a living ideology is to sanctify the present. An epoch of denial must be followed by an epoch of affirmation, and here, as a supplement to the atheism that denies the "old" gods, it would be expedient to promote a neo-paganism that sanctifies everyday social and private life. . . .

In essence, such "progress" would mean nothing but an historical regress from Marxist to Feuerbachian atheism, with its deification of worldly activity and human brotherhood on the principle that "man is a god for man." The Marxist theory of revolutionary atheism, with its denial not only of God but of such of His attributes as "spirit," "love," and "holiness," was needed for the transition from bourgeois to socialist society; but life *within* socialist society is much better served by Feuerbachian atheism, with its remarkable similarities to "Atheanism" (see under "Atheist Sects"). The obsolete, dried-up scientific atheism is now being replaced by a so-called creative atheism, spawning dozens of new religious beliefs. While denying God as a supernatural subject, it transfers His holy attributes onto man, the family, and society, displaying the full "this-worldliness" of contemporary neo-sectarianism.

It is worth recalling here those specifically Russian currents of the early twentieth century—"God-seeking" and "God-construction"— that anticipated the present range of new faiths. Communism itself arose as a quest for divine justice and the establishment of God's kingdom on earth. Communism could not be overcome "from without," but now it is being overcome "from within," on its own ground. Communism started as a religio-atheistic sect, and now that it has realized its full potential, it is becoming what it was in the first place: the sum of scores and hundreds of sects, among which, in the final analysis, it remains only one—and not even the most influential.

ROBERT COHEN
A Religious Consciousness in Distress[7]

Russia used to be a remote province of the religious world, with a narrow spiritual horizon hemmed in by eastern Orthodoxy and Marxist atheism. Now, suddenly, she has become the site of an astonishing efflorescence of new cults and sects, many of them quite exotic and entirely unknown in the West. This major information gap has now been filled by a handbook of new sects, published in Moscow and written from a Marxist point of view, but quite objective in its factual reporting on the new cults. Its six thematic sections are richly illustrated with excerpts from the Russian sectarians' own writings, the great majority of which have never before been published in English or even in Russian.

The book is composed in a two-thousand-year-old canonical genre. It could have been named *Against All Heresies,* after the work of the Christian theologian Irenaeus of Lyons (c. 130–c. 200), or *Refutation of all Heresies,* after the work of Hippolytus of Rome (c. 160 or 170–235). Wherever a single true doctrine has arisen, all opinions even slightly diverging from it can only be classified as heresies. Thus it is no surprise that the genre of the "Hereticon"—born at the dawn of our era and practiced with equal zeal by both supporters and opponents of Christianity—is now being reborn, almost two thousand years later

and in an almost identical form, in the capital of the "most progressive state on earth." What *is* surprising is that this very capital of world
atheism has provided a foothold for several religious heresies whose
existence we now learn of for the first time from the writings of their
powerful enemies.

. . . In the future we are sure to learn a lot more about the views of
these Russian thinkers who, unfortunately, remain nameless for the
time being. But history has taught us to place a very high value on
such books written "against all heresies" (in this case, against all faiths),
since through them we can often descry the earliest stages of religious
movements before they take shape in popular consciousness. And
sometimes, as we have learned from the bitter lessons of the past, all
that remains of a heretical doctrine is the polemical works directed
against it. What would we know of the Gnostics, for example, if their
Christian opponents had not taken such pains to describe at least the
general outlines of this complex doctrine? Even in the case of triumphant Christianity, our earliest historical evidence of its doctrines
is preserved in the work of one of its persecutors (Celsius). After all,
the dignity of a heresy is only enhanced when it comes down to posterity branded with contempt and rejection: "Blessed are you when
they persecute you."

But what are all these heresies, really? Each of them offers a religious
explanation of some aspect of human experience, including such things
as food, the home, love of art, fear of war, horror at blood, and wonder
at the starry heaven. This Moscow encyclopedia shows how each of
these preoccupations can become the focus of a religious group. It follows that life as a whole, consisting of many such preoccupations in
turn, is religious through and through. This is our permanent religious
situation, in which nothing changes but the concrete particulars. . . .

As the reader becomes acquainted with each of these sects, it seems
at first like some freak aberration, a bit of high-flown hokum dreamed
up by giddy crackpots. But then, gradually, the reader begins to see
in the rites of each sect one of the motifs of his own life: he too, at some
point in his life, has removed some pebble that was blocking the channel of a little rivulet, or pored over the structure of a grain of sand, or
speculated about the magical properties of glasses and mirrors, or
deified his favorite poet. Little by little, reading one article after the
next, he realizes that he himself is involved in many of these sects as

an unseen participant, a secret novice. Herein lies the indirect but compelling effect of the book: it lays bare before the reader the religious basis of his own life. In a certain sense all of us—some consciously, others without realizing it—belong to the circle of this new sectarianism.

The authors' method can be called "sectionalizing"—they separate out discrete elements of experience, endow them with religious significance, and raise them to the rank of sects. In this sense, sectarianism is simply a means of enlarging for separate examination all the microscopic particles (or atoms) of religious experience that make up human life as a whole. A sect is a socially enlarged model of individual experience in which earth and home, fire, stream, and sand have been sanctified.

It should be noted that this "sectionalizing" method—i.e., the analysis of the spiritual into discrete "sectors," each crystallized into a definite sect, existing or merely possible—is not new; it has been used by philosophers and theologians in the past. Thus Augustine, following Varro, enumerates 288 possible sects, classified with respect to the question of the highest good. The first division concerns the question whether the end of goods and evils is in the soul, the body, or both. "In his painstaking philosophic investigations within the general framework of this threefold division of sects, Marcus Varro surveyed such a great variety of doctrines that he easily brought the number of sects to 288—not such as have definitely existed, but such as could logically arise within the series."[8] The compilers of the Moscow "Hereticon" do not establish a definite number of sects, since they proceed not from strictly logical principles, as the ancient philosopher did, but from actually existing types of worldview. Incidentally, the criteria used by Varro to establish his 288 sects are so abstract and minor that the sects themselves could never have existed in reality. At most, only five or six truly distinct sects could be fashioned from them. But even the most impoverished reality is richer than the most exquisite logic.

Each of the Moscow sects has its own strict dogma, which is almost in harmony with Christian doctrine or, at any rate, with a certain generalized Judeo-Christian worldview. But the heart of the matter lies within this "almost." Authentic religious doctrine is not divisible into parts, and wherever such a division takes place, the world of heresies springs into life. A new religious worldview often takes shape through the conscious critique of heresies. This is what took place at all the church councils, where Christian doctrine was gradually built up through the critique of Arianism, Monophysitism, Pelagianism, Nestorianism, etc. In fact, by defining a particular teaching as a heresy, we imply the existence of another, integral doctrine, from which it has split off or into which it has not yet merged. The wholeness of authentic faith is inexpressible; what can be expressed is either a heresy or a critique of a heresy. Can we not conclude that this depiction of the multifarious Moscow sects bears witness to the birth of a new religious consciousness, defined for the time being in reverse perspective only because it has not yet found its direct expression?

Each of the sects described here presents an absurd, grotesque exaggeration of the object of its veneration. But everything falls into place if we define the religious consciousness as the inner unity of all those sectarian tendencies scrutinized one by one under the microscope of this encyclopedia. The authentic religious consciousness embraces all those aspects of being revered piecemeal by the various sects. All these sects are ingredients of a single religious experience, which can be theoretically described only in its parts, though it can be lived and incarnated only as a whole. One must hope for the emergence of a "sect" capable of uniting all the others within itself. Then, at last, it will lose its sectarian character and gain the dignity of an authentic religion. Thus, I would define this strange encyclopedia as the path to self-possession of a religious consciousness in distress.

EPILOGUE TO
THE NEW SECTARIANISM
Atheism as a Spiritual Vocation: From the Archive of Professor R. O. Gibaydulina

Preface

Of all the fighters on all the fronts of Soviet ideology, one group—the scientific atheists—always remained a bit in the shadows. While other groups—dialectical materialists, historical materialists, political economists, Party historians, scientific communists—adorned academic and public institutions everywhere in a blaze of life-affirming glory, there was always something pale and sepulchral about the scientific atheists. In fact, their importance was inversely proportional to their achievements, and the more progress they made in throwing religion into "the dustbin of history," the more of an anachronism they became. The phenomenon of the atheist always evoked a kind of shame in the Soviet people, a reproach: "What?! You—still here? So you haven't finished rooting out all the vestiges yet? What are you working on now?" Atheism was always dragging around the shadow of its otherworldly enemy, darkening the doors of those festive halls where the Party was busy snuggling up to the bright future. It was forever muttering about some contradictions in the Bible, pathetically picking away at some discrepancies in forgotten theological quarrels. For example, it was continually exposing the "incorrect, non-Marxist, not even strictly Hegelian dialectic of multiplicity and unity in the doctrine of the Trinity." While solid Soviet citizens were impatiently waiting to toast the communist future of all mankind and drink up, the atheists kept hammering away about the fires of the Inquisition and some monstrous parents who had actually made their child wear a cross right under the knot of his Young Pioneer necktie. While other ranks of fighters—the dialectical materialists, say, or the scientific communists—were boldly hewing a path into the unknown future, exploiting the most advanced tendencies of science and technology, the atheists were still clutching at the shadows of the past. And they themselves were shades of shadows; among ordinary Party members

there was even a superstition that an atheist could put the evil eye
on you.

The unfortunate and even disgraceful obsolescence of the atheists
was, alas, no accident; it had already been acknowledged, though in
the fine print of an early, incomplete thought, in the doctrine of the
founding fathers. In his *Economic and Philosophic Manuscripts of 1844*
(first published in Russian only in 1956), the twenty-six-year-old Karl
Marx wrote:

> Atheism in its early stages is still far from being *communism*; in-
> deed the atheism that gives rise to communism is still for the
> most part an abstraction. Thus the philanthropy of atheism is
> at first a merely *philosophic,* abstract philanthropy, whereas the
> philanthropy of communism is immediate and real, aimed di-
> rectly at *action.* . . . *Atheism* . . . loses its point, because it is the
> *denial of God* and asserts the *existence of man* precisely by means
> of this denial; but socialism per se no longer needs such tactics.
> . . . Socialism is the *positive self-consciousness* of man, no longer
> mediated by the denial of religion. . . . [1]

If atheism was already "pointless" in Marx's youth, when communism, as positive and active humanism ("philanthropy"), was still just
emerging, then it had become all the more pointless now that communism had risen to its full height and taken almost half the human race
into its embrace. What is the sense of such stubborn efforts to deny
the nonexistent God, once the Revolution has already established the
omnipotence of man? It's no wonder that the atheists, while duty bound
to the struggle with "spiritual addicts" and their seductive weed, felt
somewhat out of place in the society of triumphant socialism. Their
greatest achievement would be complete and final self-annihilation.
This is why their social stride was so uneven: by hastening their own
victory, they would be cutting off the limb they stood on. Thus they
whipped on their horses with one hand while reining them in with
the other.

But when the light of communist reason sputtered out and a new
dark age of superstition fell upon post-Soviet society, the atheists dissolved into the shadows once and for all. They were like people who
had managed to die twice: first with the withering-away of religion
and then with its rebirth. Members of other groups retooled without

missing a beat: Komsomol operatives headed up the merger of bank-
ing and mafia capital; party functionaries boldly strode into the front
ranks of committed democrats and business managers; Party ideologues took over departments of political science and culturology;
dialectical materialists went into science and technology, historical
materialists into the history of philosophy and civilization, Party historians into the history of Russia, scientific communists into public-
sector management. . . . Only the scientific atheists remained just as
out of place in the new Russia as they had been in the old, Communist
Russia. Theoretically, they should have merged into the ranks of religi-
ologists; but religious studies in post-Soviet Russia were taken over
by the religions themselves, and the atheists found themselves out of
place once again. They weren't allowed anywhere near the seminaries
and divinity schools. What became of them? Who has ever heard anything about their fate in the post-Soviet period? Who remembers them,
the twice-dead? In the face of such total oblivion and ostracism one
must feel something for them—if not respect then at least the metaphysical tenderness and concern that attends everything ghostly and
insubstantial.

The posthumous papers presented below constitute a sort of case
history, remarkable in its own way, of the fate of atheism in the post-
Soviet period. Professor Raisa Omarovna Gibaydulina was a captain
of the atheist forces of the 1950s–1980s. As author of five books and
many articles, editor of anthologies and manuals, director of scientific
expeditions, organizer of conferences and seminars, and teacher in
institutions of higher learning, she spent thirty years at the forefront
of the atheistic struggle. All the more precious, then, is the testimony
of the journals and notes of her last years, when her convictions put
her into sharp conflict with the climate of post-Soviet society. Although
I was not personally acquainted with R. O. Gibaydulina, I came into
professional contact with her on two occasions: first, when I wrote the
preface to the first declassified edition of her manual *The New Sectarianism* (originally published by the Moscow Institute of Atheism in 1985
"For Official Use Only"); and second, when she wrote a polemical response to my article "Post-atheism, or Poor Religion." Professor Gibaydulina's letter was sent to me by the editors, but I had no chance to
answer it. In the summer of 1997, I learned of the death of Professor
Raisa Omarovna Gibaydulina, Doctor of Philosophic Sciences. At the

request of the American publishing house Paul Dry Books, which is preparing an English translation of Professor Gibaydulina's *The New Sectarianism,* I contacted her literary executor and her colleagues, and received from them a set of valuable archival materials, excerpts from which are here presented to the attention of the reader.

Atlanta, 27 November 1999

Biobibliography

From the *Encyclopedia of Twentieth-Century Russian Philosophers* (forthcoming):

Gibaydulina, Raisa Omarovna
(27 October 1926, Kazan–19 April 1997, Moscow)
Specialist in religious studies, Ph.D., professor.
B.A., M.A. (1955), Ph.D. (1972)—Moscow State University, Philosophy Department.

Her M.A. thesis concerned the relation of fetishism and animism in prehistoric religions. Her doctoral dissertation was entitled "On the Epistemological Status of Religion and its Place in Social Consciousness." She was a member of the Philosophy Department at Moscow State University. In 1974, she was appointed Professor of the Theory and History of Religion and Atheism at the Moscow Pedagogical Institute. From 1989 to 1993, she was Director of the Institute for the Study of Religion in Contemporary Society. Gibaydulina's scholarly interests included the sociological and psychological roots of religion; the relationship of artistic, scientific, and religious consciousness; and the analysis of the theoretical conceptions of twentieth-century Russian and Western theologians. Gibaydulina approached the problems of religion within broad philosophic categories, not limiting herself to the narrow framework of so-called scientific atheism.

Works:
Animism and the Problem of the Origin of Religion. Moscow, 1958.
Lenin's Atheistic Heritage Today. Moscow, 1960.
"The Misadventures of Existential Theology." *Questions of Religion and Atheism* 1, 1963.

"Man's Mortality and Immortality." *Philosophic and Social Sciences* 8, 1965.
"'Christianity without Religion': D. Bonhoffer and Others." *Questions of Religion and Atheism* 6, 1970.
Marxism as the Highest Form of Atheism. Moscow, 1974.
Marx, Engels, and Lenin on Religion. Moscow, 1978.
"On the Proofs and Refutations of the Existence of God." *Questions of Religion and Atheism* 8, 1982.
The New Sectarianism: A Reference Manual. Moscow, 1985.
"The Personality of the Believer: Axiological Approaches." In *Personality in the World of Values.* Moscow, 1989.
"Religion and 'Non-classical Science': Paradigm Shifts." In *Questions of Philosophy and Methodology.* Moscow, 1990.
From Pseudoscientific Antitheism to Creative Atheism. Moscow, 1994.

R. O. Gibaydulina and the End of Communism

Raisa Omarovna Gibaydulina belonged to the generation of the Soviet intelligentsia that was born and raised under the communist regime and took its collapse as a tragedy. Although politically conformist, this was a stubborn generation, recognizing a single intellectual authority. If it sometimes wandered at the margins of the "total world-view," if it sometimes strayed in the direction of existentialism or phenomenology or logical positivism, this was only because it believed in the "living spirit" of Marxism and tried to give it the kind of "universal receptiveness" that Dostoevsky had attributed to Pushkin. The harshness of Marxist thought was tempered here by the gentleness of the Slavic soul, which is prone to keep falling under the spell of one "ism" after the next until it returns in spite of itself to its ancestral "correct unbelief"—the "ism" for all times.

But R. O. Gibaydulina always sought to preserve not a "dogma," but the purity of thought. In her writings, she reasons everything out to the end, and her vigilant eye allows not a single strand of faith to slip through the atheist patrol into the camp of "spirituality," "moral-seeking," etc. Reading Gibaydulina, one keeps wondering: how can she understand everything and accept nothing? Could any thinker be so fortunate as to win over this skeptical soul entirely, gain her complete agreement? Could Marx? Lenin? Is there anyone whose thought could have earned the indulgent caresses of this exquisite Muslim woman? (For she was good-looking; the portrait published in her classic work, *Marxism as the Highest Form of Atheism,* shows black tapering eyebrows and an enigmatic, serpentine smile.) In the casuistics of her atheistic researches there is no final resting place for thought, because every thought contains a certain impurity and the bad conscience of half-hidden faith. If the faith of some ordinary Thingwright or Domestican could evoke her merciless critique, imagine the refined sarcasm she could have brought to bear on Marx's faith in the dictatorship of the proletariat or Lenin's faith in the cook who can run the government. All that restrained her was her native sense of communist decency and the inevitability of self-censorship.

What could have been this woman's secret thoughts about the revolutionary leaders she idolized? She was smarter and slyer than her idols, and certainly knew how to take their measure: she could have written a brilliant treatise on "Karl Marx as a Religious Type." Try as we might to imagine this woman in a moment of love, submission, or self-surrender, we can never make out anyone at her side. She basks alone in the stately folds and filigrees of her unbelief. No one but Allah Himself could be the answer to this woman's atheistic inquiries—and then only if, by some miracle, he could manage to become Non-God while remaining just as strict, single, almighty, and all-punishing as the God of the Muslims. What did she need all those Marxes and Lenins for? R. O. Gibaydulina could have climbed solo up the dark cliffs of unbelief onto those sharp, icy, glistening peaks that have been reached from the sunny side only by the greatest champions of the holy wars. Her absolute unbelief exposed every thought as a servile compromise, a superstition, a prejudice. In all her critical sketches, we catch the glint of a mind as tough as Damascus steel, like the sword with which Allah's warriors cut down the unfaithful.

It seems as if Gibaydulina secretly knows that the object of her quest, *pure unbelief,* has never yet been embodied in any positive system —neither in Marxism nor in Leninism nor in anyone except herself alone, so that she herself is obliged to formulate the credo that follows from her unbelief. All the more precious, then, is the intimate testimony of this "pure," "ideal" worldview as it observes its own collapse and attempts to begin a new life—the afterlife, as it were, of the communist

idea in postcommunist society. Gibaydulina's last years were a desperate "struggle for a worldview" in a society that had come to abhor
every "general idea" as an antisocial plague. This struggle finally gave
her the right to speak out directly, no longer hiding behind Marx,
Lenin, and all the ranks of Soviet ideologues.

In her last years, R. O. Gibaydulina was working on a "Postcommunist Manifesto" in which she hoped to unite "Marx's burning contempt
for bourgeois pettiness" with "the restraint of the Stoics" and "an existential mixture of despair and hope." What is arresting in these sketches
is the unrelievedly bleak forlornness of a person who goes on raving
about the bright future of all mankind:

> The main thing is not to lose that tremendous force that once
> united us and raised us up above the earth. In Soviet times, it
> was as if we were all walking on air, raised up by our expecta-
> tions, our faith. Now we have come to know the earthly gravity
> of daily money accounts and that whole vulgar reality whose
> infatuating spell we saw in our dissidents and young people,
> infected by the West and experiencing its infection like a nar-
> cotic trance. In those days, the idea of the West saved us from
> encountering the West itself, just as the idea of materialism saved
> us from contact with matter itself. Our ideology, like an air pil-
> low, held us up above the earth. Marx's materialism was a holy
> materialism; its poetic morning freshness protected us from the
> dreary prose of the profane, money-counting sort of materialism.
> And suddenly this bright cloud of glory dissolved, and we
> fell down onto the thorny earth. Our life was emptied of that
> tremendous force that had once filled it with the awe and joy
> that resounded in our songs: "For us there is no limit, Neither
> by sea nor by land . . . " We were alone in the empty universe,
> and there was nothing but ourselves to fill it with. Our present
> pain marks the end of the Great October Narcosis, that cold, se-
> vere, and curative Narcosis that kept us in ignorance of the
> weight of time, the irresistible pressure of death. Light on our
> feet, we didn't think of bodily decay; we dreamed only of ex-
> porting world revolution on spaceships into that starry cosmos
> that glowed for us like Novalis's blue flower. Communism was
> our *eros*, and capitalism is becoming our *thanatos*. Look at this
> parade of flesh for sale all up and down the streets of our capi-
> tals, these ulcerous beggars swarming about our churches and

metro stations. Body, body, body—lewd, rotting, stinking. Our dissidents imagined themselves as noble Ivan Karamazovs proudly repudiating their tickets to the Kingdom of Communism; and now they have ended up as pathetic Smerdyakovs stuffing their credit cards into a dirty sock.

Is this the sort of matter that Marxist materialism had in mind? No—but rather a sort of dazzling, thinking matter, the Queen of the World, the Beloved of God Himself, frolicking in the circuit of His creation. With that sort of matter, we didn't need any spirit, any idealism or religion. With that sort of matter—eternal, inextinguishable, playful in all its motions, in the rotations of nature and society, in the spiraling whorls of history—we needed no life after death; we ourselves were like immortal gods, like angels of this celestial-material world. Summoned to the feast of matter, we brought the plague of nihilism upon ourselves. Only such a dull-witted idealist and incompetent "dialectician" as A. F. Losev could have written that matter is a blind, eyeless monster before whom the Marxists prostrate themselves. Matter was our mother. We didn't give her much thought, because she was so near to us. We loved her from habit, and we didn't notice how she started slipping away from us, aging, declining. . . . And then in her death throes our mother-matter went tumbling through barren fields, felled forests, poisoned waters. . . . We hadn't noticed her fragility, we believed she was immortal, and so we ignored her, like children who imagine that their mother's love will last forever. Yet we did love her, however obliviously and distractedly. Indeed, she was all we loved, all we had to love, our only comfort before eyeless death—the all-embracing mother whose conception of us was immaculate because, although she had a Creator, she had no mate, no husband to enter her womb.

In her last years, Gibaydulina was particularly interested in electronic communications and virtual space. She saw a certain continuity between the unrealized communist project and that "universal hive of minds and souls" under construction on the worldwide web. It is remarkable that in her notes she stubbornly refuses to call this network a "web" and, in defiance of the generally accepted term, insists on calling it a "hive":

Perhaps we were in too much of a hurry to introduce communism into people's social and material lives. We should have held off on the communism of property and started by cultivating the communism of minds, a selfless readiness to share ideas and symbols by carrying them home into the common stock of information, the storehouse of human knowledge. The electronic hive is the communism of minds that we never succeeded in building. Instead of fields and factories, we should have begun with numerals and signs. . . . But we didn't have the technology. If Lenin were alive today, he would describe communism not as "Soviet power plus the electrification of the whole country," but as "joint thinking plus the electronification of the whole world."

In her "Postcommunist Manifesto" she addresses the topic again, seeing communism as the harbinger, even the prototype, of the age of global communications.

Communism has receded into the past and joined those invincible spectres that will disturb the peace and conscience of humanity until the end of time. So long as communism was in the future, it could be regarded condescendingly as just one more in a series of philosophic dreams or utopian ideas. So long as it was in our present—and we had the high honor to be both its founders and its buriers—we were blinded by its huge nearness and could not see what was actually happening to us. It is only now, when communism is receding into the past, that we can make out its true scale in world history: it was the first, doomed, sacrificial sortie into the electronic information age. . . .

Everything happening now in the world of science and technology is inevitably drawing us toward a future of communism, only under a different name. The society of the future will call itself "global," "planetary," "virtual," maybe "viral" or "memetic" or even "communitarian"—anything but "communist." Soviet Communism, alas, forever compromised this name, though it foresaw and partly even set the course of history for many centuries to come. Mankind is more and more becoming a single information-processing organism. *Communism* is an early, im-

mature version of universal *communication,* and its highest goal
is the collectivization *not of material but of intellectual and spiritual property.* From the International to the Internet . . .

Atheism as a Spiritual Vocation: Gibaydulina's Papers of the 1990s

The theme of "atheism as a spiritual vocation" runs through all of
R. O. Gibaydulina's private journals and public statements. But her
views in later life were by no means always in harmony with changing political realities. Her introductory essay to *The New Sectarianism*
had presented the classic Soviet form of atheism; but faced with the
growing liberalization of the late 1980s, when Russia was celebrating
her first millennium of Christianity and Perestroika was extending religious freedom, Gibaydulina's position actually hardened, becoming
ever more uncompromising and metaphysically provocative. She
started calling for a turn from atheism to outright theomachy. At the
first Plenary Session of the Institute of Atheism's symposium on "The
Future of Atheism," Dr. R. O. Gibaydulina reported as follows:

The atheists are losing because they deny the existence of their
enemy and limit their efforts to rebutting rumors and opinions
about Him. Just imagine if, instead of fighting against the enemy's troops, we were to fight only against panicmongers at
home—people who spread exaggerated rumors of the enemy's
forces or even just acknowledge their very existence. Sad historical experience has taught us what to expect from such "denial
of the enemy" (let us recall the boastful Soviet propaganda on
the eve of the German-Fascist invasion). . . . We must do just the
opposite: recognize the enemy's strength and prepare for the
struggle with open eyes. The atheist of the future will struggle
against God Himself and not just against rumors and opinions
about Him. . . . We must gradually prepare our society to
acknowledge the reality of the Enemy. Yes, He exists; but new
scientific discoveries are constantly exposing more and more
defects in His creation. Our universe must be a pretty shoddy
piece of workmanship, if some chunk of ice from outer space

could suddenly career across the Earth's orbit and obliterate every trace of the labors of mankind. Human history has been one long attempt to correct the defects of the creation—in other words, to face up to the defects of the Creator, maybe even His malice. It's we who are conquering His disruptive diseases, rewriting His faulty genetic code, and redirecting the muddled course of His biological evolution. . . .

These are the terms in which we must put the matter if we are to inspire renewed strength and courage in our supporters. As things stand, what has thinned our ranks and dispirited our troops is the manifest absurdity of waging war against an enemy whose existence we ourselves deny. What we need is intelligence. There's a whole library of theological works that we must reread with fresh eyes if we expect to get reliable intelligence on the Enemy's forces, His attributes, His recruiting methods. It's time to direct our troops against the real Enemy, not His image. . . .

Nor can we continue to rely on science as a source of new recruits. Science itself is on the verge of acknowledging the existence of a higher being. In the West, they're already publishing research that draws parallels between the new physics and the old mystics. . . . What if science announces publicly that God exists? Will "scientific progress" compel us to become believers, or is our attitude to God still a matter of free choice? It's time for atheism to raise its own Kantian revolution! Kant, as everyone in this room knows so well, refuted all so-called proofs of the existence of God. But if there are no proofs, there are also no refutations. Our pre-Kantian atheism is obsolete. Here we are, still trying to prove that there is no God. . . . But the arguments for atheism are just as inconclusive as the arguments for God. What we need is not subtlety of argument but firmness of will. Our models should be not only Voltaire and d'Holbach but Job and Ivan Karamazov. It is time to call God to judgment! The age of atheism is over; the time has come for all-out theomachy![2]

But Gibaydulina's "theomachy" soon came to nothing; the ranks of her supporters were visibly thinning, and she remained practically alone in the field, abandoned by her former mates. Joseph Aronovich Kryvelev had been in the vanguard of atheist campaigns since his appointment to the Central Soviet of the Union of Militant Atheists in the 1930s. He kept up some rearguard actions through the mid-1980s, but finally retired altogether. Andrei Dmitrievich Sukhov abandoned his beloved studies in the history of Russian atheism and took up Slavophilism instead. Zulphia Abdulkhakovna Tazhurizina, a close friend of Gibaydulina's from the Department of the Theory and History of Religion and Atheism at the Moscow Pedagogical Institute, had been a leading specialist in medieval and Renaissance freethinking. As late as 1985, Tazhurizina published a militant essay on "Theomachy as a Social-Psychological Phenomenon" (in *Contemporary Problems in the Theory and Practice of Scientific Atheism*, Moscow), but she subsequently went into pedagogical philosophy, and by the early 1990s she was wholly engrossed in the theme of "the mutual deification of teacher and student." R. O. Gibaydulina remained alone, and even her research center, the Institute for the Study of Religion in Contemporary Society (1989–1993), survived by only one year the Institute of Atheism under whose auspices it had been founded.

Gibaydulina's later writings are marked by such extremes that they sometimes take on a tragic coloring. She writes with an almost physiological despair of religion and Soviet atheism alike, unable to find any thought that could bring relief to her overwrought soul. Below are two sketches presenting the new extremes of her tortured worldview.

11 February 1993
"There is nothing more revolting than a godlet," wrote our Atheist-in-Chief. This is hard to express, but the feeling an atheist gets from God is like a gob of oatmeal shoved in his mouth. "Shut up and eat. And say thank you!"—And meanwhile he's gagging on it. ". . . Every religious idea, every idea about every little godlet . . . is inexpressibly disgusting," wrote Lenin ("On Religion," p. 243). "Even the worship of the purest and most ideal of godlets is a type of necrophilia" (p. 242). The purer and more abstract the god, the more repulsive he is for the atheist, who would far rather have a bloody sacrifice or a savage superstition than the sort of misty intellectual faith in which atheism sees the fall of its nearest and dearest, free reason itself. For an atheist, the most sickening of all the gods are the ecumenical and synthetic ones, the ones who dissolve the hard dogmatic core of religion into a wad of wet cotton—"God in general." Unlike the believer, revolted by the endless stream of matter, the atheist is nauseated by the spongy immateriality of "the

other world." We want a fresh, vivid world, the wild bloody meat of creation—and religion offers us a loathsome gruel, already chewed over for us by a higher being as if we were toothless babies.

20 November 1994

And I would gaze, full of joy,
Into the empty heavens . . .
—A. S. Pushkin

What does an atheist live for if he doesn't believe in the next life, but also gets no satisfaction from this earthly life, rejecting pleasure in general as a sort of bourgeois decadence? Our descendants will certainly wonder what the point of all this was. Maybe it was just a method of soothing our nerves by suppressing all strivings? . . . In an effort to avoid sadness, we also did without joy. The ideal of our atheists was a sort of vegetable existence, without ups and downs. They treated the human heart like an experimental tree, eliminating every disturbance so that its rings would grow evenly from year to year; from dendrification they moved on to petrification, a regression of the organism back into the preorganic state. Life for them was just a sort of reproductive ritual: birth, education, marriage, work, death and all that—a sort of self-sufficient social form that every individual had to repeat. Our atheists were fixated on the appearance of order: they wanted a kind of truth and beauty that could be rationed out to everyone in equal measure. But the appearance of order is only an empty image of grace—no troubled depths, no prayer, no repentance. . . .

Real atheism is the bottomless abyss of man's communal aloneness before the empty eyes of the universe. Communal aloneness. Mankind is an orphan—without God, without eternity, without heavenly promises. Man's experience is in pride and suffering, hope and despair, longing and heroism—a supreme effort with no final reward, no eternal rest. And there is no one to turn to for forgiveness.

Thus, religion is "cottonwool stuffed into the mouth of mankind," but atheism of the Soviet type is also a tasteless brew, good-looking without real goodness. Where is the solution? This is the theme of

R. O. Gibaydulina's last published work, *From Pseudoscientific Antitheism to Creative Atheism*. This is not exactly a book, but a little brochure put out in an edition of 300 copies by an obscure Moscow publishing house named "The Sword." Gibaydulina acknowledges here that the atheism of the Soviet era did not really correspond to its name and was more akin to anti-theism. Genuine a-theism, as a stance of creative "outsiderhood" toward all religion, is still a matter for the future. We present here some excerpts from this brochure:

> After renouncing its ancestral religions, mankind must first pass through an ecstasy of atheism, and then through a period of atheistic despair, before emerging with a new religion of daring and creativity. The transition between the two periods of atheism may be roughly assigned to the late 1960s and early 1970s, when we first observed signs of the exhaustion and impotence of antitheism and the approach of a religious renaissance. . . .
>
> The genuine atheist will be a person for whom all religions are equally near and equally distant. Thus it is the true atheist, rather than some representative of "faith in general," who will stand at the crossroads of all faiths and be in a position to realize their potential dialogue.
>
> Our own field studies showed us just how isolated the various religious groups really are. In their jealous rivalry for the favor of the "true God," they feed on rumors and suspicions instead of meeting each other face to face. It was only thanks to us atheists that they started making contact with one another. In the city of Maikop, for example, the first meeting ever between the local Pentecostals and Jehovah's Witnesses took place in my hotel room.
>
> By bringing different faiths together, atheism may finally enable them to understand not only each other but themselves. M. M. Bakhtin's observation about human individuals applies to religious groups as well: "A person cannot see his own appearance as a whole. Mirrors and snapshots will not help him here; only *others* can grasp his true appearance."[3] Atheism is the *other* of all religions and of religion as such; it is the non-religious quintessence of religion, or, in Hegelian terms, it is not the denial of religion but the raising of religion onto a higher plane, a more mature worldview.
>
> Our mistake lay in denial. We should have acknowledged

the truth of religion as "necessary but not sufficient," needing to find its completion in atheism—which could have acted on it like a controlled thermonuclear explosion, releasing infinite new energies from the everyday fabric of existence. Of course, the word "atheism" itself has been fatally compromised, like the word "communism," by its stubborn denial of the other world. But it rightly divined the path from denial to what our descendants will perhaps come to know as "supertheism."

In the last years of her life, as her contemporaries were dying out and some of her former colleagues had started blowing in the new winds of religion and worrying about the salvation of their souls, Gibaydulina's diaries show her seeking for some common denominator of all historical faiths that might serve as the last bulwark of her own "worldly faith" as well:

30 September 1996
As more and more of my contemporaries go off to join various cults and confessions, the empty place where we used to stand together is witnessing the birth of a new, worldly faith. Indeed, the only thing all these new converts still have in common is this place, this worldly world which they all abandoned and now despise. What do they know or want to know about each other, all these Lutherans and Orthodox, Hare Krishnas and Scientologists, Mormons and Taoists, Buddhists and Jews? Nothing! They're in different worlds, different universes. What are the "goyim" to the Jews, the "unbelievers" to the Muslims? The only outsiders recognized by all believers are the unbelievers, the "world." Out there in the world there are still people to be converted and saved, while those who have already accepted another faith are irremediably lost. The world abandoned by them all—the world of childhood, parents, nature—is all they still have in common.
  While all faiths preach love for other persons, not one preaches love for other faiths; they all regard each other as errors and heresies. This is where atheism will find its true vocation: to offer equal love and equal understanding to all faiths.

When can we expect the transition from Soviet antitheism to the new, creative atheism, "worldly faith"? According to Gibaydulina, it will take at least another two or three generations until the whirlwind of denial raised by the Revolution plays itself out, and religion finally yields to atheism as to the pure self-creation of mankind.

Polemics on "Poor Religion"

Toward the end of her life, Gibaydulina's reflections took the form of a critique of so-called "poor" religion, which she developed in a polemical letter to the editors of *October* in November 1996. The letter was in response to my article "Post-atheism, or Poor Religion," which itself had relied on materials taken from Gibaydulina's earlier reference manual, *The New Sectarianism*. Below are some excerpts from my article:

> Imagine a young person from a typical Soviet family, completely cut off from all religious traditions for three or four generations. Now, suddenly, this young person hears in his soul a summons from on high, the voice of God; and he does not know where to turn. The voice seems to be coming closer and closer, but all the traditional religions seem equally far from him. He goes to an Orthodox church, and finds there a set form of rites and dogmas that doesn't seem to answer to his feeling. He goes to a Catholic church, a Baptist church, a synagogue . . . and everywhere it's the same: he wants to know God whole, but he finds only particular historical forms of worship.
>
> Here, in this gap between emergent faith and the existing faiths, is the source of "poor religion"—religion without books, rites, or rituals. The number of people leaving atheism is much greater than the number arriving in churches. By promiscuously categorizing the followers of all religions simply as "believers," Soviet atheism gave rise to precisely this type of contemporary person, someone who cannot be said to be "Orthodox" or "Jewish" or "Muslim," but who is simply "a believer." The faith of such "believers" might well be called "poor religion." It is religion without further specification—simply "belief," simply "in God." The soul of the "poor" believer is empty of all those religious habits or preferences that are formed by long historical usage or a strong family tradition. Unlike the ecumenical or universalizing movements of the West, which are built on foundations of already existing, richly developed religious traditions,

the universalism of "poor religion" is a uniquely post-Soviet phenomenon, founded on nothing but the vacuum of an atheistic past.

Some recently published statistics are suggestive in estimating the proportion of "poor believers" in Russia. According to a survey conducted in December 1995 by the Center for Sociological Research at Moscow State University, 12.8% of Russian believers defined themselves as "Christians in general," not belonging to any specific confession. Another 2.7% said they saw no essential difference among the confessions, and 2.5% claimed to have their own personal idea of God. Thus, religion outside of the confessions (71% of respondents identified themselves as Orthodox, 0.2% as Catholic and 0.7% as Protestant) accounted for about 18% of believers—a not insignificant proportion.

Even more striking are the figures presented by Lyudmila Vorontsova and Sergei Filatov in their article, "Religion and Political Consciousness in Post-Soviet Russia": ". . . Orthodoxy's main competitor is not other religions, but the swiftly growing category of people with no denominational adherence: 'just Christians.' They grew two and a half times over the three years 1989–92 and in 1992 made up 52% of the population, while the number of Orthodox (of all jurisdictions) decreased" (*Religion, State & Society* 22, no. 4 [1994]: 401).

There is obviously a large gap between the statistics in these two studies—18% of believers as opposed to 52% of the entire population; but, in any case, it seems clear that "poor religion" has become a significant factor in Russian society.[4]

In reply to this article the editors received the following letter from Professor Gibaydulina:

6 November 1996
To The Editor:
In issue number 9 for 1996, the journal *October* published an article by Mikhail Epstein entitled "Post-atheism, or Poor Religion."

Epstein claims to have discovered nothing less than a new religion, which, in his view, arose from the atheism of the Soviet era. Epstein's attitude to this religion is ambiguous. On the one hand, he clearly understands its "poverty"—its lack of rituals, books, traditions—in comparison with the historically developed religions. On the other hand, evidently, he is not only sympathetic to this empty and abstract religion, but comes forward as its apologist and even its theologian.

Unfortunately, instead of taking into account important historical evidence that would have enabled him to connect his observations with concrete popular beliefs, Epstein has made up a new religion out of his own head. Without entering into theological disputes, I would like to present some materials which, while corroborating the existence of "poor religion," cast it in a completely different light from what Epstein imagines. These materials are based on field studies carried out by the Institute of Atheism in the 1960s–1980s in the Yaroslavl, Vologda, and Arkhangelsk regions. Many middle-aged respondents replied to our surveys in terms of views that were widespread in the Russian countryside in the 1920s. According to the norms of professional ethics—almost forgotten, alas, in the post-Soviet press—I omit the names of the respondents.

Arkhangelsk region, June 1972
"After the revolution we gave God the nickname 'Po',' since he was now the ruler of the poor instead of the rich. And we started praying to Him like that: 'Po', our Po', come to the poor, save us from our troubles.'

"People in our parts started praying to Po' back in the 1920s. My Sanka once came home from a party and said, 'Why are you all praying to God? There are no more rich people. We have to pray to Po' now—he's the one who helps the poor.'[5]

"Write down what I want to say: There is no God anymore. The Soviet regime is doing a lot of good for people, but God never did a thing. I pray for the Soviet regime, and I've hung a star in my house to please the eye of my soul. When I took down the icons I tried slicing cabbages on them at first, and then I gave them away to the neighbors. As a Russian, I don't need anything. Rich people used to believe in God, but we kicked them all out. And their God too. Now we're all poor, and we believe in Po'."

Vologda district, August 1972
Notes of a conversation with a former schoolteacher trained in philology:

"Among us they used to say: 'Pray to Po',' 'Po' will help,' 'Go with Po'.' 'Those who were poor with God are rich with Po'.'

The name Po' is more ancient and correct, since it comes from the same Indo-European root as the Greek 'pistis' and the Latin 'fides.' But in ancient times it was forbidden to pronounce this name, so as not to 'bring the evil eye.' The real names of God were taboo among many peoples, including the Jews. Later, the name Po' was replaced with its opposite, 'Rich.' They did this in order to flatter him, to get a better deal in life. Gradually, the old name was forgotten. This is just like what happened with the Slavs in the case of bears. The bear was called 'arktos' in Greek and 'ursus' in Latin, but the Slavs were afraid to mention the bear directly, so they called him 'honey-eater.' But then they became afraid of this term as well and started referring to the bear obliquely as 'Misha' or 'Bruin.' Euphemism is a typical form of taboo. People thought that if they called Po' 'Rich,' he would bring wealth rather than poverty. . . . But now in our time, the end of the world is at hand and the real names are being revealed. God is revealing His real name to the true believers so they will be able to call out to Him at the gates of the Kingdom."

"When did God become Po'? When He heard about the death of His son. His hair turned white from grief, and He turned His suffering face to us. In our hearts, when we think about the Lord, we see His image through a blur of tears. The world is drowned in tears, and each teardrop reflects the image of Po'."

"We didn't understand the destiny of our people. We prayed to 'God'—but this was a false, flattering name that we thought up ourselves. And where is our reward? We're the poorest of the poor. Now the word 'God' is hardly used anymore among the poor. That 'God' they used to pray to, the rich one—did he ever share their troubles? Po' comes in poverty and every beggar knows that Po' will never abandon him. This is how one should pray: 'Po', Po', accept the sacrifice of our poverty! We used to call you by the wrong name, but we didn't know any better! We are yours, poor Po', we are poor like you, come to us in our poverty!' This is how people pray now in Vologda and Arkhangelsk, and they're even starting to use this prayer in Petersburg and Moscow."

As these surveys clearly show, "poor religion" is not what Epstein takes it for—some abstract, empty form of "faith in general" or equal acceptance of all faiths. It is a concrete religion of poverty that arose in particular historical circumstances, an inversion of the notions of wealth and abundance that had previously been associated with belief in God. For all its naive theology, "poor religion" represented a socially and psychologically mature reflection on the crisis of the traditional religions of the ruling social classes.

Once this popular religion of Po' receives adequate analysis in the scholarly literature, it will of course shed significant light on current discussions of "the Russian idea" in this period of the primary accumulation of capital. For what "idea" are we actually talking about—a "Russian" idea or a merely "Muscovite" one? Moscow intellectuals may be suffering metaphorical torments at the crossroads of "universal faith," but elsewhere in Russia "poverty" has quite a different meaning. The people out there are actually *poor*, and it's only a matter of time until they bring their condition to the attention of the capital.

Thus, Epstein has missed the true meaning of the phenomena he describes. His so-called "poor" religion is merely the last gasp of the Russian intelligentsia, which has always been noted for its tendency to criticize "reality in general" by the standard of some "ideality in general." Even those anti-intellectuals like Berdyaev, who attacked the vagueness and abstraction of their own class, still paid tribute to it in the cloudy form of their own religious ideas. While the "progressive" Marxist intelligentsia attacked religion "in general," the Berdyaev crowd came back at them by inventing a religion "in general," some supremely abstract religion of the "Third Testament" or whatever. "Poor religion" as presented by Epstein is just the latest twist in the generalizing ambitions of the Moscow intelligentsia. The fall of communism has given them free rein, for now, to promote their favorite neutered concepts of "God in general" or "faith in general."

I propose that you open your journal to a broad discussion of the popular religion of Po' as opposed to the intelligentsia's "poor religion." Such a discussion is especially timely now, with four-fifths of our country's population living far beneath the poverty level. This is where we should be looking for the germs of a new religious consciousness—not in Moscow but out in the provinces, where pathetic and shameful poverty is the present breeding ground of popular beliefs. This is what Osip Mandelstam was getting at back in 1921, when he wrote that material

conditions had reached such a degree of destitution that nothing remained but to live by the Holy Spirit. "Culture has turned
into a temple. . . . Worldly life no longer affects us. In place of
food, we have a sacrificial altar, in place of housing, a monastery,
in place of clothing, vestments. . . . Apples, bread, potatoes—
from now on these must satisfy not so much our physical as our
spiritual hunger." Although Epstein cites this profound remark
in his article, he unfortunately does not develop it. It could well
become the starting point of the discussion I am proposing.

I hope that the editorial board of *October* will publish this
letter either within the framework of such a discussion or as a
spur to it.

> Respectfully,
> Professor R. O. Gibaydulina
> Doctor of Philosophic Sciences

Gibaydulina's letter was forwarded to me by the editors, but the
discussion never took place. In April 1997, Gibaydulina died of heart
failure.

Last Notes

Gibaydulina's last notes of 1997 testify that in spite of her critique of
"poor religion," she nevertheless gradually came to accept this "abstract faith" as a necessary historical transition to "creative atheism."

21 January 1997
Not so long ago, it still seemed as if history had brilliantly cor-
roborated Engels' scientific prediction: "All the possibilities of
religion have been exhausted. After Christianity—the absolute,
i.e., abstract religion, 'religion as such'—no other form of religion can arise" (Marx and Engels, *Works*, v. 1, p. 591). But *is*
Christianity really "the absolute, i.e., abstract religion"? After
all, its revelation includes such historically concrete details as
the name of Pontius Pilate.

Perhaps the truly absolute religion is emerging only now,
with the collapse of scientific atheism? Perhaps this is what is
heralded not only by our "poor religion" here in Russia but by
the various "universal" religions developing in the West, move-

ments such as the "Unitarian Church" and "cyber-religion"? All these religions may be absolutely false, but they do seem to reflect a true shift in popular consciousness, a move from "anti-theism" to "uni-theism." Of course, it's impossible to disagree with Engels' argument that the final form of religion must be, as he put it, "religion as such." But perhaps he didn't realize that pre-atheistic Christianity was not yet this "religion as such," but only another one of the particular historical religions. Perhaps Christianity had to pass through the "Kingdom of the Anti-christ" before it could start its final metamorphosis into "religion as such"?

If this is so, then Engels was premature in his judgment that "all the possibilities of religion" had already been exhausted in his time. He didn't realize that the era of atheism ushered in by his own work would only be a prelude to the final "religion as such." This is how the cunning of history deceives its own prophets! Only the triumph of this final "religion as such" will exhaust the last possibility of religion and lay the foundation for the ultimate transition to creative atheism!

Gibaydulina observed that man's progress toward abstract religion is at the same time a regress from the highly developed historical religions to the most primitive stages of animism and fetishism, which she saw as "the ruling forms of Western religion in the age of postmodernism." Judging by the mock-perplexity of her marginal notes, Gibaydulina did not have an easy time reading postmodern texts, but she still managed to formulate her own response:

25 January 1997
We thought atheism was the most powerful foundation of humanism: God retires and man rules. But it has turned out that atheism can just as well lead to antihumanist conclusions. Here at the end of our century, the steering wheel is slipping out of man's hands; suddenly he finds himself at the mercy of linguistic structures, the id, epistemic fields, genetic codes, or some viruses of consciousness ("memes"). When you read the "post-" thinkers, you get the impression that men are so terrified of their own freedom that they can't run fast enough to lay it at the feet of one idol or another. . . .
Contemporary movements are possessed by their quest for

the "other," someone or something to relieve people of their own freedom and responsibility. Anything will do—a gene, a sign, a machine. . . . Post-structuralism is swarming with little automatic mechanisms, poltergeists that kick up some mischief as soon as your back is turned. These impish creatures are full of pranks and naughtiness, but they're not capable of serious harm or evil. They're just sign systems at play, frolicking traces and differences—they do disappearing tricks and throw pies in your face. Contemporary thought has a lot in common with ancient animism, which endowed each thing with its own particular spirit. Genes, molecules, language, all of them act independently. . . . After expelling God from the universe, the "post-" thinkers have taken on thousands of distracting little godlets who not only can't be controlled, but aren't even capable of entering into serious moral relations. They just buzz around and whistle mockingly behind your back.

Foucault, Deleuze, Baudrillard—this is not just the dehumanization of thought, but its fetishization. As soon as humanism gets a foothold in the struggle against theism, the pendulum swings back toward animism and ultimately fetishism —incomparably more vulgar forms of superstition than theism. Marx exposed commodity fetishism, the alienated form of human relations that comes to rule over man in the mystical power and authority of "property." Now, after the transition from industrial to informational society, the time has come to expose the informational fetishism in which signs and sign systems are elevated into self-subsistent essences and acquire mystical power over man. Atheism's role in the so-called postmodern age is the same as ever: to destroy idols and fetishes, whether in the form of wooden amulets, monetary tokens, or "systems of signifiers."

It would appear that Gibaydulina stuck with her idea of "creative atheism" to the end, proclaiming its victory over "the historical forms of theism," over "poor religion," and over "the theoretical fetishism of postmodernism." But precisely as an *idea*, in the end she seems to have found creative atheism less and less satisfying, as shown in this note of 12 February 1997:

As an idea, atheism is worth very little—it is just theism turned inside out. But as a kaleidoscope, an optical display instrument,

creative atheism gives us the whole spectrum of possible images of life in all their brilliance. Atheism is the optics of the natural illumination of things. It preserves that healthy color of
things that gets bleached out under the light of divine revelation: the green of leaves, the violet of amethysts, the grey of dust.
Natural light is invisible to us, but it is the only medium in which
we can see with true clarity.

It was the error of a whole epoch to think of atheism as an
object. As a result of this objectification, we got "anti-theism"
as the opponent of theism. But atheism is opposed to nothing;
it is, rather, the pure medium of thought. Oversalted food loses
its own particular flavor. Religion, the "salt of the world," over-
salts everything, so that all we taste is the salt itself. Atheism is
not some specific flavor or fragrance; it is the medium in which
we can savor the true taste and aroma of the things themselves.

Project: "Spiritual Movements of the Future"

In her retirement, Raisa Omarovna was working on a series of sketches
which she tentatively called *Spiritual Movements of the Future*. This
book was intended to become a "panorama" of creative atheism—a
"nondiscursive," purely "optical" method of presenting it. Stylisti-
cally, these sketches are reminiscent of her work in *The New Sectarianism*,
although without the critical commentaries. Gibaydulina explains her
choice of genre in her draft preface:

Since the sectarian mentality is so deeply rooted in the traditions
of Russian spiritual culture, I have ascribed to the spiritual
movements of the future the conventional forms and "religious
coloration" of sects. In this sense, religion is being treated as a
phenomenon of style. While the sectarian prophets of the past
clothed their religious doctrines in political, scientific, and artistic forms, in the present case, scientific and ethical ideas are presented in the guise of religious movements. Such a reversal of
form and content corresponds perfectly to the present post-
communist moment, when the capitalist past—to borrow from
the language of chess—is being castled with the communist future. Capitalism and religion are being restored in our country
in the manner of stage scenery or, as they say now, "simulacra."

Everything is on display, everything is for sale, everything is one endless presentation-masquerade. Religion appears as a phantom of a phantom, with God as an image of an image. . . .

It is hard to judge whether *Spiritual Movements of the Future* reflects some familiarity on Gibaydulina's part with actual postcommunist movements, or whether it is an imaginative projection into the future of the material she had collected for a second edition of *The New Sectarianism*. The Institute of Atheism was dissolved in 1992, and the projected second edition was never published.

We present here three excerpts from Gibaydulina's drafts of *Spiritual Movements of the Future*. These three movements—the Conscience-keepers, Foam-brewers, and Gift-givers—are characteristic of the three primary positive transformations of Gibaydulina's negative atheistic patterns:

1. *Humanism:* conscience as the principle of moral self-regulation, in contrast to religious belief where human behavior is regulated by an external supernatural force;

2. *Materialism:* a poetic vision of matter in its spiritual-symbolic density and richness, in contrast to the abstract, diluted visions of idealism;

3. *Communitarianism, with donatism as its manifestation:* gift-giving as the mode of creative and individual exchange in contrast to the market-inspired "circulation of commodities."

CONSCIENCE-KEEPERS. A spiritual movement bearing witness to "the call of conscience." "Conscience is neither religious nor atheistic; it is prior to this distinction. In some epochs, conscience moves people to religion, in others—to atheism. It is against conscience to live by the belly alone, but it is also against conscience to give God the responsibility for improving human life. Conscience is what moves people, prevents them from coming to rest either in bodily satisfaction or in passive prayerfulness." (Yu. M., "The Tribunal of Conscience")

The Conscience-keepers disagree with both the Social-Moralists and the Existential-Moralists about the nature of morality. "Conscience is not merely the right of free choice, but the responsibility for it before all mankind. Existentialism claims the sovereignty of the individual above the masses, as represented by Sartre's saying, 'Hell is other people.' But, in truth, the 'masses' are present within each individual. The voice of conscience is 'the others' in me, all of mankind within a single man." (S. V., "Mass Existentialism")

One branch of the Conscience-keepers is called Chekhovism. This is an authentically atheistic (as opposed to antitheistic) worldview that gives supreme importance to the concept of "decency." As D. Sh. puts it in "The Ordinary Ones of This World": "Not to deceive, not to betray, not to lie, not to pretend . . . This is the whole basis of all values. . . . Tolstoy and Dostoevsky are far too insistent and grandiose, always addressing us either in a scream or a beyond-the-grave whisper. Pushkin's voice rings clear, of course, but it's somehow *too* smooth and harmonious. The real ideal is Chekhov, precisely because he was afraid of all ideals and couldn't endure the very word 'ideal.' It's in Chekhov that we can recognize the true measure of man: neither a god nor a slave, neither a king nor a servant, but simply himself, simply a human being. . . . It is said that 'Man is the measure of all things,' but what is the measure of man himself? Ordinariness! Neither to rule nor to obey, neither to swagger nor to grovel. This is the teaching we find in Chekhov: fortitude, but not invulnerable, sensitivity, but not lachrymose. This is why we call this ideal 'decency,' in the sense of being neither great nor small, neither above nor below, but within the ordinary proportions of men. Courage, but not to the point of harshness; modesty, but not to the point of cowardice—a constant process of self-correction, canceling out all extremes for the sake of the golden mean. Chekhov is our own homegrown Aristotle. This calm and dignified Chekhovian bearing is what is needed by the Russian people. They have been run ragged by the demands of their civil and ecclesiastical authorities to 'struggle for greatness' or to 'sink into humility.' But who, after all that, will be left to be ordinary?"

FOAM-BREWERS. A spiritual movement that arose from the ranks of the "Beer Party," formed in 1995 with the slogan "Beer is the best policy," which the Foam-brewers replaced with "Beer is the new metaphysics."

"Foam is the perfect state of matter, the play of liquid with air and light. As symbolically expressed in the myth of Aphrodite's birth, it was foam that gave rise to life in the be-

ginning, and from foam a new spiritual universe will arise in
the end of days." (V. M., "Foam of Ages")

The Foam-brewers trace their doctrine to certain discoveries of contemporary vacuum physics, according to which the
universe consists of foamy waves of nothingness. The Soviet
physicist K. P. Stanyukovich compared the universe to an ocean
full of little bubbles—but instead of an ocean of water, it is an
ocean of emptiness, a gravitational vacuum. Matter itself is a
bubbly brew in an ocean of emptiness, and spirit, a bubbly brew
in an ocean of matter. This process of world-fermentation is the
source of all energy and the spring of cosmic evolution. . . .

The Foam-brewers are conscious participants in this process.
In their terminology, "brewing foam" means stirring up the
heavy lower layers of matter, bringing them up to the surface
where they can be touched by air and light. Foam is the prototype of the final transfiguration of the world. There seems to be
a contradiction among ancient sources, some saying the world
will end in a new flood, others in an all-consuming fire. But perhaps both prophecies are true, and will be truly understood
only when the future world turns out to be an ecstatic foam of
fire and water. . . .

Beer, of course, produces the best and thickest foam, the truly
royal foam; but other kinds of foam are not to be sneezed at. In
principle, any substance can be induced to foam, and Foam-
brewers experiment with the possibilities in a growing number
of specialized fermenting studios where they produce foams of
sugar, flour, birch bark, raspberries, etc., each with its own characteristic color and index of refraction. For guidance, Foam-
brewers look to materials such as sponges, lace, and snow—all
types of porous, permeable, or leaky substances. Their task is
to rarefy each thing as far as possible and then whip it up into
a thick foam or, as they put it in the ancient treatises, "make the
cradle of Aphrodite."

GIFT-GIVERS. A spiritual movement that considers ordinary
gift-giving a type of sacrificial offering. Gift-givers devote their
lives to thinking up gifts and presenting them to all their acquaintances—sometimes even to strangers, for "a gift from the
blue is a double gift." In their view, every thing is a potential
gift and every person a potential recipient; the discipline of Gift-

giving lies in matching up the qualities of the things with those of the people. . . .

"True Gift-givers are capable of the most harmonious orchestration of the interactions between people and things, suggesting the perfection our world would have if only each person got what he truly needed and each thing were owned by someone who could make the most perfect use of it. This sort of elective affinity between people and things cannot receive full expression in purchase, because a person negotiating a purchase is closed in on himself, while a person receiving a gift is open to the giver." (E. A., "The Art of the Gift")

Of course, there are mechanisms of exchange for the coordination of people and things, but they regulate only the impersonal quantity and price of goods without reference to the actual people involved. When a thing is made a gift, it acquires a personal quality that it could never have had as merchandise. Merchandise is exchangeable, but a gift is a gift only when it is given to its intended recipient.

"By uniting the individualities of the giver and the receiver, the gift becomes a symbol in the literal, unsymbolic sense of the term. In ancient Greek, "symbols" were the two parts of an unevenly broken object which, when matched, could testify to the relationship of friends or relatives. In religion, art, and poetry, the term "symbol" has taken on a purely conventional sense, which barely hints at that original union of two individuals through the medium of a unique thing." (E. A., "Toward a History of the 'Symbol'")

The giving of birthday gifts is a ritual deification of the recipient: his first appearance in the world is memorialized with sacrificial offerings. The birthday is the emblematic holiday of the atheistic age. In the Soviet period, the place of Christmas, the holiday of God-become-man, was taken by the birthday, the little one-day religion in which each person is honored as a god.

Gift-givers are priests of the Personality; they specialize in bringing to each individual the sacrifice that most exactly corresponds to his individual qualities. And the poorer the material life of a given society, the greater the dignity and holiness of the gift. In Russia, the material level has always been lower than in the West, but the culture of the gift is proportionally higher. As E. A. writes in "On the Art of the Gift": "Gift-giving is an exact science. It has no place for approximations. The correct gift to one person cannot be given to another without turn-ing into merchandise or a bribe rather than a gift. The correct recipient of a volume of Lermontov cannot be given a volume of Pushkin. . . . The maker of a thing is a connoisseur of that thing, but its giver must be a connoisseur of the human soul as well, able to make fine discriminations among those delicate links that connect the world of the soul to the world of things. Gift-giving is the most democratic of religions, the applied sci-ence of practical ethics, aesthetics, and psychology."

Spiritual Movements of the Future is an unfinished and perhaps, as Gibaydulina herself wrote, an "unfinishable" book, "a journal in which new movements will go on entering their own doctrines into the indefinite future" (note of 3 December 1996). It is sometimes thought that in the face of approaching death all the elements of a thinker's worldview are finally drawn together, but in Gibaydulina's case, they instead fell apart, like a river entering the sea. Perhaps this is because she was not a real philosopher but a champion of certain views. In her last notes, there is no diminution of the emotional force of her think-ing; if anything, it actually increases, as all her efforts to construct an integral worldview break against some invisible barrier.

"In my old age I seem to be turning into a hydra. I keep cutting off my own head, but other, new ones grow back even faster," she writes in a sardonic note of 31 December 1996. Indeed, it looks as if one of her heads is working out the final socio-electronic theses of the *Post-communist Manifesto,* while another is reflecting on Russian poverty and the ultimate meaning of the religion of Po', and yet a third is criti-cizing the "universal religion" of the Russian intelligentsia while simul-taneously promoting it as a necessary preparation for creative atheism.

Spiritual Movements of the Future was the work that allowed Gibay-dulina to use all her heads at once in an overarching kaleidoscopic survey. She worked on this book until the end of March 1997 and took her notes to the hospital with her. After the section on Gift-givers there is only one more entry:

12 April. Am I afraid of death? It would seem not. I'm not sorry to surrender myself; in this surrender I myself will disappear, so I won't lose anything—But what if something remains? Some shadowy substance, some cloud of particles flitting about in

agony? The terrible thing is not death but the possibility of some trick form of immortality. What if death, so far from being inevitable, is actually unattainable? People have always prayed for immortality, but maybe they would have done better to pray for death. Of course, if there is nothing *there,* then there is no one to pray to. . . . But still, maybe death is not so easy, and some special prayer is needed to attain it.

I look out the window and try to take my leave of everything, I tell myself that this is "for the last time"—and I cannot, something is pushing against my soul. The impossibility of death. Nausea—there's some inner thumping that will not leave you, release you.

R. O. Gibaydulina died in the First Municipal Hospital of Moscow on the night of 19 April 1997.

Afterword
The Comedy of Ideas

The Age of Ideas

The twentieth century may well go down in history as the Age of Ideas. Never before have people's minds been ruled as in our century by ideas in the form of national and class ideologies, state ideocracies, personal ideomanias and ideophobias. An idea is an abstract concept turned into an impulse of the will, an insistent thought turned into an urgent desire. Ideas rule over the consciousness of masses; they become a material force and replace the world around us. Never before has our planet been enveloped in such a thick ideosphere: unlike the blue atmosphere, this is a red sky hovering over our heads. How else to explain the tremendous slaughters of the twentieth century than by the participation of great ideas in military affairs? An arrow kills one man, a bomb hundreds or thousands. Only an idea can wipe out millions.

But the very super-saturation of life by ideas of various kinds—political, pedagogical, economic, administrative, religious—is assuming more and more of a tragicomic character. Ideas, and the people who become their instruments, are guilty of the most terrible crimes of the century: world wars and civil wars, death camps, atomic explosions, ecological catastrophes, political terror. But gradually, as the end of the century approaches, the power of ideas is being reduced to nothing. Mankind is becoming convinced that there are more important values to be preserved and developed: love, life, nature, the ability to be enchanted by everything unique, individual, unrepeatable.

Ideas are not merely dying out; they are making room for a new freedom of thought which goes under the ancient name of "wisdom." In the Proverbs of Solomon, Wisdom says of herself: "The Lord possessed me in the beginning of His way, before His works of old: I was set up from everlasting, from the beginning, or ever the earth was" (Prov. 8.22–23). But with each generation, a new experience of wisdom develops out of the "being of the earth." A century gripped by the absurd power of ideologies is becoming wiser toward its end. A new spiritual environment is taking form, a sphere of understanding and agreement among all beings living on earth—the Sophiosphere.

In this new sphere, embracing the whole planet, ideas look like relics of gigantic fossils that once inhabited the earth but died out in a climate of spiritual overheating. All these mammoths, dinosaurs, tyrannosaurs, these colossal monsters that once ruled over the minds of millions of people, are now being turned into museum pieces categorized by decade: the twenties, the thirties, the forties. . . . "Collectivization," "Trotskyism," "Enemy of the People," "Socialist Realism," "The Struggle with Cosmopolitanism," "The Conquest of Outer Space," "The Doctors' Plot," "Workers of the World, Unite," "The Red Front," "Blood and Soil," "The Aryan Race." . . . We gaze at them with curiosity, amazed by their powerful muscles, their gigantic organs, their taut joints. Yet at the same time we are perplexed: how could these dusty stuffed animals once have inspired so much terror and ecstasy; how could they even have supported their own weight and not been destroyed by the mere gravitation of the earth? Their former vitality still poses a melancholy puzzle for us; but a sense of pure absurdity vies with our melancholy and even starts to crowd it out. We are standing in a Kunstkammer of ideas, each obligingly labeled and tastefully displayed in its own bottle of formaldehyde.[1]

Some of the monsters have a heavy teardrop frozen in each eye— a sign of their torment beyond the grave and their disgust at their own ugliness. The crooked, jeering grin on their faces, combined with the mournful, tear-stained expression of their eyes, gives them a certain unnatural stateliness. Will the temples of the third millennium perhaps be decorated with these chimeras of the twentieth century, as the Cathedral of Notre Dame in Paris was decorated with the chimeras of the pagan Dark Ages?

Pars Pro Toto

The Comedy of Ideas is the title of a cycle of my works that reproduces not so much the content of twentieth-century ideas as their form.[2] This is a world of ideological dreams and speculative phantasmagorias. Each of the ideas is followed as far as possible to its logical end or limit, as if it were *sui generis* and determined the fate of the world. In other words, each idea comes forward in its totalitarian character, as self-sufficient and all-embracing. This is the source of its inner comedy. The greater its pretensions to being the ultimate law of universal order and the only means of universal salvation, the more comic it becomes: it starts remodeling the world, mobilizing millions of people, herding them into their assigned grooves in the one and only "correct" world order.

The comedy lies in the gap between the partial, "partisan" content of each idea and its all-embracing "totalitarian" form. Partisanship and totalitarianism are just as closely bound to each other in the ideologies of the twentieth century as in the ancient Latin expression *pars pro toto,* "the part for the whole"—from which, indeed, the concepts of *partisanship* ("partialness") and *totalitarianism* ("wholeness") arose. This is the principle of ideological thinking, which promotes some particular party to the position of an absolute.

If, for instance, there is a system consisting of two elements, a nut and a bolt, then there are two possible ideologies: boltism and nuttism. Boltists think that the bolt has to be screwed into the nut; nuttists, that the nut has to be turned around the bolt. Boltists prefer using screwdrivers, nuttists wrenches. The former proclaim the primacy of "pointedness," the latter of "roundedness." The former go by the method of "perforation," the latter by the method of "circumrotation." The former hold that the criterion of truth is linearity, the latter, all-embracingness. And although any actual interplay of nut and bolt presupposes the truth of both boltism and nuttism, on the level of ideology these two truths defy each other in mortal enmity. As soon as we split the whole into parts and attribute wholeness to each part, a host of ideologies springs forth fully armed, cutting and hacking at each other with all the passion of splinters.

By applying the same principle to the seasons, we can come up with a series of "calendrical" ideologies along the lines of "Aprilism":

This outpouring of life from beneath its snowy shroud, this intoxicating tang in the air, this saffron eiderdown on the trees, these plumes of ice-banner in the piercingly blue sky—all this is life in its purest expression, awakened but not yet coarsened, revealing its deepest secrets with the mysterious tenderness of infancy. March is still too stiff and frost-bound, May is already

overexuberant and overfamiliar, in comparison with the perfectly delicate, subtle charm of April.

So might write the ideologue V. L. in his *New Aprilist Theses*. Every
ideology involves a "pro" and a "con," and if the qualities of April are
all marked by plus signs, the other months, both preceding and following, are arrayed on a descending scale. And beside the furthest of
them, October, stands the biggest minus sign of all: "hideous October,
dark, denuded, and desperate, too late for the gold of autumn leaves
and too early for the silver of winter snow, as barren of the charms of
blossoming life as of the mysteries of dormant death—this hideous
blemish at the ragged edge of the year's graveyard" ("Thesis 12").

One can equally well have an ideology of May ("Mayism") and of
every other month as well, for each of them in turn is a culmination
of something in the cycle of the seasons, a sort of peak from which
one can see the other months as stepping stones leading up to or down
from it. August is the peak of maturity, the height of fruitfulness before the first signs of running to seed. October is the peak of exposure
and nakedness, when all the golden and silver masks of life and death
are torn away. February is the peak of severity, the cruelest experience
of the will to live pushed to its limits in a frigid waste. And each of
these calendrical ideologies, just like any political or religious ideology,
could be supported by its own sacred scriptures, its own authoritative
witnesses.

Such is the strange ideological sickness of a mind that takes the
part for the Whole. Every ideology is a sort of tangent to the circle of
life rather than an arc of that circle; arbitrarily taking some one point
as its origin, it promotes that point as the "key point," the "foundation,"
and proceeds to erect upon it a staggering superstructure—staggering
more and more perilously, the further it goes off on its tangent. Thus
it turns out that some one nation, or one class, or one theory, or one
technological or medical scheme must reform, save, regenerate, and
beatify the whole world. An ideology is a strategem by which one of
the parts captures the Whole. This is why every ideology is a cross between the partisan and the totalitarian: it begins with a party and ends
with totalitarianism, and in this metamorphosis lies its whole aim and
essence.

How Many Ideologies Can There Be?

Totalitarianism is in our blood. This has been shown not only by the post-Revolutionary decades but the previous centuries as well. No sooner does an idea arise than it takes on all the attributes of totality —all must devote their whole lives to it, all other designs and aspirations must be harmonized with it, it must capture the hearts and determine the fates of multitudes, of all mankind. Perhaps this is a feature not only of Russian thought but of the Russian land itself: whatever arises on the steppe is immediately conspicuous from afar, from all the points of the compass. A plain is the generalizing and amplifying thought of nature herself; anything that appears upon it immediately swells out into infinity. It has no room for the discrete, the particular, the relative. It recognizes only the absolute and the universal.

But could it be that this totalitarianism, the age-old bane of Russian liberty, also has within it a positive potential? What if we have not yet had *enough* totalitarianism, and we still need a little more?!—But in such a way that the world-saving idea would come not just from politics but from aesthetics, music, technology, sports, literature; from Pushkin, Chekhov, Fedorov, Tsiolkovsky, Khlebnikov, Bulgakov, Vysotsky! From every profession, every science, every occupation, passion, interest, amusement, from every month and every date in the calendar! From grass and flowers, from seas and mountains, from children and fathers, from sunrises and sunsets, from ants and bees, from things and words, from nooks and crooks and empty lots, from heights and depths, from doubts and beliefs! From bemused reveries and idle glances out the window!—Then, among so many other totalitarian groups, fellowships, and societies, the one-and-only political totalitarianism that formerly ruled supreme would simply dissolve and vanish. After all, it was not a perfect totalitarianism but a partial, defective, misshapen one—the totalization of the political part alone at the expense of all others. But what if we were to remove all obstacles from the path of this innate totalism of ours, if we were simply to stop struggling against it and give it free passage through all occupations and trades?

Then, in this full, all-embracing, truly total totalitarianism, we would find a path of salvation from the destructive state totalitarianism. Every group would have its own messianic idea. Every set and circle would have its own way of saving the world.

Wouldn't you like to join the Flower Fellowship? Here, take a copy of our program, our bylaws, our manifesto. We've discovered that horticulture is the key to all social-historical and scientific-technological progress! Take Japan, for instance, or Holland . . . Our slogan: "A Flower in Every Bed." Our mission: to develop the flora of the underdeveloped countries until everyone everywhere on our planet will always be within hailing distance of a flower. Then better feelings and thoughts will blossom in men's souls! Flowers are organs of fructification, and the human soul is invisibly interlinked with all the processes of the vegetable world—fertilization, budding, and blossoming. The fragrance of a flower is an aspect of the flowering of a soul.

Looking ahead, we can make out the features of the perfect man of the future, the Flower-Man, harmoniously uniting beauty of face, strength of body, subtlety of aroma, and loftiness of aspiration. The future Flower-Man will come in every variety: rose-men, orchid-men, daisy-men, each as highly differentiated as the flowers themselves. (From the catalogue-manifesto "Flowers of the Future")

Tailors and bus drivers, stamp collectors and chess players, cleaning ladies and astronauts would all have their own missionaries. Why should it be only the priest in his vestments, the worker in his overalls, the general in his uniform who are called to reform the world and redeem mankind? What about the gardener with his watering can, the biochemist with his microscope, the bookkeeper with her abacus, and the photographer with his flashbulb? Tens, hundreds, thousands of totalitarianisms—and in the end we get pluralism: our own peculiar pluralism, achieved in the agony of atomizing reality and heroically rising from each least atom to bring the Glad Tidings. "Here I stand, Lord—there is nothing whole in me, just a mass of scars and wounds, but by them will the world be healed!"

The question is whether it is possible for the one-and-only pluralism to consist of a thousand different totalitarianisms. For the time being, it would seem, we have nothing better to work with than this agonizing spread of one and the same totalitarianism into every area of life. Every group, every leader, every idea becomes a caricature of itself, a monstrous and absurd exaggeration. We are approaching pluralism in a non-Western manner, through the mutual friction and modification of different points of view; and precisely through the radicalism of each we cancel out the domination of any. Our redemption from totalitarianism lies in totalitarianism itself, but only if it is carried through to the end. By spreading through all professions and occupations, it attains the ultimate totalism—and splits its sides laughing at the realization of its own relativity. The comic utopia. The totalitarian grotesque.

Ideosophy

But let us remember that "comedy" originally meant not only something laughable but also something positive and illuminating. Comedy begins from the depths of the universe and ascends to its heights. So too with the *Comedy of Ideas:* in its overall design there is a descent into the infernal abysses of ideology but also an ascent to the heights of consciousness, an ascent that can be called "ideosophical." The point is that every idea, however comically incongruous in its pretensions to total dominion, still contains a positive, life-enhancing moment. However risible its pretensions to be the salvation of the world, it evokes sympathy as one of the little attempts to save, support, justify some one particular particle of life. Every nation and class, every flower and pebble, every fragment of reality has its positive value, and in this sense its own idea, which it can reveal as "this" particular one of "these little ones"—solitary, isolated, of limited potential. By rights it is just a common parishioner in the long file of communicants, but it tries to climb up onto the altar and speak in God's name, to usurp His veneration and worship.

   The task of ideosophy, as we define this sphere of knowledge, is to bring the form of an idea into correspondence with the partiality of its content. By collecting various ideas with all their limitations and giving each the chance to express itself, to reach its inherent limit, ideosophy draws out their absolute content, makes a humiliating farce of their claims to totality, and thereby restores their authentic meaning.

Ideology knows only one attitude to the truths it pronounces: the triumphal-assertive. Ideosophy embraces a whole spectrum of successive attitudes that arise with the unfolding of each idea:

1. The neutrally scientific, trustfully serious attitude toward the strictly intelligible aspect of the idea

2. Rapture at the heroic thrust of the idea, its colossal potential, its rush to explain and change the world

3. Seeds of doubt, dissatisfaction with the idea's bombastic and tendentious character, rejection of its totalizing sweep, its inflexible and oversimplified approach to reality

4. Derisive ridicule of the idea, of the farcical incongruity between the absoluteness of its pretensions and the poverty of its actual content

5. The prick of pity, the shudder of love for this poor lost idea, limited and doomed, like every creature of the human mind

6. A glad and sympathetic grasp of the bit of truth that actually is contained in the idea and that justifies the idea's original impulse to come to the defense of a bit of reality, to make sense of it from within, and thus to lift it into the "pearl of creation"

7. Sober contemplation of the idea in the light of wisdom, which has assigned it a unique place in the design of the world order

Ideas are the transmutations undergone by integral wisdom when it is split into particles, each deified in itself. Guided by wisdom, which extends over thought in its wholeness, in the intelligible harmony of all its parts, ideosophy restores the integrity and mutual connection of the ideas.

It is important here to draw a clear distinction between ideology and religion. Whereas for ideology the supreme value is the objective idea, fully accessible and knowable, for religion the supreme value is the subjective Person, inaccessible in the mode of knowledge or mastery, but disclosing itself in the mode of revelation. Although ideology sets up certain absolutes, such as "freedom," "equality," "power," "dictatorship" etc., these are in fact ideas merely posited by ideology itself. This is why ideology, regardless what absolutes it sets up, is itself its own only absolute. This is why it is possible, for the sake of ideology or in the name of an idea, to sacrifice everything real, including the lives of thousands of people and entire nations; for they are all partial and relative in the light of the absolutism of ideology itself. Religion, so long as it does not turn into ideology, can never be reduced to totalitarianism, since it acknowledges the existence of an Absolute outside itself, beyond the limit of its own knowledge and mastery—which means that it admits its own imperfection in relation to Him, its partialness, finitude, and liability to error.

The critique of ideology can be truly radical only if it acknowledges for *thought* the existence of an *Unthinkable One,* such an Absolute as would be not merely an Absolute Idea, but an Absolute Person. Such a Person—and not just the personification of an Idea—is Sophia, Divine Wisdom, who says of herself: "Then I was beside Him as a master workman, and I was joy every day, rejoicing before His face at all times, rejoicing in His inhabited earth, and my delight is with the sons of men" (Prov. 8.30–31). Ideosophy is joyful Wisdom, and part of her joy lies in smashing the idols of consciousness with laughter.

In a certain sense, one can regard ideosophy as a therapy for the traumas of consciousness, just as psychoanalysis is a therapy for the traumas of the unconscious. In psychological terms, every idea is a hyperconscious fixation on some trauma. The trauma of wounded national pride calls to life a nationalistic ideology; the "inferiority complex" of one or another class produces an ideology of its own class superiority and future supremacy; the trauma of technological backwardness gives rise to the ideology of cosmism, the exploration of interstellar space and dominion over the resources of other planets. Rich, successful, untraumatized societies are free from the compulsion of ideologies. The vocation of ideosophy is to work with the ideological consciousness, emancipating it from the cruel afflictions of obsession, from its subjection to *idées fixes.*

Consciousness can be liberated from the dictatorship of ideas, from attachment to absolutized points of view, only when it acknowledges the mystery of the Absolute as a Person and not an Idea; that is, only when it acknowledges the impossibility of fixing the Absolute in consciousness itself. The Absolute cannot be dissolved in the world of ideas, and this is all that limits the claims of ideology. Only the unknowability of the Absolute emancipates the consciousness, frees it to confront the endless variety of values, and consecrates this very variety. The acknowledgment of unknowability is the path to the liberation of consciousness. But when consciousness claims to embrace and contain everything in itself, totalitarianism arises on the margins of its rationalistic strivings as the denial of mystery and the claim to violence (for violence is the activity that abolishes mystery).

This is why Sophia is not only wise but chaste: she keeps the source of her wisdom under seal. Unlike the harlot who tears off her clothes to certify that knowledge need have no limit, Sophia sets a limit to knowledge and thereby turns it into wisdom in the face of the inaccessible, the concealed. "Whence then cometh wisdom? . . . She is hid from the eyes of all living. . . . God knows her path, and He knows her place" (Job 28.20–21, 23). "We preach the secret and hidden Divine Wisdom . . . which no one of the rulers of this age has known" (1 Cor. 2.7–8). The entry of Sophia into the kingdom of ideas, over which it is hers to rule, is manifested chiefly in the consecration of mystery, while in ideology, it is the ideas themselves that are consecrated.

Thus, ideosophy does two things: it removes mystery from the realm of ideology, and hands over to ideology all the rest of the visible and variegated world, in whose every cell new and unheard-of ideologies are multiplying and dividing: "Good-belief" and "Sinner-ism," "Bloodbrothership" and "Foodnikism," "Steppiedom" and "Domesticanism," "Atheanism" and "Khazarism," "The Red Horde" and "Glazierism" (these are some of the ideas that appear in the first book of our *Comedy*). Ideosophy is a copying device that takes prints of ever-new ideologies from every sphere of being. The more of them there are, the less is the power of ideology itself. When some phenomenon claims supreme value and all-explanatory power, when everything becomes ideology, separate ideologies vanish, for the very fabric of being itself, in all its subtlest interconnections and subdivisions, turns out to be the inexhaustible source of ideas. The subject matter of ideosophy is the ceaseless and superabundant overflow of wisdom into a world dismembered by our jealous mental passions, each of which, marshalling its own lines of cause and effect, turns into a particular ideology. Yet among them all is the unity of an all-connecting providence, an incessant flow of meanings. By leading us through and then beyond the circuit of multiple ideologies, near to the center point of wisdom, ideosophy alters our consciousness, accustoms it to universal flexibility, delicate changes of emphasis; and it does so in order to root all ideas in the immutable priority of the First and Last.

The heroes of this ideosophic work, unlike those of pure philosophy, are not abstract concepts but ideas—ideas that force concepts ("thing," "emptiness," "food," "house") out of their self-identity, furiously dragging them off somewhere and inciting them to transform the world. An idea is the explosion of a concept, passion's mining of the field of universality. An idea is a passion intensified to the point of universalization, thereby gaining an all-compelling and imperious force. Not "fire," but the necessity of burning, the sanctity of the conflagration; not "home," but the necessity of building and settling, the sanctity of the threshold. This book is a survey of human passions elevated to the level of concepts, blazing now in the head and not only in the heart. Like all ideas, they are scattered particles of wisdom; like all passions, they are scattered particles of love. And when these mental passions reach the highest pitch of incandescence, we suddenly see that they are sparks flying out of the one sun, out of the love that spills over the whole world and everything in it.

Every idea is only a nostalgic longing for a world liberated from ideas, a thirst for wholeness, aimlessness, health, a longing to abide in being itself.

The Third Comedy

The French poet and thinker Paul Valéry once said that after Dante's *Divine Comedy* and Balzac's *Human Comedy*, it was time to start a third, "intellectual" comedy treating the adventures and transformations of human thought.

Comedy, in the Dantean and Balzacian sense, is the most monumental of all genres, the genre depending least on the will of its author and most on the condition of his society, which, as it were, dictates to him, turning him into its literary secretary (this image comes from Balzac's preface to his work). Every society gets the comedy it deserves.

Valéry himself did not write the "third" comedy, although he had all the necessary qualifications for it: the broadest erudition, the subtlest intellect, and a great artistic genius. But he still lived in the Balzacian world of the "human comedy," where the moving force of all events was human beings, their characters, passions, interests. Dante, for his part, had lived in a society welded together by Christian faith and organized on the model of the church. Its moving force was the authority of the divine Revelation, which had laid out the path leading from the sinful depths of earthly life to the bright crystal heavens of paradise.

The *Divine Comedy* was as much a necessary expression of medieval, "feudal" society as the *Human Comedy* was of property-owning, "bourgeois" society. And these works were written in the very countries that were the classic models of the corresponding social-spiritual organization: pre-Renaissance Italy and post-Revolutionary France.

The model of the third type of society, which we may tentatively call "socialist," appeared in post-Revolutionary Russia. It was precisely here that a new moving force appeared at the foundation of society: the force of *ideas*. It was ideas that brought the Revolution, waged the Civil and Great Patriotic Wars, established plants and factories—not only in order to produce something material, but also to assert the productivity of the ideas themselves. Socialist society is the only society constructed according to a previously laid plan based on ideas born in the minds of its thinker-founders; it is the most speculative and "premeditated" society on earth. Socialism is society without God and without things—spiritually and materially poor but rich in ideology, built on ideas alone—the kingdom of ideas ruling in its own name, where a ruler rules only in the name of an idea or as the impersonation of an idea, the triumph of its truth.

In socialist Russia, the things that feudal and bourgeois society lived by lost their prestige and reality. A tense and conscious battle is waged against God—or, rather, against the *idea* of God, since His actual existence is denied. Likewise, a struggle is conducted for the idea of plenty, although articles of material luxury and even necessities themselves disappear. But in any case, only ideas—ideas of what is, ideas of what is not—have an acknowledged and felt reality, ruling over human beings. Everything that exists outside of ideas, whether acknowledged or denied, loses its living reality and recedes into the background. There is a struggle *against* the idea of God, though there is no actual God; there is a struggle *for* the idea of plenty, though there is also no actual plenty. Ideas are all there is. They neither save us in the next life nor feed us in this one, but they do give us the feeling that our life is rightly lived and our death not in vain.

Thus, the third comedy, the comedy of ideas, arises precisely from the self-consciousness of socialist society, whose inner spring is neither the will of God nor the private interests of human beings, but ideas in which the faith and passion of immense human masses are concentrated. The whole life of socialist society revolves not around the "divine" and not around the "human" but around some third thing, for which no suitable name has yet been invented, but which can be defined as the "ideational"—life according to the idea.

Ludicrous and terrible—in the highest sense comical—is a human being who has fallen away from God into sin, living by merely human laws. Just as comical is a human being who is possessed by the passion for things, who has fallen away from everything human, living by the laws of the material world, in the interests of wealth, career, acquisition. Such are the characters of the Dantean and Balzacian worlds: the venal Bonturo and the usurious Gobsec; Ugolino the Elder and Père Grandet, fathers who devour their own children; the thieves de Pazzi and Vautrain, Pope Nicholas III and the careerist Rastignac. But the characters of the *Comedy of Ideas,* perhaps, need no names—they are well enough served by initials, abstracted from concrete names as ideas are abstracted from concrete persons. As comical as the falling away from divinity and from humanity may be, there is nothing more comical than the idea, for in it the human being falls away from everything substantial and even from himself, from whatever is individual and unique in himself.

The idea promises everything—and takes everything. There is no subject more worthy of comic representation, more distracted and addled, than the idea, for it is both more than and less than itself. It is at once heroic and parodic, surpassing what is and laying claim to what is not, full and empty, virtuous and vicious, an envoy to the Future and an abortion of Non-being. An idea is a something raised to the highest power, and for that very reason it corresponds to nothing and means nothing. Ideas: to unleash and intensify the class struggle for the sake of the classless society; to wipe out the wealthy for the sake of the common wealth; to devalue labor in support of the value of labor; to dry up the sea in the wilderness and pour it into flourishing plains; to fight militantly in the struggle for peace; to die of hunger in the struggle for the harvest; to annihilate matter in the struggle for materialism. Every idea bears within itself a staggering comedy that has cost millions of people a tragic life.

But what is tragic on the level of individual destinies underlies the comedy of Destiny itself. Ideas have destroyed the people who asserted them, but at the same time, through the tragedy of the generations, they have revealed their essentially comic nature. This is why comedy need not blush to tumble onstage in the still-warm tracks of tragedy, on the same boards, perhaps even simultaneously with tragedy, in the same roles. Alongside the *Gulag Archipelago*, the tragedy of the tortured and guillotined, grows its enormous shadow—the vaudeville of the very ideas that had played the roles of the torturers. People were sacrificed to the Idea; but while these sacrifices were heaping up before the Idea in its priestly role, it started clowning and winking, bustling around the bloody arena in whiteface, puffing up its cheeks and breathing its last; in the role of the hangman-buffoon, it would grab its own head by the hair and drag it to the scaffold. One and the same act of the historical drama is played both as the tragedy of living people and the comedy of the specters that rule them.

Tragedy, as the literary treatises say, moves from a happy to a sad situation, comedy from a sad to a happy. Tragedy embraces that period of our history when people, apparently made happy by the triumph of their ideas, turned out to be caught in their tightening trap: "from the happy to the sad." Comedy embraces the period when the ideas, having taken people captive, suddenly emerged from behind the prison walls as a vaudeville stage set, a bunch of crumpled cardboard junk: "from the sad to the happy." Each took place through the other. The ideas had to be painted in blood so that history could later pour out its bile on them.

Thus it is by the steps of the three comedies that the comic descends into the destiny of mankind: first the human without God, then the person without humanity, finally the idea without the person.

Encyclopedia as Genre

In this sense, comedy is a genre whose contents may be embodied in completely different forms depending on the epoch. The *Divine Comedy* took the form of a poem, to which it was disposed by its very subject, the ascent of the soul seeking nearness and union with God. The *Human Comedy* took the form of a series of novels, since the novel is defined precisely by its concentration on the fate of the isolated man, the private individual—not in his relation to the highest will, as in the poem, but in his struggle with external circumstances.

What form would best correspond to the contents of the third comedy? As a poem is directed to the heights of the divine and a novel to the depths of the human, so an encyclopedia is directed at the breadth of the variegated world of ideas. If the poem of Dante unfolds in the timeless space of the three worlds beyond the grave, on the hero's path through hell, purgatory, and heaven; if the novels of Balzac unfold in historical time, in the serial plot of actions and events, in the intrigues and conflicts of the characters; then the third comedy can unfold only in that timeless and spaceless continuum where ideas coexist and communicate among themselves—not by means of spatial or temporal connections but exclusively by means of references, citations, ideal attractions and repulsions. This intelligible continuum of ideas, all existing and calling out to one another at the same time, is the encyclopedia.

As a collective genre that preserves and displays the sum of received knowledge, this genre is beloved of socialist society and answers the needs of its transhistorical nature. There is no time in the kingdom of ideas; it abides in itself, indexed in an invisible card catalogue where all the ideas that society acknowledges as worthy of existence are fully cross-referenced. And it makes no difference whose name is signed to the exposition of these ideas: the more authoritative an encyclopedic publication, the more likely the authors' names are to be omitted. After all, it is not individuals who answer for the ideas, but the ideas that govern the individuals.

It is not only in the sphere of officially sanctioned ideas that the encyclopedic method works so well, but also in that of hostile ideas, which are ground by encyclopedic citation into a hash of little excerpts, interlarded with authoritative and infallible commentaries. Not only in its politics but in its textual practice as well, ideology acts by the old, tried and true method: it *divides* the text into convenient fragments and *rules* over the meaning of each of them. From all the critical-atheistic encyclopedias the reader gets an impression of world culture as a fine dust of citations—ragged, disjointed voices emerging at random from the single-minded noise. The authors' names say very little; they are just conventional signs personifying incorrect views. In some books on atheism the names of believers, even reeducated ones, are abbreviated into initials. After all, is it worth vilifying people under their full names when they are in any case suffering the torments of their own errors?

This is why the author of this book, having taken on the role of an encyclopedia editor and having abridged all the "selected" texts into citations, has also condensed the names of their presumptive authors into initials. An initial is a citation from a name. Initials produce a sort of algebraic play of ideas and concepts, purged of any concrete allusion to the question of who expressed these views, when, where, and why. In this way, a cosmic sterile culture is produced, beyond the reach of any history or biography, clear and enigmatic as the alphabet.

The expression of the encyclopedic ideal in socialist society is by no means limited to encyclopedias in the narrow sense of the term. On the strength of their generic anonymity and citatory, countless treatises, articles, monographs, textbooks, anthologies, and chrestomathies in all fields and on all subjects have made up a great Encyclopedia which, though having a finite number of volumes, is infinitely more capacious than any "bourgeois" encyclopedia. Our entire culture has turned into a huge, million-volume work of the encyclopedic genre. Socialism led unswervingly to the collectivization of intellectual, as of all other, property. Thought, as the means of spiritual production, was removed from private hands and put into general use by the government, which stamped it with its own official seal of order and control. An encyclopedia lacks the stamp of authorship and for that very reason comes to represent authority itself. The encyclopedic rule is that ideas are presented not by their authors, with authorial passion and transport, but by people who have already done the job of transposing them into a generalized, anonymous language.

The fact that the encyclopedia originally functioned as a strictly scientific and documentary description of reality has hindered its recognition as a literary genre on the level of the poem and the novel. For centuries, for lack of a better method, the encyclopedia was compelled to perform this factographic task, just as painting was compelled to compile a visual record of the world. But just as the paintings of great artists cannot be reduced to photography, so the great encyclopedias of the past cannot be reduced to factography: they contain a system of global conceptions, a creative method of explaining and evaluating the world. After the invention of photography, painting could devote itself more freely to its own fantasies, burrowing its way into the sphere of pure inner vision; thus, we find the swift emergence of impressionism, cubism, and all the other styles that deviated further and further from objective renderings of the visible world.

In the same way, the invention of computers and systems of electronic memory has finally liberated encyclopedias from their former honorable but cramped role as preservers of information. The encyclopedia is now a genre open to creativity as never before, capable of every sort of metamorphosis in the spirit of various intellectual styles. Like painting, released by photography from the obligation to represent anything but the possibilities of representation itself, the encyclopedia too has been released by the computer from the obligation to convey any actual facts and ideas; it is now free to move on to possible or fantastic facts and ideas. We can conceive of various encyclopedias treating one and the same subject in different styles: impressionistic, abstractionist, surrealistic, existentialist, structuralist. Even a conceptualist style is possible: it would consciously reproduce all the forms of the socialist worldview in the spirit of the grotesque.

Because of the deeply citatory and anonymous style of the type of thinking accepted in socialist society and reflecting its ideocratic structure, it is entirely natural that the *Comedy of Ideas* should take the generic form of the encyclopedia. But it must literally "take" this encyclopedic form—appropriate it, exploit all its conventions and stereotypes—in order to produce something as far as possible from an informational archive. The ultimate goal of the encyclopedic genre is a comedy of ideas to be performed on the vast stage of Eurasia but behind the curtains of official ideologies. These latter, in the spirit of socialist pluralism, now include not only Marxism but also "liberalism," "democratism," "capitalism," "ecologism," "conservatism," "Westernism," etc. But all these acknowledged political ideologies are not the real drama. Behind their clumsily painted curtains, a comedy is being performed by ideas far more subtle, supple, and strange, ideas emanating from the depths of the collective unconscious. In the head and heart of each one of us are hundreds and thousands of ideologies silently awaiting their cue.

The official ideologies are already speaking for themselves from every loudspeaker. Who, though, will say a brief word on behalf of those little, out-of-the-way, still unconscious or half-conscious ideas, hardly yet differentiated from simple feelings, from the merest twitches of the cardiac muscle? Are the crazy ideas of a Niels Bohr needed more by physics than by metaphysics? Here before the reader is a collection of metaphysical crazes in which everyone can recognize something of himself, something familiar—but taken to such an extreme as to be almost unrecognizable. It's a set of stretching exercises for the mind and the heart. Once you master the use of this home apparatus to produce any ideology you like, no ideology will any longer be able to make you an ideomaniac, an ideophile, or an ideocrat. . . .

Of course, the honorable role of editor of this encyclopedia had to be assigned to a seasoned expositor of others' opinions and exposer of their flaws—a professor of scientific atheism. The direct voice of the Correct Ideology had to be heard first, before being drowned in the chorus of voices announcing all the hitherto clandestine currents of contemporary thought with all their fantastic deviations, sectarian extremes, and heretical distortions. The opening remarks are delivered in the voice of Ideology itself, the past master of the "analysis and critique" of other ideologies—until it finally dissolves into them altogether and all trace of it is lost. The socialism of content, the socialism of the one idea with the right and power to dictate to others, is dead; but its death has brought to birth the socialism of form, a socialism which, with impersonal liberality and hospitality, invites all ideas to the great feast of ideas, where they may finally leave their authors' voices behind and merge into a single encyclopedic chorus.

The ideas of all minds, ages, and peoples; the ideas of all arts, sciences, and professions; the ideas of all the kingdoms of nature and all the social classes; the ideas of every drop of water and blade of grass; the ideas of constellations and galaxies; the ideas of all heads, hearts, bellies, and breaths; the ideas of friendship, love, jealousy, equality, brotherhood, and rivalry; ideas exalted and ordinary, complex and simple, deep and ingenious, smart and eccentric, clear and obscure, credible and incredible—separated in ideologies, they seek unity in wisdom.

Notes

From the Author

1. Vladimir F. Odoevsky, *Russian Nights* (in Russian) (Leningrad: Nauka, 1975), 192. Odoevsky (1803 or 1804–1869) was a Russian prose writer and aesthetic thinker.

2. Alexander Herzen, *My Past and Thoughts*, vol. 2, trans. Constance Garnett (New York: Knopf, 1968), 415.

3. The author directed the Club of Essayists (1982–1987), the "Image and Thought" Association (1986–1988), and the Laboratory of Contemporary Culture at the Experimental Creative Center (1988–1990).

4. A. S. Prugavin, *Raskol sverkhu: Ocherki religioznykh iskanii v privilegirovannoi srede* (Schism from above: Outline of religious quests among the privileged classes) (St. Petersburg: Obshchestvennaia Pol'za, 1909), 42, 47–48.

The New Sectarianism

1. One sectarian offered us a justification of the parody and intentional "earthiness" of the new theological texts by appealing to the Eastern and Western Church Fathers, Pseudo-Dionysius Areopagiticus, and Thomas Aquinas. Pseudo-Dionysius says in his work "On the Divine Hierarchy" that low similes are more suited to divine truths than high similes, since they present less danger of mistaking the likeness for the Divine itself. This is why it is more appropriate to liken the Divine to darkness than to light, to unreason than to reason. And indeed, what God is not is much more intelligible to man than what He is. Finally, a veil of low similes helps to shield divine truths from unworthy people who would either laugh at them or distort them. In the section of the *Summa Theologica* known as "On The Nature and Sphere of Sacred Doctrine," Thomas Aquinas cites this discussion with full approval in Article 9, "Ought the Holy Scripture to Use Metaphors." On this passage, S. A. observes that "all theology is really but a parody of That which it studies, since in the case of God, what is said is always the opposite of what is really meant" ("On Sacred Parody").

2. Karl Marx, Friedrich Engels, and V. I. Lenin, *O religii* (On religion), 2d ed. (Moscow: Izdatel'stvo politicheskoi literatury, 1983), 243.

231

3. Ibid., 247.

4. Ibid., 237.

5. Vladimir D. Bonch-Bruyevich, *Izbrannye sochineniia v 3 tt.* (Selected works in three volumes), vol. 1 (Moscow, 1959), 153. Bonch-Bruyevich (1873–1955), a prominent Bolshevist and associate of V. I. Lenin, collected vast materials on sectarian movements in pre-Revolutionary Russia.

6. Bonch-Bruyevich, *Materialy k istorii i izucheniiu russkogo sektantstva* (Materials for the history and study of Russian sectarianism), 2 vols. (St. Petersburg, 1901–9).

7. Bonch-Bruyevich, ed., *Zhivotnaia kniga dukhobortsev* (Dukhobor anthology) (St. Petersburg: Tip. B. M. Volfa, 1909).

8. Sometimes we find repeated variations on the same motifs and even similar wording in excerpts from different authors belonging to one sect or version. The editors have let such repetitions stand in those cases where they signal the fundamental importance for the sectarian worldview of a particular postulate, or an "inclination to a favorite thought."

9. From the poem *"Ia slovo pozabyl, chto ia khotel skazat'"* ("I have forgotten the word that I wanted to say") by Osip Mandelstam (1891–1938), a great Russian poet and essayist.

10. Nikolai Karamzin (1766–1826), Russian historian and poet.

11. When Moses asks God His name, God answers, "I am that which is," or more literally, "I am that which I am" (Exod. 3.14).

12. From the poem *"Umyvalsia noch'iu na dvore"* ("By night he was washing himself out of doors") by Osip Mandelstam.

13. "Adama" in ancient Hebrew means "earth," "clay," "dust" (cf. Gen. 2.7).

14. This is the Khazars' name for the Volga.

15. Ararat.

16. The reference is to John the Baptist, who baptized people, including Jesus, in the water of the River Jordan. Cf. the "third baptism" (among the Bloodbrothers), viz. the baptism in blood spoken of by the other John, the apostle and evangelist.

17. In the Old Testament, as St. Augustine observes, sin-offerings were actually called "sins" (Hos. 4.8). What wisdom! One and the same deed—a murder, for instance—is a sin for one man (the sinner) and a sin-offering for another (the Sinnerist). For the sinner, it is a temptation of the flesh in pursuit of pleasure; for the Sinnerist, it is a sacrifice of the soul in pursuit of suffering.

18. St. Augustine, *De Genesi ad litteram* (The literal meaning of Genesis), bk. 2, chap. 33, 8.

19. "And I looked, and behold, a Lamb was standing on Mount Zion, and with him a hundred and forty-four thousand, having his Father's name written

on their brows. . . . They sung as it were a new song before the throne, and before the four beasts, and the elders; and no one could learn that song but the hundred and forty-four thousand, who were redeemed from the earth." (Rev. 14.1, 3)

20. "Gehenna" was the ancient Hebrew name for a valley near Jerusalem where apostate kings sacrificed to pagan gods, as a result of which it became a municipal dump where garbage constantly burned. This is the source of the Gospels' interpretation of Gehenna as an image of hell: "Fear rather Him who can destroy both the soul and the body in Gehenna" (Matt. 10.28). For the Defectors, Gehenna symbolizes not so much the judgment of the world as its purification, "the fiery spirit of God, descending into the pit of darkness."

21. Vladimir Benediktov (1807–1873).

22. "White angel"—in Russian, *belyi angel*. These lines belong to the Russian poetess Bella Akhmadulina (b. 1937).

Selected Reviews of *The New Sectarianism*

1. Ivan Dedov, "The Dal of Russian Thought," *Our Times* 12 (1986): 198–203. This title plays on the double meaning of the Russian word *dal*: as a common noun it means "horizon, distance, depth"; as a proper name, it refers to Vladimir Dal (1801–1872), the greatest Russian lexicographer and the compiler of the four-volume *Dictionary of the Living Russian Language*. The reviewer implies that the handbook of Russian sects published by Gibaydulina embraces the "horizons" of contemporary Russian thought and can be compared with Dal's dictionary in the breadth of its encyclopedic design.

2. *Repentance*, dir. by Tengiz Abuladze, Georgia Films, 1986.

3. Pierre Daniel, "The First Socialist Philosophy," *Recherches dans la Fois* 4 (1987): 163–166.

4. "Whereof one cannot speak, thereof one must be silent." Ludwig Wittgenstein, *Tractatus Logico-Philosophicus*, n. 7 (the concluding aphorism).

5. Gustav Schneider, "From Atheism to Paganism," *Der Philosophische Glaube* 8 (1987): 72–75.

6. Because of the dark color of his face, Marx was called "the Moor" at home.

7. Robert Cohen, "A Religious Consciousness in Distress," *God and World* (Philadelphia) 10 (1987): 26–30.

8. St. Augustine, *De civitate Dei* (The city of God), bk. 19, chap. 1.

Epilogue to *The New Sectarianism*

1. Karl Marx and Friedrich Engels, *Iz rannikh proizvedenii* (Selected early works) (Moscow: Gospolitizdat, 1956), 589, 598.

2. The full text in Russian was published in *Our Newsletter* 7 (1988). This newsletter, the internal organ of the Institute of Atheism, was entitled *Storming the Heavens* until 1988.

3. Mikhail Bakhtin, *Literaturno-kriticheskie stat' i* (Literary-critical articles) (Moscow: Khudozhestvennaya literatura, 1986), 507.

4. Mikhail Epstein, "Post-ateizm, ili Bednaia religiia" (Post-atheism, or poor religion), *Oktiabr'* 9 (1996): 158–165.

5. This section on "poor" and "rich" religions plays on the Russian etymology of the word *Bog* (God), a cognate to *bogatyi* (rich). This suggests that the poor people should have a different God, or, rather, no God at all.

Afterword

1. The Kunstkammer, located in the center of St. Petersburg, opened to the public in 1714. The museum's purpose was to collect natural and human curiosities, and it initially exhibited grotesque aborted fetuses and freaks of nature that Peter the Great had brought from Amsterdam. Known today as Peter the Great's Museum of Anthropology and Ethnography (Kunstkammer), it contains over one million artifacts and reflects the diversity of traditional cultures in the Old and New World.

2. *Cries in the New Wilderness* is the first volume of the cycle *The Comedy of Ideas*. Parts of a second volume, "Thinkers of Our Time," were published as "Uchenie Iakova Abramova v izlozhenii ego uchenikov" (The teachings of Yakov Abramov in the interpretation of his disciples), in *LOGOS* (Leningrad: Leningrad University Press, 1991), 211–254; "Razmyshleniia Ivana Soloviev ob Erose," *Chelovek* 1 (1991): 195–212, partially translated as "Ivan Soloviev's Reflections on Eros," in *Postcommunism and the Body Politic: Genders 22*, ed. Ellen E. Berry (New York and London: New York University Press, 1995), 252–266; and the preface to "Messianskie rechi" (Messianic speeches), by Ivan Soloviev, *Oktiabr'* 7 (1998): 148–167. For discussion of a projected third volume, "A Book of Books: An Anthology of Alternative Ideas," see my "Interactive Anthology of Alternative Ideas: An Introduction," in *Transcultural Experiments: Russian and American Models of Creative Communication*, ed. Mikhail Epstein and Ellen E. Berry (New York: St. Martin's Press, 1999), 290–301.

Index

Mikhail N. Epstein was born in Moscow and graduated from Moscow State University *summa cum laude* in philology. He was founder and director of the Laboratory of Contemporary Culture in Moscow. In 1990 Epstein moved to the United States, where he spent a year in Washington, D.C., as a fellow at the Woodrow Wilson International Center. He is now Samuel Candler Dobbs Professor of Cultural Theory and Russian Literature at Emory University.

Epstein's recent books in English include *After the Future: Paradoxes of Postmodernism and Contemporary Russian Culture; Russian Postmodernism: New Perspectives on Post-Soviet Culture* (with two coauthors); and *Transcultural Experiments: Russian and American Models of Creative Communication* (with Ellen Berry). He is the author of 15 books and approximately 400 essays and articles, translated into 14 languages.

In 2000 Epstein was awarded the Liberty Prize, given each year to prominent Russian cultural figures who have made outstanding contributions to American society. He has also received, among many other awards, the 1995 Social Innovations Award from the Institute for Social Inventions (London) for his electronic Bank of New Ideas, and the 1991 Andrei Belyi Prize (St. Petersburg) for his literary criticism and scholarship.

Eve Adler is professor of classics at Middlebury College in Vermont. She is the translator of Leo Strauss's *Philosophy and Law*, coauthor with Vladimir Shlyakhov of the *Dictionary of Russian Slang and Colloquial Expressions*, and author of *Vergil's Empire: The Political Thought of the Aeneid*.